DEATH IN A BLACKOUT

Also by Jessica Ellicott

The Beryl and Edwina mysteries

MURDER IN AN ENGLISH VILLAGE
MURDER FLIES THE COOP
MURDER CUTS THE MUSTARD
MURDER COMES TO CALL
MURDER IN AN ENGLISH GLADE
MURDER THROUGH THE ENGLISH POST

DEATH IN A BLACKOUT

Jessica Ellicott

SEVERN
HOUSE

First world edition published in Great Britain and the USA in 2022
by Severn House, an imprint of Canongate Books Ltd,
14 High Street, Edinburgh EH1 1TE.

Trade paperback edition first published in Great Britain and the USA in 2022
by Severn House, an imprint of Canongate Books Ltd.

severnhouse.com

British Library Cataloguing-in-Publication Data
A CIP catalogue record for this title is available from the British Library.

ISBN-13: 978-1-4483-0652-7 (cased)
ISBN-13: 978-1-4483-0659-6 (trade paper)
ISBN-13: 978-1-4483-0658-9 (e-book)

All Severn House titles are printed on acid-free paper.

Typeset by Palimpsest Book Production Ltd.,
Falkirk, Stirlingshire, Scotland.
Printed and bound in Great Britain by
TJ Books, Padstow, Cornwall.

ONE

Barton St Giles
June 1940
Dear Father,
   *I hope somehow this letter reaches you and that you
will agree with my decision despite the risks . . .*

Wilhelmina Harkness stood several yards from the makeshift recruiting center, feigning admiration for a display of irreproachably serviceable and singularly unattractive shoes in the window of the shop while reminding herself to breathe. She looked over her shoulder to reassure herself that she could approach the building without attracting any notice. A group of recently arrived evacuee children raced up the street and provided a convenient distraction should anyone take it into their heads to wonder what the rector's daughter was doing loafing about in the middle of the afternoon when there was so much to be done.

She could scarcely believe she had worked up the nerve to defy her mother's vehemently expressed wishes. Perhaps it had been the fact that in the hours since her lifelong friend Candace Palmer had pressed a rousing recruitment pamphlet into her hands, she had read it over so many times she could recite it word for word. Maybe it had been the sound of the train whistle bearing young men from the village off to a military base at the crack of dawn. She thought it likely she was spurred to action by the reports still flooding in via the newspapers bearing the news of Dunkirk.

The call to action was clear. The services were more than eager for fit young women to do their duty and enlist. Every woman who volunteered freed up a man to serve overseas. The pamphlet had made the work sound noble and important. What was more, Wilhelmina could learn a skill or trade that just might provide her with the sort of opportunities in the future that were usually only offered to men. But a future where such things might be possible was of little importance compared with the present and doing one's bit to help the Allies win the war.

Regardless of her reason for doing so, she had raced through her morning chores, gobbled down her luncheon and scurried off towards the recruitment office that very afternoon, determined to volunteer for whichever branch of the services would have her.

Glancing about one last time, she hurried across the street, pushed open the heavy glass door and slipped inside. Frances Hughes looked up from her desk, a faint spark of surprise flitting across her face before she offered a welcoming smile.

'Good afternoon, Wilhelmina. What brings you in today?' she asked.

Wilhelmina dismissed her mother's face from her mind's eye and stepped forward, thrusting the recruiting pamphlet in front of her. 'I would like to enlist in one of the women's auxiliary services. That is, if you think one of them will have me.' There – she'd come out and said it. She released her grip on the pamphlet slightly and noticed the edge of it was stained with perspiration.

'We can most certainly find a place for you in one of the service branches. I'm sure if there is no place available in the WAAF, we can find space for you in the ATS.' Frances rose and stepped out from behind her battered wooden desk and looked Wilhelmina up and down as though she thought it unlikely she would make it into the coveted Women's Auxiliary Air Force.

'Now I know the Territorials are not terribly popular with the girls, but I can assure you that the khaki-colored uniforms are nowhere nearly as unattractive as some would make them out to be. With a bit of tailoring and a touch of Tangee lipstick, I think you'll find the women in the Territorials cut quite dashing figures.'

'The uniform is the very least of my worries. I am only concerned with doing my bit for the war effort. Besides, when it comes down to it, a country rector's daughter's wardrobe isn't exactly known for its glamour either,' Wilhelmina said with a shrug.

'Very sensible of you, my dear. Speaking of rectors, have you had any more word about your father?'

The chilling news of her father's internment in a prisoner-of-war camp had spread over the village like a hoar frost. His name had been broadcast over German radio along with a number of others from his unit the week before. Wilhelmina's mother had refused to believe that the man mentioned was her husband until his name appeared in the local newspaper along with the detail of his rank as chaplain.

'Not a thing.'

'Please pass along my condolences to your mother. It is very generous of her to support your decision to join up in light of the contribution your father and brother have made.'

Wilhelmina's stomach clenched into a hard little knot. Her mother had been unwavering in her resistance to the notion of her only daughter signing up for any branch of the services. Martha Harkness had little use for the notion of the modern woman and had a particular antipathy for those in uniform. Whenever Wilhelmina broached the subject, her mother muttered darkly about moral degradation, then swiftly changed the topic of conversation.

Still, she told herself, she was of age and as such had the right to decide how best to make her own contribution. There was no need to enlighten Frances on her mother's views. It would only serve to make things awkward in the present and surely her mother would have to come round once the deed was done. It was not as though she needed her mother's permission. Despite her upbringing in the Anglican Church, she found she had a rather shocking attitude towards telling the truth when it made little sense to do so. She often found lies of omission entirely justifiable in service of the greater good.

'As soon as we heard he had been detained, I decided the time had come for me to enlist. I cannot stand idly by any longer when there is so much that needs to be done for the war effort.'

'That's the spirit. And should your mother express reservation, you could mention to her that there's no better place to meet eligible young men than in the services,' Frances said. 'If she is like most mothers, I am sure she has been urging you to marry and settle down.'

'I'll be sure to mention that to her,' Wilhelmina said. 'But I wouldn't want you to think that was my reason for volunteering. I am eager to do something of real value for the country.'

'Of course you are.' Frances bustled back behind the desk and pulled out a stack of forms. 'Let's get the paperwork started. Do you have any special skills that I should make a note of when determining where to send you? I seem to recall that you are an experienced driver.'

Wilhelmina felt her heart leap. She loved the sensation of freedom she derived from being behind the wheel. 'I've had my motoring license for some time. Is that of any use?'

'It can be. I don't suppose you have any skills at repairing vehicles, do you?'

She wondered what exactly defined *any*. She had once mended a puncture with a patching kit and on another occasion hammered a small dent from the rear fender of her father's motorcar before her recklessness could be noticed. Surely that constituted enough knowledge to mention. She straightened her posture and nodded. Frances smiled and carefully made a note on the form in front of her.

Frances quickly completed the necessary paperwork and assured Wilhelmina that her application would go out by the evening post. She promised that she would be informed of her assignment in less than a week. Frances even went so far as to produce a measuring tape in order to procure a correctly sized uniform. All that remained was the most difficult thing of all: how and when to break the news to her mother.

As Wilhelmina exited the recruitment center, she looked up and down the street once more. She released a deep breath she had not realized she was holding as her friend Candace hurried towards her and reached out for her arm.

'Did you actually do it?' Candace asked, her voice barely above a whisper.

Candace was well aware of Martha Harkness's stance on women in the services and how difficult it would be for her friend to oppose her mother's wishes.

Wilhelmina nodded carefully, as though she still couldn't quite believe it herself. 'I did. I went in and signed my name on the paperwork to join the ATS.'

'That's marvelous,' Candace said. 'Perhaps you will end up being assigned to my unit.' Her friend gave her arm an enthusiastic squeeze.

'Have you received your orders already?' Wilhelmina asked. Her stomach fluttered with nervous excitement.

'They came in late yesterday. I'm on my way now to the recruitment center to pick up my uniform. I am so excited I think I shall burst.' Candace tipped her head to the side and gave Wilhelmina one of her brilliant smiles.

'That must mean you'll be leaving soon,' Wilhelmina said, a lump forming in her throat.

'I head out by the afternoon train.'

'As soon as that? There will be no time for a going-away party, will there?'

'I shouldn't have wanted to have one anyway. I would prefer not to have any fuss,' Candace said.

'Shall I come to see you off at least?'

'I wish you wouldn't. I've asked my parents not to, either. It sounds silly, I'm sure, but I think that it will make it harder to go if I am waving at what I am leaving behind.' Candace's scarlet-tinted lower lip wobbled. 'But don't worry, you'll be right behind me, I'm sure. And we'll write just as often as we can, won't we?'

There had been so many leave-takings of late. Wilhelmina's thoughts flicked for a moment to her mother and the sorrow she would feel at her daughter's departure. She drove the thought from her mind and snapped open her handbag in search of the small notebook and pencil she always carried with her. She opened it to a blank page, telling herself her friend's address deserved better than a spot at the end of a chore list, even amidst paper shortages.

'Of course, we will. Just write down your address and I will send you mine as soon as I have it,' Wilhelmina said, pressing the notebook into Candace's hand.

Candace jotted it down carefully and then wrapped Wilhelmina in a tight embrace. 'Wish me luck,' she said as she let go.

'Of course. But I expect I'll need more of it than you. I still have to tell my mother what I've done.'

'I'm sure she'll come around eventually. You can tell me all about it in your first letter,' Candace said. She lifted her hand in a cheery wave and then turned and strode up the street to the recruitment center and out of sight.

As she mulled over how to best break the news to her mother, Wilhelmina found her feet had carried her to the door of the reading room. Whenever she found her life weighing her down, she delved between the covers of a book in search of an escape. The heat of the afternoon sun faded away as she pushed open the door. She let out a sigh of pleasure to find herself alone in the cool, silent space.

The reading room had been endowed by a local man who had sought and found his fortune in the Victorian era like the hero of a Dickens novel. While the dedication plaque on the front of the building always struck her as a bit condescending with its mention of expanding the villagers' collective vistas through reading, she could not but be grateful for his generosity.

She strode to the fiction section and ran her finger slowly along the irresistible spines of books. Old, familiar favorites and potential new loves sat side by side, jockeying for her attention. She pulled several off the shelves and carried them to a wingback chair tucked beside a long window. She stacked the books on a nearby table and settled in for a few stolen moments of reading.

A nagging thrum of guilt pulsed through her as she eyed a thick manual on the art of automotive repair. Perhaps she had been foolish to exaggerate her mechanical abilities in the hope she might be selected for a job that involved something other than office work. She had spent more hours than she cared to remember typing up her father's sermons, his correspondence and minutes of various church meetings.

Still, the lure of an unfamiliar novel, *Rebecca* by Daphne du Maurier, proved too strong to ignore. Just as she had finished the third chapter, the door to the reading room burst open and Wilhelmina's stomach turned over like a well-tuned lorry engine. Her mother swept her blazing gaze around the small room and raised an accusing finger in the air as it landed on her daughter.

'I know you are inclined to be impetuous and to launch

yourself into things without seeking proper counsel, but I never thought I would live to see the day when my own child would go behind my back as you have done. You know I expressly forbade you to enlist,' Martha Harkness said as she barreled towards her. 'Did you not even consider how I would feel should you, too, end up missing or killed?'

'It was precisely the danger Father and Frederick are experiencing that convinced me that I could no longer excuse myself from my duty, no matter who might object,' Wilhelmina said.

She braced herself for a torrent of angry words but instead was surprised to see her mother's eyes shimmering with tears. Her father was the only one of her parents given to the occasional expression of tender emotion. Martha could be counted on to give vent to displeasure, even occasional praise, but never tears. Wilhelmina felt a lump rise in her own throat to realize that her actions had caused her mother so much distress. She almost regretted what she had done. She scrambled to her feet and clutched the book to her chest.

'I'm truly sorry to have upset you, Mother, but I just cannot see how I could, in good conscience, remain here in the familiar comfort of the village when there is such a need for women to be willing to join the services.'

'Comfort, is it? I see you've made yourself quite comfortable indeed, taking your ease here with your nose in a book. But I'll soon set that to rights. I'll speak to Clementia Burrows about having you assist her with the evacuated children. Seeing what those little tykes are enduring might help you appreciate remaining in your own home with your mother.' A scarlet flush crept up Martha's neck, and Wilhelmina imagined she could slot a halfpenny piece into the furrow between her mother's brows.

'The country has an overwhelming need for women like me to be willing to sacrifice our own comforts for the greater good. Surely, if you consider it calmly, you will understand why I volunteered,' Wilhelmina said. 'Besides, aren't you always mentioning that I ought to marry? The recruiter said that joining one of the services is an excellent way to meet eligible young men. That would please you, wouldn't it?'

'It most certainly would not.' A crimson flush surged up from below Martha's collar and spread towards her cheeks. 'The women in the services have scandalous reputations. I shan't have any daughter of mine exposing herself to such scorn. Which is just what I said to Frances,' Martha said, jabbing her finger at Wilhelmina once more.

Wilhelmina felt her throat constrict. 'You spoke to the recruiting officer?'

'As soon as Mildred Dawes told me she spotted you slinking out of the recruitment center, I hurried over there and told Frances in no uncertain terms that you were not to go. I insisted she withdraw your application,' Martha said.

Of course, Mildred Dawes had been the one to carry the tale to her mother. Mildred was the most devoted gossip in the village.

'But you can't have done that,' Wilhelmina said, feeling the blood in her temples begin to pound.

'I can and I did. I had to become rather more forceful than might have been strictly ladylike, but, in the end, she came round to my way of thinking. I am sure, in time, you will do the same.'

'You had absolutely no right to interfere with my plans. If Father and Frederick were willing to make important contributions, I see no reason why I should not do the same.'

'Your father and Frederick are men and, as such, are expected to place themselves in harm's way, as much as I wish it wasn't necessary. Women are not properly equipped to do any such thing.' Martha reached out a hand and clamped it around her daughter's arm. 'It's time we got back to the rectory. Ronald will be expecting his tea shortly, and I haven't yet prepared a thing since I've spent the better part of my afternoon remedying the trouble you tried to get yourself into.'

Wilhelmina yanked her arm away. 'I'm not going with you. I am going back to the recruiting center to tell the officer to go ahead and submit my application.'

'I wouldn't waste my time if I were you. I assured the recruiter that I could make things exceedingly difficult for her in this community if she went against my wishes.' Martha flashed a triumphant smile, and Wilhelmina felt something inside her crack open. It was as if the months of wishing there was more she could do to help came tumbling out all at once.

'Mother, be reasonable. Surely you agree that we must all do whatever we possibly can to support our men overseas. I beg you to think of Father and Frederick and all the men like them.'

Before she knew what was happening, she felt a sharp sting as her mother's palm struck her across the cheek.

'How could you possibly imagine I do anything but think of your father trapped in that prison camp? Or that I am not consumed with worry about what has become of Frederick?'

Wilhelmina dashed to the reading-room door, her hand cupping her smarting cheek. She felt the tears she had managed to hold back since news of her father's capture and the telegram reporting that Frederick was missing tumble freely down her face. Her mother's voice called after her, the urgency in it slowing her flight for a moment on the steps in front of the building.

'Promise me, Wilhelmina, that you won't ever join the services,' she said, her tone shrill with desperation. 'Promise me.'

Wilhelmina broke into a run and tore off across the rolling fields leading away from the village and the rectory.

She paused her flight at the base of a towering beech tree standing sentry at the center of a lush hedgerow and sank down to settle against its smooth, sturdy trunk. The whistle of a train wafted across the fields, announcing Candace's departure. From a wealth of experience, she knew it would be some time before she would feel capable of apologizing and longer still before her mother would have calmed sufficiently to be willing to accept her apology if offered. Wilhelmina would have to be the one to back down. There would be no other way equanimity would be restored.

In all her twenty-two years, she could not think of a single time her mother had been the one to admit she had been wrong. She certainly would not be the one to broker peace in this case. No, it was better for Wilhelmina to spend as long as she possibly could off on her own collecting her thoughts and convincing herself that it would be more desirable to apologize than to suffer an extended and silent battle with her own mother. After

all, it was difficult enough spending so much energy being at
war with the Germans. Fomenting discontent in her own home
seemed almost an act of treason.

TWO

Hull
Special Constable Upton's Police Notebook

He paused on the pavement in front of number twelve
as memories of the place washed over him like the cold
waves slapping against the nearby docks. The modest
brick homes still stood cheek by jowl; not even the color of
paint on the wooden doors differentiated one from another. The
narrow, cobbled street wended as unevenly as it had always
done. The same briny tang floated in the air. Children raced by,
shouting and jostling one another as he had done at their age.
Bracing himself for what he might find once inside, he mounted
the steps, then pressed down firmly on the latch on the front
door.

His mother, as was her habit, must have been listening for
him with the vigilance of a trained guard dog. She bustled out
from the kitchen at the end of the cramped hallway, wiping her
small hands on a faded floral pinny.

'Peter, love, you'll never guess what I've made for tea,' she
said as she closed the space between them and wrapped her
short arms around him in a firm embrace.

He looked down at the top of her head, noticing glinting
threads of silver in among the deep auburn strands of her youth.
He squeezed her back, inhaling the homey scents of fresh bread,
cinnamon and washing powder. For a moment he was engulfed
in the memory of a time when the house held just the two of
them.

'You always manage to surprise me, Mum,' he said. She
released him and tipped her head back to look him in the face.
He peered down at her face in turn, relieved to see it devoid of

the heavy layer of pancake makeup that was a sure sign she was trying to cover fresh bruises.

'You'd best just come to see, then,' she said, taking him by the hand and pulling him along behind her. They passed the wall of framed photographs hanging above the hall table, and Peter's lips pressed tightly together as he tried to ignore the faces peering out at him as she hurried him along.

The kitchen table was set with two thick white mugs and a chipped Brown Betty teapot. His mother filled the kettle and placed it on the hob before opening the oven door and pulling out a plate heaped high with beans on toast, a rasher of crisp bacon and three sausages.

'Sit yourself down and tuck into this,' she said, pointing at the chair closest to the door. 'You look just about done in.'

He sank into the same spot he had occupied as a child as she placed the food in front of him. She settled into the chair opposite and nodded at him encouragingly.

'Aren't you eating?' he asked.

'I'm not particularly hungry, so I'll just join you for a slice of cake once you've got all that down you,' she said. 'I've been saving up the sugar and butter ration, so I made one this morning in honor of your visit.'

'You didn't need to do that,' he said. He hated to think of her going without on his account. It wasn't as if he was still a growing boy. If anything, he should be looking after her. He suspected her bacon and pork ration for the week was on his plate as well. But there would be no arguing with her. A lifetime of experience had taught him that much.

'It is a mother's privilege to make treats for her children. You wouldn't deny me that pleasure, now would you?' she asked, pointing once again to the plate.

He lifted his fork and cut the end from a sausage. His landlady was pleasant and kept a tidy house, but she wasn't much of a cook, and the government rationing had simply made that fact harder to ignore. He hadn't had a sausage, at least not one he could recognize as such, since the last time he visited his mother.

'I wouldn't deny you anything within my power to grant,' he said before taking a bite.

'If that's so, then I'd ask you to gain a few pounds and try getting a bit of a kip now and again.'

'I'm just fine, Mum.' He winked at her reassuringly before spearing another bite of sausage.

'You're looking peaky and the bags under your eyes could be filled with enough sand to hold back a river. I know you want to do your bit, but I can't help but wonder if you aren't putting in too many shifts with the constabulary,' she said.

'Everyone in the country is putting in extra effort. I shan't be an exception,' he said.

Peter had been surprised when war had been declared, and even more so when he had rushed to the Royal Navy recruitment office a day later to enlist only to be told he was ineligible to serve overseas. As a dock inspector, his was a reserved occupation. No matter how he had tried to convince the older man behind the recruiting desk to make an exception or to turn a blind eye, he had not been able to do so. The recruiter explained that there were some home front occupations of such import that their workers could not be removed from their posts. To do otherwise would be illegal. He would have to remain in Hull, performing his duties, for the duration.

'But why the constabulary? Why not fire-watching? That would give you the chance to sit down while doing your duty at least.'

The kettle whistled and she jumped to her feet to fetch it, distracting her and sparing him the need to explain his decision to answer the call for special constables as soon as it went out to men like him employed in reserved occupations.

It had taken him by surprise when his mother had impulsively married Len, a member of the merchant navy, shortly after war had been declared. She had never shown any interest in putting aside her role of widow until she met Len at an ambulance corps fundraiser. Peter had tried to warm to the man, telling himself that his mother had every right to happiness, especially since she had put him first throughout all the long years she had raised him on her own. But something about Len and his faint air of possessiveness had left him feeling leery of the older man.

Peter's concerns were confirmed when he unexpectedly

dropped by to visit his mother upon her return from their honeymoon trip. He had let himself into the house to find her huddled in bed, one eye swollen shut and her jawline covered in bruises. If not for the fact that Len had been back out at sea, Peter doubted he could have refrained from thrashing the man senseless.

When he urged her to have the marriage annulled or to divorce him for cruelty, she completely dismissed the suggestion. His mother believed in the sanctity of marriage regardless of the circumstances and refused to discuss it further. He stayed with her that night and the next, fetching her cups of Bovril and aspirin tablets. On the third day, when she shooed him out of the house, he had made straight for the nearest police station and volunteered to serve as a special constable. Even though she wasn't prepared to do anything to protect herself, he most certainly was.

Peter had made a point of meeting Len's ship as it returned to the docks. He would never forget the way the blood roared in his ears and the rest of the world seemed to fade from view as Len swaggered down the gangway and raised a hand in greeting, no sign of regret on his face. Before Peter had realized what was happening, he felt his fist reverberate against Len's jaw. His stepfather's body swayed and toppled from the dock and down into the murky water of the dock basin with a tremendous splash. Peter watched him thrash about for a long moment before tossing him a length of heavy rope lashed to a nearby piling.

Len's eyes had narrowed as he stood dripping on the dock, a group of fellow sailors gathering about him. One of the other sailors had shouted that Len ought to report him to the police. Peter had retrieved his shiny new warrant card from his jacket pocket and held it up for Len to see. Without a word, he turned his back and strode off. They hadn't spoken since, but Peter faithfully visited his mother at least once each week just to be sure Len hadn't forgotten the warning.

He watched her as she lifted the lid from the pot and poured the steaming water over the tea leaves. They sat in companionable silence as it steeped. As she poured them each a cup, she changed the subject, if only slightly.

'People are saying that crime has been on the rise ever since the war began. The police are lucky to have you, I'm sure,' she said, pushing the sugar bowl towards him.

He wasn't at all sure how to respond. The truth of the matter was that crime had escalated of late, but officials did not want to advertise that fact. It was thought that there were enough demoralizing aspects to life during wartime without admitting to the public that they were in more danger from their neighbors than they had been before the hostilities had commenced.

The blackout had provided cover for those intent on mischief and worse. And then there was the reduced number of officers on the force. Even with the voluntary special constables like him, the ranks were thin enough that it made it easier to get away with any manner of crimes. He didn't want to alarm her or to add grist to the rumor mill, but his mother always could tell when he ducked the truth.

'I wouldn't listen to everything you hear in the shops or on the street, but I would take special care to lock the doors and windows and to hold your handbag close when you go out, especially after dark,' he said.

'You know I take care with such things, even more so after what happened to Father O'Connell's bicycle,' she said, crossing her arms across her chest.

Peter lowered his fork and gave her his full attention. 'What about his bicycle?'

'It was stolen. I don't know what the world is coming to when there are those roaming about who will steal from a priest.'

Peter was far from convinced the world had ever been the sort of a place where even men of the cloth could be assured their lives would be shielded from crime, but that didn't mean he was not angered at the news. Father O'Connell had been their parish priest since he was a small lad and had taken a particular interest in Peter, filling in as a sort of a surrogate father figure when his own had been lost at sea.

'When did this happen?' he asked.

'A day or two ago, I suppose. You could look into it, couldn't you? That is the sort of thing constables do, isn't it?' She lifted her teacup to her lips and gazed at him wide-eyed over the rim as she took a sip.

Perhaps that was why she had rung up the boarding house and left word that she wished he would visit. It had been less than a week since the last time he had stopped by and he had been surprised to hear from her as soon as he had. He had chalked it up to a general sense of worry caused by the war. Knowing her, it was a desire to help Father O'Connell that had motivated her.

'Did he report it?'

'He told me about it. And I'm mentioning it to you. Isn't that enough?'

He couldn't help but suspect that this was her latest attempt at getting him to take an interest in the church. Despite her efforts, he wasn't one for attending mass or making confession.

'That's not really how it's done.'

She waved her hand dismissively. 'I promised Father O'Connell that he could count on you to get it back for him.'

He shook his head at her. Did she have any idea how difficult it might prove to find a single bicycle in a city the size of Hull? He didn't want to disappoint her, but the odds weren't in favor of retrieving it.

'I wish you hadn't made a promise I likely cannot keep.'

'Nonsense. With you looking for it, I am sure it is as good as found.'

'Did he have any idea who could have taken it?'

'No. Why would he?'

'We both know that Father O'Connell has some questionable contacts.'

She crossed her arms over her chest and shook her head. 'I know no such thing. I should like to think I raised you better than to make such a wicked suggestion about a man of God.'

Peter couldn't find fault with his upbringing and so did not see a reason to contradict her over something she found so distressing. It didn't change his opinion that Father O'Connell had some less than entirely law-abiding connections. It would be best to conclude the visit before any ill-feeling arose. He scraped back his chair and rose.

'I should be going. My volunteer shift starts soon, and the

sergeant is a stickler for timeliness. Thanks for the meal. It will set me up for the long night ahead.'

She nodded and held up a finger. He watched as she deftly sliced off a thick slab of cake and placed it in a small tin. She pressed the lid into place, then turned and held it out to him. As he reached for it, she pulled it just out of reach.

'Promise me you will look into the father's missing bicycle,' she said.

He leaned towards her and met her steady gaze. Fine lines ringed hazel eyes filled with a look of faith and expectation. 'I promise.'

THREE

Barton St Giles
Dear Frederick,
   If only you were here, perhaps Mother would be more reasonable . . .

It was the unnerving cry of a fox that woke her. She had fallen asleep to the sound of the droning of bees after indulging in a hearty bout of crying far from the prying ears of her fellow villagers. When she awoke, a heavy dew had drenched her garments and her exposed skin, and she felt almost chilled. The moon was new, and no light, save that of a few faint stars, reached her eyes as she stretched and got stiffly to her feet. She squinted to get her bearings in the dense shadows, made deeper still by the blackout. By the time she reached the door of the rectory, she heartily regretted her decision to head so far out of the village. Her mother was bound to be even more furious with her for staying out past dark.

The rectory was shrouded in darkness as she mounted the front steps and cautiously pressed down on the door latch. Although the heavy door swung quietly on its sturdy iron hinges, Wilhelmina held her breath, expecting to hear her mother's irate voice calling out to her. Instead, only the sound of the clock ticking on the mantlepiece and the creak of the floorboards under her own feet met her ears. Baffled, she moved on tiptoes from room to room, searching for her mother. The argument seemed less important somehow, and Wilhelmina was overcome by an eagerness to make amends. She would even make a peace offering by promising to work a shift with the Women's Voluntary Service later in the week. Surely that would go a long way towards softening any hard feelings between them.

But look as she might, her mother was nowhere to be found. Wilhelmina called out to her and only succeeded in attracting the attention of her father's curate, Ronald. At the sound of her voice, his balding head appeared at the top of the stairs.

'Your mother isn't here,' he said with a note of chiding in his voice.

'But she never goes out after dark if she can help it. Where can she be?' Wilhelmina asked.

'When I arrived back at the rectory after visiting some parishioners, I found a note from her on the kitchen table saying she had gone out in search of you. She said something about a quarrel and not wanting to go to bed angry.'

'I'm sure she'll be back soon. I'll just sit up and wait for her here,' Wilhelmina said.

A look of relief passed over Ronald's face, and he retreated up the stairs. Wilhelmina waited until she could no longer hear the curate's footsteps moving along the corridor above her, then settled herself in a chair near the window in the drawing room, which faced the street. She switched on a small lamp placed on a low tea table, then plucked a ball of navy-blue worsted from her workbasket. Heavy blackout curtains shrouded the window, but she was certain she would hear the moment her mother returned home.

Usually, the rhythm of a simple knitting project would work its soothing magic on her mind, and she would feel calm and capable of handling whatever came her way. But this evening, beset by worry and regret, each stitch felt like a struggle. She let the project fall abandoned into her lap as she went over and over again the cross words she had exchanged with her mother. She knew that she would have to apologize for being disrespectful, but truth be told, she did not know how she would bring herself to offer an apology. After all, she still felt like a wounded party. She regretted the incident with her mother, but as she replayed the argument in her mind, she could not honestly say that she felt any differently all these hours later than she had in the heat of the moment. She still wished to contribute something more than knitted caps for soldiers and fundraising efforts for the local fire brigade.

She was still mulling it over when she heard the clatter of feet on the steps outside the front door of the rectory. As she tucked her knitting back in its basket, she heard a knock. Had her mother forgotten her latchkey? She hurried across the room and turned the lock, flinging the door open wide. Constable Bridges stood on the steps, twisting his helmet around and around in his hands. Mildred Dawes hovered closely behind him.

'May we come in, Miss Harkness?' Constable Bridges asked.

Mrs Dawes pushed past him and rushed into the foyer. She reached out and grasped Wilhelmina's hands in her own, squeezing them so hard Wilhelmina winced.

'Oh, my dear, the most dreadful thing has happened. I knew I should be the one to come along and comfort you,' Mrs Dawes said. 'I'm sure it's what your mother would have wanted.'

Wilhelmina tried to take a step backwards, but Mrs Dawes's hands held her firmly in place like some sort of oversized bird of prey.

'Has something happened to my mother?' Wilhelmina looked over Mrs Dawes's shoulder and addressed her question to the constable. She knew from the look on his face that she did not want him to answer. Just then, Ronald descended the stairs and came to stand next to her.

'I'm afraid that your mother has been involved in an accident with a motorcar,' Constable Bridges said. A feeling of relief washed over Wilhelmina.

'You must be mistaken. My mother doesn't know how to drive. She went out for a walk earlier, didn't she, Ronald?' Wilhelmina said. Mrs Dawes tightened her grip even more.

'Yes, that's right. She left a note saying so,' Ronald said.

'Well, that's just it, you see,' Mrs Dawes said. 'Your mother was struck down by a motorcar as she was out walking. At least, the constable assumes it was a motorcar. You couldn't say for sure, could you?' Mildred Dawes turned towards the constable.

'Miss Harkness, I'm afraid there is no mistake. Your mother was struck down by some sort of vehicle which fled the scene of the accident. If it is any comfort, it seems unlikely that she suffered,' Constable Bridges said. Wilhelmina yanked her hands away from Mrs Dawes and stumbled backwards.

'Are you saying she was killed?' Wilhelmina asked, feeling as though she was floating over the scene and looking down on it from above.

'I am sorry but yes, she died at the scene of the accident,' the constable said. 'It's the blackout. We've had so many more incidents of injuries in the last year than ever before. Motorists simply can't see pedestrians until it's too late, especially on a moonless night like this one.'

'I blame the Germans,' Mildred said.

'Do you know why your mother went on a walk this evening?' Constable Bridges asked.

Wilhelmina's knees felt weak, and the sounds around her seemed to be coming from a great distance off. She thought she felt Ronald place one hand on her upper back and the other below her elbow. She vaguely felt herself being steered towards the parlor and urged into the chair in which she had waited in vain for her mother to return. She felt shell-shocked with shame. If only she had been forthright about her plans rather than sneaking off to enlist, perhaps her mother would have adjusted to the idea and none of this would have happened.

'She said something about parish business,' Ronald said. 'I cannot say more than that.' Wilhelmina felt his hand rest upon her shoulder. He gave it a slight squeeze as he lied to the constable.

'Is there anyone else we should inform? Do you have any other family you would like us to notify?' Constable Bridges asked. Wilhelmina's mind went blank. 'Other than your father, of course.'

'It's a very small family, Constable,' Mildred said. She had followed them into the parlor without Wilhelmina noticing. Her voice came as a surprise as it drifted across the room from the doorway. 'Martha had no family to my knowledge.'

'What about the rector?' Constable Bridges asked. 'Do you know how I can reach him?'

Wilhelmina felt a fresh wave of misery wash over her as she thought of her father receiving such terrible news while so far from home. Her breath caught in her throat as she noticed that the constable hadn't even asked about contacting Frederick.

'We've been sending letters to the War Office. Maybe they might be able to arrange word to him at the prisoner-of-war camp,' Wilhelmina said.

'Is there any family on your father's side that could come to be with you?' Constable Bridges asked.

'My father has a few distant cousins, but we've never met. I can't imagine troubling any of them to come,' Wilhelmina said.

'They ought to at least be informed,' Mildred said. 'It is only proper.'

Wilhelmina pressed her hands against the arms of the chair but felt Ronald's hand upon her shoulder urging her to remain seated.

'Your father's address book will be in his desk, won't it?' Ronald asked.

When Wilhelmina nodded, he exited the room and returned a few moments later with the small leather-bound volume in his hand. He passed it to the constable who carefully copied the information he needed into a small notebook before handing the address book back to Ronald. Wilhelmina noted the details carefully as though the entire world had slowed down to half speed.

'Of course, you will need me to stay, Wilhelmina,' Mildred said matter-of-factly as though Wilhelmina was a child.

Wilhelmina could think of nothing she needed less than Mildred Dawes fluttering about, spouting platitudes. Ronald must have felt the same. As Mildred made to sit, he stepped forward and placed his hand beneath her elbow.

'I think it would be best if Wilhelmina had some time to herself – a chance to take in what has happened. If you are needed, I will be sure to call on you,' he said as he propelled Mildred to the doorway.

Wilhelmina was hardly aware of Constable Bridges patting her on the shoulder before following the others out of the room. She waited for the sound of the heavy door swinging shut behind the visitors before she allowed herself to burst into tears.

In the days following the accident, evenings were the worst. Only a week earlier, the prospect of being cooped up in the dark night with her mother seemed an impossible chore. Now, the idea of spending that same evening alone, or in the presence of Ronald, was overwhelmingly bleak. Before, Wilhelmina would have headed out into the night for a walk or to socialize with someone else from the village. But somehow, after what had happened to her mother, she could not bring herself to leave the house once darkness fell.

Instead, she took up her customary position in the same armchair in the parlor and tried to concentrate on knitting up a helmet liner for some soldier stationed overseas. The night was a warm one and the wool slipping between her fingers felt sticky with each stitch begrudgingly moving across the knitting needles. In the past, she had found such an activity to be meditative, almost prayerful. Something about the motion of her hands in a smooth and steady rhythm allowed her mind to soar freely and to untangle any knotty problems that weighed her down. But since her mother's death, no such comfort could be found in the simple act of knitting or anything else. She knew she needed to think of a way forward, but she had no idea whatsoever how to do so.

She heard the front door latch followed by the sound of footsteps along the hallway. She looked up from her knitting as Ronald entered the room, a pile of correspondence clutched in his hand.

'The evening's post,' he said, holding it out to her.

'Just put it on the table there and I'll open it later,' she said.

'Really, Wilhelmina, I think you had best take yourself in hand a bit more,' Ronald said. 'At the very least, you could stir yourself sufficiently to take an interest in your letters.'

He crossed the room and thrust the sheaf of letters beneath

her nose. He stood waiting, rather too close for comfort, until she reached up and relieved him of them. With a nod of approval, he took a backward step and began pacing the room. Her heart squeezed with guilt as she spotted another letter addressed to her in Candace's familiar, rounded hand. She really must make a point of keeping her promise to write to her friend.

'I don't believe that being behind in my correspondence is worth getting yourself worked up about. Nor is it really any of your concern.'

Ronald halted his pacing and spun about to face her. 'It reflects poorly on me as the temporary rector and the Church as a whole for you to be so unable to face life's daily tasks. Refusing to deal with the post in a timely manner is just one example of how you have allowed yourself to become beset by melancholy.'

'I can't see that's the business of anyone besides me,' she said.

'Indeed, it is a matter of concern to others. Your behavior affects those around you far more than you seem to realize. In case you had forgotten, there are others who are losing loved ones unexpectedly on a daily basis. What sort of example does it set for the community if the rector's daughter is unable to lean on her faith and provide a moral example for others?' Ronald said, staring down at her.

Ronald had put his finger on one of the main difficulties a rector's family faced. Everything one did was a matter of public scrutiny. From the time she could talk, her parents had admonished her to think of the example she set for those around her. It was a heavy burden at the best of times and one that seemed impossible to shoulder since her mother's death.

'Are these your own thoughts or has someone encouraged you to reprimand me?' she asked.

She peered up at Ronald and glimpsed a thin sheen of perspiration clinging to his upper lip. So, she thought, he had been taken to task and she suspected she knew by whom.

'Certainly, it had occurred to me that you have been handling things poorly since the funeral. After all, we do reside under the same roof and it would be difficult for me not to have noticed your suffering. Mildred Dawes only reinforced my own thinking when she happened to broach the subject with me today,' Ronald said.

Of course, Mildred had an opinion on how the bereaved should comport themselves. And she would, of course, have shared that opinion with anyone within earshot. Wilhelmina marveled that it had taken so long for Mildred's comments to reach her.

'Did Mildred happen to have anything else to say on the subject of my behavior?' she asked.

Ronald dropped abruptly into the chair next to hers and once more leaned uncomfortably close.

'I'm glad you brought that up. Mildred impressed upon me the damage being done to both our reputations by dint of our living arrangements.'

'But nothing's changed about our living arrangements. How can they possibly have become objectionable?' she asked.

'Something important has changed, Wilhelmina. I have been made aware that the entire village is being corrupted by our example. It is thoroughly inappropriate for the two of us to live together under the same roof without the benefit of a chaperone.'

Wilhelmina's mind reeled. It had not occurred to her in the slightest that anyone with a ha'penny's worth of sense could possibly consider one might need to be chaperoned while in the presence of Ronald Kershaw. Certainly, he was a man who was not without his merits, but he was so rigorously upright in his comportment that the idea of any stain of scandal attaching to his snowy-white soul was impossible to entertain.

'Surely Mildred does not expect for us to move in a sort of guardian. Who does she propose would be qualified to serve in such a role? Herself?' she asked.

'No, she offered a rather more practical solution and one I am rather ashamed to say I had not thought of on my own,' Ronald said.

He leaned even closer and swallowed with apparent difficulty. Wilhelmina felt a knot gather tightly in her stomach.

'While I realize that this is not the most romantic of courtships, I believe that you could develop into a suitable wife who could be of much use to me in my career. And, if I may flatter myself, I am not without value to you as well. My profession is an honorable one, and while I could not promise you a lavish lifestyle, I can certainly assure you that you would want for none of your earthly needs. The Church would provide us with housing, as it has always done for your family, and we would be sufficiently fed and clothed. A marriage would provide you with far more financial security than does your current circumstance.'

'You have taken me completely by surprise. I have never considered such a match,' Wilhelmina said.

She hoped he would not be offended by her candor, but the words were out of her mouth before she considered them. While she had been relentlessly considering the direction her life would take in the weeks and months to come, she had never entertained the idea of becoming a rector's wife. Her mother's tasks and obligations had not been the sort that appealed to Wilhelmina in the least. In fact, they were among the reasons she had been so eager to join one of the services. The idea of stepping into what amounted to her dead mother's shoes sent chills running up her spine.

'I understand completely but hope you will give the matter careful consideration. I do not wish to alarm you, but I think you should know that your position at the rectory cannot remain assured. With your father unable to return to the parish indefinitely and your mother, sadly, no longer fulfilling her duties, your place here is a tenuous one and the appearance of impropriety between us has placed my own position here at risk,' he said.

She fixed her eyes firmly on Ronald's large Adam's apple to anchor the room that had begun to spin before her eyes. She had been so eager to leave Barton St Giles when she signed her name at the bottom of the enlistment form. But she had always expected she would return on leave and that her family and all the rest of the village would be much as she had left them. While she knew that things were irreparably altered, she had not considered she might have no place at the rectory.

Undoubtedly, Ronald's suggestion had merit, but even though she had never been the sort given to flights of romantic fancy, Wilhelmina was firmly of the opinion that a marriage should be built upon more than simple convenience and propriety. Ronald's proposal could not have been delivered in a less tantalizing manner.

She could not, however, simply state such a thing to Ronald. She needed to give more thought to her next move before giving Ronald an answer. Fortunately, he was just the sort of man who valued caution and contemplation.

'Thank you for bringing this to my attention and for your generous offer of marriage. I would ask you to allow me some time to think it over before I give you an answer. I am sure you will agree it is not the sort of thing one should rush into,' she said, getting to her feet.

Ronald rose and nodded. 'Your level-headedness does you credit. I am more certain than ever that we would make a fine match. But, whatever your answer, I insist that this is the very last night we remain under the same roof unwed. Mildred has kindly offered you the use of her spare room as of tomorrow and I have accepted on your behalf.'

Wilhelmina felt his watery blue eyes boring into her back as she gathered up the post and hurried out of the door and off towards the relative peace of her own bedchamber.

FOUR

Hull
Special Constable Upton's PNB

Although it was growing late and Peter was due for his shift with the police, he couldn't shirk from fulfilling his promise to his mother to stop in and speak to Father O'Connell about the theft of his bicycle. Not for the first time, he felt grateful for the fact that he had spent all his life in Hull, much of it roaming the streets as an unsupervised young boy with more time on his hands than sense. Peter's pace slowed as he turned down the avenue leading towards the church steps. Although he would not call himself a lapsed Catholic, he would have to admit he had not made a priority of attending services ever since war had been declared.

He could have blamed his lack of attendance on an over-filled schedule, but he knew in his heart of hearts that there was more to it than that. The truth was, there was just something about the atrocity of war that made the idea of an all-knowing and all-powerful God difficult to swallow. As much as he found the notion of someone robbing the local priest of his prized possession to be repugnant and worthy of police attention, Peter found himself wishing he was not the officer who had agreed to look into the matter. Although he felt he owed Father O'Connell an enormous debt of gratitude for his kindness throughout Peter's childhood, both to him and to his mother, he couldn't help but wish he did not feel a need to explain to the priest why he had not been at mass of late.

Still, there was nothing for it but to do his duty. His mother would surely ask him about his progress the next time she saw him. Peter mounted the shallow steps that led up to the large carved doors of the church. He had no need to push them open as they always stood wide and welcoming as long as the weather permitted it. As Peter entered the sanctuary, he squinted through the low light in search of the priest. As his eyes slowly adjusted, he spotted Father O'Connell's slim form emerging from a door at the far end of the church, his long arms clutching a stack of books.

'Is that you, Peter? I hardly recognize you after so many weeks without darkening the church's doors,' the priest called out in a voice that had not quite lost all traces of his homeland. Peter's mother had said that Father O'Connell always reminded her of the men back home with his warm smile and melodious voice. 'I don't suppose you've come to confess some misdeeds, now have you?'

Peter crossed the sanctuary to meet him at the halfway point and extended his hands to relieve the priest of some of his burden.

'No, Father, I'm here on an errand for my mother,' he said.

'I suppose if anything would bring you into the church nowadays, it would be an errand for that good woman, bless her soul,' Father O'Connell said. 'So, what is it that I can do for the two of you?'

He pointed to a pew and waited while Peter sat down on it and placed his uniform cap on his knee. The seat felt hard and a slight chill seeped through Peter's trousers despite the summer warmth in the evening air. Father O'Connell settled in on the creaking wooden boards beside Peter and draped a gaunt arm over the back of the pew.

'Actually, I'm here about something that my mother hoped I could do for you,' Peter said. Father O'Connell cocked his head slightly and his eyes widened beneath his bushy gray eyebrows. 'She mentioned that someone seems to have helped himself to your bicycle.'

Father O'Connell grimaced and nodded. 'A sore trial it's been to have lost it, I must admit,' he said. 'Not for myself, mind, but for the people who have come to depend upon its use.'

'Why don't you tell me what happened?' Peter said.

He slipped his hand inside his vest pocket and removed his small police-issued notebook and the stub of a pencil. He flipped to the next fresh sheet of paper and turned his gaze towards the priest's face.

'I don't want you to have the impression that the boy was careless in any way because I don't believe that was the case,' Father O'Connell said. 'If anything, I would say that he took better care of the bicycle than I did myself. He was always washing it or polishing the chrome or making sure that the tires were properly inflated.'

'Which boy was this?' Peter asked.

'Young Mickey Jamison,' the father said.

'Why did he need to borrow it?' Peter asked.

'He'd got a job as a delivery boy at Folsom's butcher shop and a bicycle was necessary in order to keep it. His family needs the money he could bring in, and when I heard about his difficulties, I offered to lend it to him on the days that he worked, providing he returned it for my use in the evenings. You know that I rely upon it to pay calls on the elderly and the shut-ins in the parish,' Father O'Connell said.

Peter nodded. The priest was a familiar sight as he swooped through the streets of Hull on his bicycle, his long, thin legs pumping and his cassock flapping about him.

'Was the bicycle stolen while it was in Mickey's possession?' Peter asked.

'It was taken on a day he had borrowed it, but as I understand it, it was stolen while he was in a residence making a delivery,' the priest said.

'So it was stolen right in broad daylight?' Peter asked.

'Indeed, it was. I don't know what the world's come to that a body cannot leave a bicycle unattended for a few moments and expect to find it still there upon one's return,' the priest said, shaking his head slowly. 'Young Mickey was beside himself over the whole affair. He didn't want to come to tell me for fear of what I'd say. I'm rather afraid he thought I might ask him to pay for a new one out of his wages.'

Peter knew a little bit about the Jamison family, and he could not say he found it all that surprising that young Mickey would be anxious about being suspected of complicity in the bicycle theft. His family was not one of the most criminally inclined that Peter had heard tell of at the police station, but they had had more than their fair share of run-ins with the law. One of the reasons that any wages Mickey was able to bring home would be so useful to the family came down to the fact that his father was in jail as often as he was out of it. From petty theft to drunk and disorderly conduct, he was hauled up before the magistrate at the Hull police court often enough that there was no way he could be relied upon to bring in a steady wage.

He did, however, seem to be home often enough to help produce more mouths for his wife to find some way of feeding. Mickey, who couldn't have been more than fourteen, was one of the older Jamison children. If Peter remembered correctly, there were at least four others younger than him. No matter how hard the delivery boy for a butcher worked, earning enough to make amends for a stolen bicycle would have felt a daunting task.

'When did this all happen?' Peter asked.

'Three days ago. But Mickey only told me about it a day later when his mother marched him in here, dragging him by the ear. The poor boy was scared half to death, although I'm not sure if he was more concerned about telling me my bicycle had been stolen or frightened of his mother who seemed to be in a white-hot lather about it all,' Father O'Connell said with a chuckle.

'Did he tell you exactly what happened?' Peter asked.

'To tell you the truth, I was more concerned about smoothing Mrs Jamison's ruffled feathers than I was about questioning young Mickey. As I didn't expect anything he had to say would lead to me getting it back, it seemed a foolish waste of time and energy to fret over the details. You don't expect you're going to be able to find it, do you?'

'I'm certainly going to give it my best try. But I'll have to speak to Mickey myself since you haven't anything else to tell me,' Peter said. 'Do you happen to have his current address?'

The Jamisons were the sort to move house regularly, often a few steps ahead of a bailiff. Every time Peter had seen Mr Jamison up before the bench, he had given a different address.

Father O'Connell nodded. 'He and his family have moved over to Jarrett Street, number forty-three, I believe. But you'll get more out of the boy if you manage to speak to him away from his mother,' Father O'Connell said.

'I'll stop in at Folsom's to have a chat with him,' Peter said. 'You haven't heard of any other crimes lately, have you? My mother said there has been some trouble in the neighborhood.'

'You know I cannot tell you what I know about that sort of thing, lad,' he said as he crossed his arms over his chest.

'I'll take that as a yes. You might consider locking the church doors for at least a portion of the day or the evening,' Peter said.

Father O'Connell shook his head vigorously. 'The troubles of our times make it so that people need unfettered access more than ever to the one who knows all our destinies. I could not possibly consider locking the doors of the church, no matter what the reasons,' he said.

'I just hate to think of you getting coshed over the head one night because some hooligan takes the notion to make off with the brasses,' Peter said.

'I know how to take care of myself, you know. I've had plenty of practice, whether holding my own against civilian ruffians or those who were members of the constabulary,' the priest said.

Peter felt chagrined. While it was not something about which they spoke with any degree of frequency, Peter did know that Father O'Connell had not been at all pleased when Peter volunteered for the police department. Prior to his migration to England, Father O'Connell had presided over a parish where all of his congregants had reason to say that an English policeman was the worst form of enemy.

'I won't offer you any more unsolicited advice. And I'll make every effort to locate your bicycle.' He picked up his cap and brushed off a bit of dust from the brim. Father O'Connell stood and stepped out into the aisle to allow Peter to pass. The older man extended his hand and Peter grasped it. Before he could pull away, the priest spoke again.

'I hope to see you again before long,' he said. 'I know you are working yourself to the bone, inspecting the docks and performing your duties as a constable, but there is no excuse for missing mass for so many months in a row. By now I expect you have a great number of things you would feel better for confessing,' he said with a wink.

FIVE

Barton St Giles
Dear Mildred,
   Ronald has apprised me of your concerns and your offer of hospitality . . .

Alone in her room, Wilhelmina found she could not stop herself from pacing, despite the unnerving creak of the floorboards beneath her feet. Ronald's offer was as unwelcome as it was unexpected. While she would not be so foolish as to disregard the value of a marriage built upon the firm foundation of common interests and complementary temperaments, she had never expected to accept an offer made with no pretense of affection whatsoever. That said, she was alarmed to consider the precariousness of her situation. Until now she had not considered how the loss of her mother might affect her role in the community. Ronald had correctly assessed her financial situation as well.

The modern view of marriage seemed to favor impetuous decisions and a spirit of adventure rather than the sort of cut-and-dried practical arrangement Ronald had suggested. In fact, marrying a soldier who was about to ship out was almost a fashion at present. Not that she was inclined to be swayed by that sort of pressure, but it did throw Ronald's proposition into stark contrast. There was more to her resistance to his offer than simply a lack of romantic interest, however. While Ronald had every right to take measures to preserve his reputation, it was not his place to accept Mildred's invitation on her behalf without consulting her first. If he felt at ease acting so high-handedly while in a position of a mere housemate, she shuddered to think how he might behave as her husband. No, it was clear to her that a life with Ronald would be a mistake from the very beginning.

Her mother had always chided her for being too eager to launch herself into situations without considering the consequences or taking advice from others. She desperately wished she had someone with whom she could mull over her options. In better times, Frederick or Candace would have been the ones she would have turned to if she found herself unsure of which path to take. Her brother was nowhere to be found, but she did owe Candace a letter.

She dropped into the seat at her small writing desk and opened the letter from her friend to take her mind off Ronald's proposal and her own precarious living arrangements, if only for a short while. Candace's note was filled with newsy tidbits from her new life, including descriptions of the other recruits and the officers to whom she would report. It was clear from the content of the letter that news of Wilhelmina's bereavement had not yet reached her. She really ought to let Candace know not to expect her to join her in the ranks of the ATF, but somehow she couldn't muster the energy to pen such painful news, at least not yet. Despite her interest in signing up and her need for employment as well as a new place to stay, she could not bring herself to ignore her mother's insistence that she refrain from joining the services. She was simply going to have to think of something else.

She reached for the remaining pile of letters. Her heart sank as she quickly flipped through the stack of post. No envelope bearing her brother's tidy hand was tucked in among all the others. It would be a miracle if such a letter had arrived. She turned her attention to the rest of the correspondence.

Carefully, she slid open one thin envelope after another. As she read through the cards, it once again became clear to her how many lives her mother had touched with her simple acts of thoughtfulness and her unrelenting willingness to turn her hand to whichever tasks needed doing, no matter how thankless or menial.

Wilhelmina had always seen her as someone who was acutely aware of her duties and unflinchingly determined to carry them out. Looking down at the surface of the desk covered in condolence notes and remembrances from those lives that her mother had touched, she felt overwhelmed with a new perspective of all that she had given to others.

Wilhelmina thought once again of Ronald's proposal and felt all the more miserable about her disinclination to accept it in light of how much value the life of a rector's wife could have, at least if she behaved as her mother had done.

Towards the bottom of the stack sat an envelope, thicker than the others and made of higher-quality paper. The handwriting was unfamiliar to her, as was the address. She had no notion of connections her mother might have had in the city of Kingston upon Hull. She slit the envelope carefully in order to preserve the address. Given the effort the writer had made, a note of response would be required. Instead of the usual half sheet of thin, wartime paper, she discovered a handsome card depicting a young woman in a brightly colored dress standing at the seashore. It was quite unlike any other note of condolence she had ever seen.

My dearest Billie (I do hope you will indulge the nickname. I cannot help but think Wilhelmina rather a mouthful, and unfortunately Germanic at present, don't you agree?),
    When I received word of your mother's passing, I was

overcome with the desire to make myself acquainted with you. I feel it has been remiss of us all to have allowed the branches of our family to have grown apart over time through a mere lack of bother. Between your mother's death and the newspaper notice of your father's recent internment overseas, I feel the lack of connection all the more acutely.

Which brings me to the practical purpose of my desire to contact you. I am eager to provide any support within my power at what must be an immensely difficult time. I have always found that nothing does one so much good as a change of scenery. While I cannot pretend to have any notion of your present attachments and obligations, I should be very surprised if an excursion, especially one of some distance, would not do you incalculable good.

Should you feel inclined to make the journey to Kingston upon Hull, please know there is always room for you in my home at any time. I most eagerly look forward to making your acquaintance.

Your cousin,

Lydia Harkness

Wilhelmina leaned back in the chair, feeling a wave of surprise flow over her entire being. While it had never been a secret that her father had a cousin named Lydia, she was almost never spoken of. When asked about his extended family, her father would always say that his own father and his uncle had drifted apart through no fault on the part of either of them. As a result, she knew very little of his uncle's circumstances or his descendants.

Wilhelmina and Frederick had enjoyed speculating about what their far-flung cousins might be like and what sort of lives they might lead. Frederick, in particular, was a remarkably imaginative person and would occasionally make up outrageous stories for them all. She had particularly liked one he had invented casting them as a troupe of circus performers traveling the world and dazzling the masses with a renowned fire-eating trapeze act.

But there, revealed in a confident, elegant hand, was an

invitation to discover what at least one of them was really like. Wilhelmina was overtaken by an urge to race down the hallway holding the letter aloft, calling out her brother's name as she did so. Frederick would be utterly delighted to have the opportunity to meet Cousin Lydia in the flesh. But although she could picture an impish look of glee on his face when she told him of the letter, the sad fact remained that he was nowhere she could reach him.

She pushed back her chair and crossed the room to a bookcase tucked beneath the eaves. Selecting an atlas of the world she had pilfered from the rectory library after her father and Frederick were shipped overseas, she carried it to the bed and opened the page featuring a detailed map of the United Kingdom. She swept her gaze carefully over the names printed on the nation's familiar outline, searching carefully for the city of Kingston upon Hull. She knew from Lydia's invitation that it must be along the coast somewhere. Wilhelmina had some notion of it being to the north. She ran her finger from her own village in Wiltshire almost as far as York and found it tucked along the river Humber a few miles in from the northeast coast of England.

She returned to the bookcase once more for a train timetable. With the faintest stirring of excitement, she checked for trains leaving a few hours hence. The next available train was scheduled to depart in only six hours. Without hesitation, she crept quietly out of the bedroom and along the passageway past the room that had so recently been occupied by her mother. She held her breath as she made her way down the stairs, carefully avoiding the treads most inclined to groan loudly underfoot. In a cupboard beneath the stairs, she located a dusty valise. She crept silently back to her room and placed it on the bed before turning to the wardrobe and emptying it of most of its contents.

For the first time in her life, Wilhelmina was grateful that a rector's daughter did not have the wherewithal to afford a larger, more glamorous wardrobe. All of her clothing fit neatly into the bag. At least, all the clothing that would be appropriate for the season. She left her winter coat and hat as well as a sturdy pair of boots in the wardrobe. She could always send for them if it became clear that her stay would be of long duration. She once again looked over the bookcase and selected a number of her favorite volumes to tuck in alongside a pad of sketching paper and a tin of charcoal pencils.

She changed into a traveling outfit, retrieved her handbag and evaluated the contents of her purse. If she was careful, she had sufficient funds to purchase a ticket for the journey and perhaps some refreshments along the way. She snapped her purse shut and tucked it back into her handbag before seating herself at the desk once more.

She penned a note to Ronald, thanking him for his generous offer. She wished him well and hoped he would find a wife far more suited than she to the life he had in mind. At the bottom of the note, she included Lydia's address in case of emergencies and also for her post to be forwarded for the time being. Then she lay down on the bed fully clothed and far too excited to sleep, waiting for the dawn to break and her journey to begin.

SIX

Barton St Giles
Dear Sirs,
Please suspend my subscription to the Wiltshire Woman's Weekly *until further notice as I will be away for some time . . .*

As soon as the morning light began to creep through the merest crack at the bottom edge of the blackout curtains covering her bedroom window, Wilhelmina swung her stockinged feet from the bed and rested them quietly on the floor. The small clock on her bedside table indicated it was not yet five in the morning. She fastened the buckles on the valise, double-checked the contents of her handbag and gathered a pair of shoes into her hand.

The doorknob turned smoothly in her grasp and the hinges made no sound as she eased the door open. She made her way down the hallway and on to the stairs without any sign she had roused Ronald. She placed the note she had written to him on the blotter in the room that had been her father's study. Ronald had made himself very much at home there during the rector's absence, and she felt certain he would see it that morning.

With a lump in her throat and a final glance around the room, she took her leave of it, unsure how much time would pass before she returned. Or, for that matter, whether she would return at all. As things stood, there was no guarantee her father would be able to take up his duties as the rector there again. She slipped down the hallway and out of the front door, stopping on the stone steps to slip on her shoes before striding off in the direction of the train station.

During the long hours of the night, she had worried she might encounter a tradesperson or the milkman on his delivery round who would make so bold as to inquire as to her purpose, but not a soul was about between the rectory and the train station. Although the man selling tickets behind the glass partition raised his eyebrows when she approached, he was too well mannered to ask for details as he handed her a second-class ticket to London. No other passengers boarded the train when it pulled up half an hour later.

As she settled back in her seat, clasping and unclasping her hands in her lap, she wondered if she was making the biggest mistake of her life. But no, she thought, she had already done that when she had stayed out so late the night of her mother's death.

She must have fallen asleep – hardly any wonder after the wakeful night she had passed. She awoke when the train lurched to a stop and the clamor of other passengers gathering their possessions filled the air. She got to her feet and retrieved her luggage, worried she might miss her connecting train. While she had been to London once before, it had been many years before, and she had never undertaken a journey to a large city on her own. In truth, she had never undertaken any journey by herself.

A wave of nervousness swept over her, setting her stomach aquiver. She scolded herself and imagined what Frederick would do, before reaching for her bag and stepping off the train. She looked about her in an effort to get her bearings. Throngs of people of every sort streamed past her, going about their business with an urgency she rarely encountered in Barton St Giles. A man bumped into her and tipped his hat in apology as she made her way towards the center of the station, where she consulted a large sign indicating train platforms and the destinations. Her gaze landed on a sign marked *Tickets* and she hurried towards it to join the end of a long queue. Upon reaching the front of the line, she was confronted by an elderly man with a scowl etched deeply into his face.

'Where to, miss?' he asked.

'I'd like a second-class ticket for the next train to Kingston upon Hull, please.'

'Hull is in the defense zone. Any holiday-making trips to the seaside are no longer allowed, young lady. Do you have legitimate business there?' he asked, leaning forward and peering at her with an intensity she rarely felt from strangers or even her intimates.

Her heart thumped wildly in her chest. Of course, she had read about the new regulations governing the defense of the coastline stretching from the far north all the way down to the southernmost boundary of the nation. But like so many people who lived in the interior, the coast seemed a nebulous sort of delineation. Was it possible that Kingston upon Hull could be included in the rules governing the coastline? It was several miles inland, surely, and not one of the places one associated with being under immediate threat of invasion from the sea.

If the city was included in the regulations, would her cousin's letter serve as a legitimate matter of business in Kingston upon Hull? She had no idea whatsoever which sorts of matters fell under such a description. The ticket seller drummed his gnarled fingers on the scarred wooden counter stretching between them and cocked an unruly white eyebrow at her. She felt the woman in the queue behind her take an impatient step closer. Ronald's face flitted past her mind's eye and she stiffened her posture.

'My cousin is in residence there and has need of me,' she said with what she hoped was far more confidence than she actually

felt. The man shrugged his bony shoulders and reached his hand
out for the fare.

'Suit yourself. Mind you, there are no refunds should you
arrive in Hull and discover you aren't permitted to leave the
station. There will be no free fare from there to anywhere else
either.'

He slid her change along with the ticket under the glass
partition and barked for the next customer before Wilhelmina
had time to place her ticket and the few remaining coins into
her handbag.

SEVEN

Hull
Special Constable Upton's PNB

The police station buzzed with activity. Officers streamed
in and out through the front door and along the corridors.
Benches lining the long hallway opposite the sergeant's
desk were stuffed cheek by jowl with the citizens of Hull who
found themselves in need of assistance, had a crime to report
or simply wished to make a nuisance of themselves. At least
that's how it appeared to Peter as he made his way towards the
front desk.

'A long day at the docks?' Sergeant Skelton said, peering
down at Peter.

The sergeant was a skyscraper of a man with an extra two
or three stone of solid home cooking spread over his vast frame.
The overhead lights bounced off his gleaming pate as he cocked
his head to one side and raised an eyebrow questioningly at
Peter.

'It wasn't dock business that kept me. I had a stop at St Brigid's
I needed to make on my way in this evening,' Peter said.

'Did you now? I hadn't taken you for much of a churchgoer,'
Sergeant Skelton said, crossing his long arms over his beefy
chest.

'I'm not, as a rule. I stopped to ask Father O'Connell about a theft,' Peter said.

The sergeant looked up at him sharply and leaned across the desk.

'There was a theft at St Brigid's?' he asked. 'The little bastards. What won't they get up to next? Kids have been running amok since the schools closed. I knew it would come to something like this before long. I say evacuate them all to Canada and make it a problem for the provinces. What did they take?' he asked.

Peter shook his head. 'No one broke into the church. It was about a bicycle,' Peter said.

'You're late for your shift because of a bicycle theft?' Sergeant Skelton asked.

'A theft is a theft, isn't it?' he asked.

Peter could see no reason why the theft of a bicycle should be of any less importance than a break-in at the church. Besides, if it came down to it, stealing a priest's bike was tantamount to steeling from the Catholic Church.

'There's a difference. Breaking into a church takes a special sort of nerve and rarely occurs. Bicycle thefts are commonplace. Do you have any idea how many bikes go missing every year in the city?'

'I've no idea, sir.'

Peter had never given it any thought. He had never had a bicycle of his own to worry about it being stolen. He supposed he ought to have given it some consideration since he was well aware of how much those who owned them relied upon them. With petrol rationing, bicycles were more useful than ever.

'I don't know the exact number, but I can tell you it is a lot. More often than not, it comes down to juvenile deviltry and high spirits. I expect the priest's bicycle will show up before the end of the week, abandoned not far from where it was taken.'

'The end of the week may be too much time. It's not just Father O'Connell who has been affected. He lent it to Mickey Jamison for his job as a butcher's delivery boy. But the lad cannot keep his position with nothing to make his rounds on. It seems to me that that's just as important as whether or not someone nicked a chalice or some other useless metal object from the altar at St Brigid's,' Peter said.

'Mickey Jamison,' Sergeant Skelton said, drumming his fingers on the patrol roster laid on the counter in front of him. 'He's not related to Jimmy Jamison, is he?'

Peter nodded. 'He's his eldest son.'

Sergeant Skelton let out a sigh and shook his head. 'What I wouldn't give to once again be an idealistic young copper like you. Have you considered the possibility that young Mickey takes after his old man? He could have pretended the thing was stolen and then flogged it.'

The sergeant's suggestion left Peter feeling uneasy. Father O'Connell had a habit of seeing the best in his parishioners, especially young boys. Peter had benefited from that attitude himself on more occasions than he could recall. But the fact that Father O'Connell only saw the potential in the young people he encountered did not mean they were all worthy of such expectation. Peter himself had disappointed the priest from time to time, and there was nothing to say that Sergeant Skelton was mistaken in suggesting Mickey might have stolen the bicycle himself and sold it on to another. Still, a crime had been committed, and Peter wasn't one to brush such things under the rug.

'No matter who stole it, the fact remains that Father O'Connell has been deprived of its use. I'd like to look into it one way or another. If Mickey is responsible, maybe an early run-in with the law will discourage him from following in his father's footsteps any further. You could consider it a form of preventative policing.'

Sergeant Skelton raised an eyebrow at him again, then offered a rare, weary smile. 'You know, I was worried that all of you special constables might end up being more trouble than you were worth, but it sounds as though, at least in your case, we might just make a proper copper of you.'

It was a familiar concern and not one only voiced by Sergeant Skelton. Nobody had been entirely sure why the powers that be had made the fateful decision not to make police officers a reserved occupation. Perhaps someone in the War Office thought that the sort of man who was used to the physical danger of being a constable would be the ideal candidate to serve as a soldier as well. What they hadn't considered was how wartime conditions would provide ideal breeding grounds for criminality on the home front.

At a time when the police were more needed than ever, those who were willing to serve were less prepared than in the past to do so. As a special constable, Peter was a part-time volunteer who squeezed in his efforts around the hours of his full-time reserved occupation at the docks. There were members of the constabulary and even the general public who held the opinion that the special constables were only playing at being police officers.

But Peter could not agree. To his way of thinking, every officer seen out and about in the city served as a deterrent to criminal behavior. He believed that just his presence in uniform on the streets of Hull gave a much-needed boost of morale to law-abiding citizens. And if he could make it at least a little bit harder for those bent on crime, he would consider it a job well done.

'Does that mean you think I should look into it?' Peter asked.

'If it doesn't keep you from patrolling your patch, I don't see why you shouldn't see what you can find out. With any luck, you'll recover the good father's bicycle and discover that young Mickey isn't to blame to boot. Now, get on out there before I change my mind and ask you to deal with this lot.'

With that, he beckoned one of the men sitting slouched on a bench opposite to stand before him. As the man staggered up beside him, Peter could smell the spirits wafting from his breath, his skin and even his clothing. Peter took the opportunity to make his escape just as the man started to retch and Sergeant Skelton hollered for someone to fetch a bucket. He felt a surge of purpose swell up in his chest. He shot one last glance at the sergeant's desk where the drunkard was making even more of a mess of things, then strode back out through the police station door.

EIGHT

London
Dear Candace,

I am so sorry to have been so delayed in writing to you. Much has happened since I said goodbye to you in front of the recruiting office. Perhaps by now you have received word from someone in the village of my mother's accident. I still cannot believe that she is gone and that our last words were ones of anger. Each morning when I awake, even before I open my eyes, my first thought is that she is still dead and there is nothing I can do to change what I did and what I said.

You of all people will see the irony in the fact that, as a result of her passing, Ronald has made me an offer of marriage. I am quite certain my mother would have been utterly delighted by such a turn of events. Before you begin shouting at this letter, allow me to assure you that I have no intention of accepting. In fact, I have received an invitation from my mysterious cousin, Lydia, to stay with her at her home in Kingston upon Hull. I leaped at the chance for a change of scenery and the chance to grieve out from under the kind but watchful eyes of the village. They have been very good to me, but I must confess to feeling hemmed in by their well-intentioned concern.

But enough about me. Your life as an enlisted woman sounds so interesting, and I appreciate that you were able to spare the time to write to me. I so enjoyed hearing about the routine, the other girls and your terrifying sergeant.

When you have time, I hope you will write to me at my cousin's address. I will be in agonies wondering if you managed to sneak back into the barracks after curfew as

you planned or if you were caught. You made the conse-
quences sound dire indeed!
   Love,
   Wilhelmina

The second leg of the journey was far less restful than the first. The train was not crowded, and apart from a middle-aged man in a fawn-colored suit who devoted the entirety of his attention to a paperback detective novel, there was no one in Wilhelmina's compartment. Field after field of English countryside slid past the window as she wondered if she would be able to complete her journey and what she would do if she was turned away.

She had sufficient money to cover the fare to Kingston upon Hull with too little left over for a return ticket. Contacting Ronald to ask for money was out of the question. She would not like to trouble her cousin for funds as they were not yet acquainted, and Lydia might feel uncomfortable as she was the one who encouraged Wilhelmina to place herself in the predicament in the first place.

As the hours passed, she was glad to have remembered a book of her own to read. Even though she had no complaints about the story, she found herself restlessly abandoning the volume in her lap again and again, too distracted by thoughts of what her arrival in Hull might hold to concentrate on the storyline. Finally, she surrendered all pretense of reading and gave herself over to simply staring out of the window.

As the hours went by, the landscape began to change subtly. The villages with their low buildings and surrounding woods gave way to larger buildings pressed more tightly together. The inside of the train compartment grew warm as the day progressed, and her traveling companion thoughtfully opened the window in order to let in a cooling breeze. As she felt the train slow to a halting chug, she noticed a sort of a briny scent wafting through the cabin. From her perusal of a map of the area the night before, she knew that Kingston upon Hull, while connected via the river Humber, was several miles inland from the sea. She had not expected a salty tang to fill the air.

It was late in the afternoon as the train pulled into the station and her traveling companion offered to lower her valise from the rack above their heads. Then he tipped his hat at her and was gone. Even though they had spent no time in conversation, Wilhelmina suddenly felt more alone than she had all day as she watched his back retreating down the platform.

She gripped the handle of her bag tightly and stepped out of her compartment. As she approached the steps leading off the train, she noticed soldiers all along the platform near each of the train doors. The station was crowded with people bustling from one spot to another. A sort of amorphous queue formed around each of the soldiers as they waved those disembarking from the train towards them.

Wilhelmina paused at the bottom step. The soldier nearest her held his hand out for papers from a fellow passenger. While his head was bent over what an elderly woman placed in his hand, she felt the temptation to try to sneak past. She quickly edged off the step and stepped in behind a broad man wearing a wide-brimmed hat.

Her heart hammered in her chest as she worked her way along the platform, shielding herself from view by carefully choosing one large man after another to serve as a screen. The noise of the street grew louder and louder as she closed the gap between herself and the station door. Just as she was close enough to feel a breeze from the street blow across the threshold, a hand shot out and wrapped around her arm.

'You didn't really think a girl as pretty as you would slip past a group of soldiers without notice, now did you?'

She stopped and turned, hoping she appeared surprised to have been halted.

'Whatever do you mean?' she asked, widening her eyes as far as she could.

'I mean I feel a great swell of hope about our chances of beating the Jerries if someone with so little ability to sneak about has been hired to spy for them. Please make my week and tell me you are an enemy agent,' the soldier said.

A wave of righteous indignation swept over her and drove off the low growl of anxiety that had plagued her ever since the ticket seller in London had warned her of difficulties entering Hull. She had never entertained the notion that anyone could mistake her for a spy. She thought of herself as altogether too British for such a possibility. And if she was to be entirely truthful, a bit too ordinary to boot. 'What an absurd suggestion.'

'Absurd or not, I shall need to see some identification.' He stared down at her, his hand still tightly clutching her upper arm. His uniform was a bit too large for him, and a dollop of some sort of brown sauce clung to the front of his shirt. He reminded her uncannily of a boy with whom she had attended primary school.

Wilhelmina lifted her handbag and pulled out her identification card. 'I am a visitor to this city, and I can assure you this is not the sort of welcome that would recommend a second trip,' she said, hoping he would be as easy to influence as her former schoolmate had been.

From the way he cocked an eyebrow at her, she thought it unlikely. He tightened his grip ever so slightly as he read over the information printed on her identity card.

'Well, Miss Wilhelmina Harkness, I am duty-bound to inform you that visitors to the defense district are strictly forbidden. Without a legitimate reason for entering the city, I shall have to require you turn yourself right around and board a train bound for the interior.'

'And what exactly constitutes legitimate business?' she asked, placing her free hand on her hip and tilting her face up to stare straight back at him.

'Traveling salesmen with business cards from their employers, armament factory workers with the papers to verify their positions, servicemen and women with orders to report to Hull. Even residents who have been traveling outside of the city and are returning home. But holidaymakers and sightseers are not allowed.'

'What about someone here to join the household of one of the city's permanent residents?' she asked.

'Perhaps that sort of person might be permitted to enter. Are you planning to move here for the long run?' he asked.

Wilhelmina dug into her handbag and drew out the envelope containing the letter of invitation from Lydia. She handed it to him and held her breath as he released his grip upon her person and read through the message.

She forced herself to exhale as he folded the letter and handed it back to her.

'I am sorry to have had to question you, miss, and to know about the troubles with your parents. I meant no offense,' he said.

'I'm sure you were only doing your duty when you stopped me,' she said.

'Just because something is a duty doesn't mean it cannot also be a pleasure, Wilhelmina. Or is it Billie?'

A warm flush spread up the back of Wilhelmina's neck. She hoped it had not also appeared on her cheeks. Most of the young men in the village had been reluctant to make flirtatious remarks to the rector's daughter. She had little experience of such banter and felt tongue-tied. But mixed in with the flirting comment was an appealing question, although perhaps not the one he intended. Kingston upon Hull represented a new chapter in life, an opportunity to become more than she had been in the past. With a jolt, she realized she could be anyone she wished.

'My friends call me Billie,' she said.

'Billie it is, then. If I wasn't on duty, I would offer to escort you to your cousin's house in order to leave you with a better impression of the people of Hull,' he said, giving her arm a gentle squeeze before releasing it.

'That is more than kind of you, but your duty must come first, of course,' she said, relieved not to have to take him up on his offer.

An unwelcome overture from a man was what had sent her to Hull in the first place. She had no intention of encouraging another the moment she arrived.

'Do you know how to find your way to number seventeen, Linden Crescent?' he asked.

So he had memorized Lydia's address. She was not entirely pleased with the notion he could seek her out if he so chose. He seemed a nice enough sort, but she had been looking forward to being in a place large enough that no one knew the particulars of her comings and goings. Still, with the steady stream of passengers disembarking the trains, there must be a chance plenty of other girls with other addresses would fill his mind.

'I've no idea whatsoever. This is my first time in Hull.'

'You'd best consult the map over there in the glass case beneath the clock. That will be sure to help you find your way.'

With that, he touched his uniform cap and turned his attention to another passenger trying to leave the station.

She stepped towards the map and squinted at the small print denoting unfamiliar streets and squares. Her heartbeat quickened to discover Kingston upon Hull was far larger than she had realized. Perhaps it was a good thing she had been so ignorant of its size. Otherwise, she might have been intimidated about so impetuously striking out in its direction. Finally, after a good deal of searching, she spotted Linden Crescent. As her valise was not too heavy and her purse was lighter still, she determined to make her way there on foot.

In a small pocket notebook, she wrote out the turns for the streets between the station and her cousin's street. She hoped that she would find her way there before the night drew in. And she fervently hoped as well that Lydia would be there to greet her when she arrived, preferably with a pleased look upon her face. She read the first three street names through several times to commit them to memory, then tucked the notebook into the pocket of her skirt.

She nodded to the soldier as she passed him once more and pushed out into the open street.

NINE

Kingston upon Hull
Dear Mrs Reed,

I am sending along this picture postcard from the train station in London as I know how much your Timmy loves trains! Please tell him I thought of him as I found myself surrounded by a bewildering number of platforms,

placards and uniformed attendants. It was quite an
adventure!
    Love,
    Wilhelmina

A s she stepped out on to the pavement, the thrum of the
    busy city filled her ears. She had thought she understood
    how enormous Hull was in comparison with her own
small village, but the reality of the difference struck her forcibly
as a constant flow of automobiles whizzed past along the wide
avenue. Throngs of pedestrians clogged the junctions, and the
clang of trolleys competed with the shouting and jostling of
boys running past in gangs.

She wondered what they could possibly be doing gathering
on the streets during the school day and then realized that school
might have been suspended. Had they evacuated children from
Hull? She supposed it was likely that it was one of the cities
where it was considered prudent to do so. It seemed strange to
be in a place that might be sending its children away instead
of being in one scrambling to locate places to house evacuated
children.

Billie felt a renewed sense of purpose as she considered the
possibility that the people of Hull were taking the war far more
seriously than those back home in Barton St Giles. With a
wrench, she considered that perhaps it would not be home to
her any longer. Who was to say that her father or brother would
be able to return there? Still, there was no sense concerning
herself with such things.

She cast her gaze towards the skies where clouds had gathered
menacingly dark as the train had pulled nearer and nearer to
the railway station. She joined the crowd at the corner after
surreptitiously consulting her list of directions and crossed the
broad avenue along with them. Her heart thudded unexpectedly
in her chest as she reached the middle of the street. She had
never felt particularly alarmed at the sound of an automobile
before her mother's accident. Here in Hull, with so many motorcars and lorries speeding this way and that, she found herself
feeling the slightest bit uneasy.

With relief, she reached the pavement opposite and readjusted her grip on her valise. Her palm felt slick with perspiration and she told herself not to be so foolish. It was not yet dark, despite the threatening clouds, and surely no one would run her down in broad daylight, especially not in the middle of a crowd. The day was cooling rapidly as the winds picked up and the skies grew grayer. She quickened her pace, hoping to reach her cousin's home and to be welcomed inside before the skies opened. The distance between the station and her destination seemed far greater on foot than it had when looking at the map. She heard a low rumbling noise but was not sure if it was a lorry moving down the street or a roll of thunder that she had heard. She moved more quickly, each step urged on by an ever more ominous-looking sky, as well as a thinning of the crowds ahead of her.

According to her directions, she was only about six streets away from Lydia's home when a flash of lightning and a loud clap of thunder appeared too close for comfort above her head. The first few drops of rain splattered down upon her hat and raced along the side of her neck as she reached yet another crossroads. She dashed across the street and ducked beneath the striped awning of a café.

Behind her, another clap of thunder filled the air and the skies opened. Despite the lightness of her purse, she decided to take refuge inside the café until the worst of the rain had passed. Window boxes filled with cheerful mounds of petunias lined either side of the door, and as she yanked it open, the comfortingly familiar scent of damp soil rose from the planters.

Billie looked around the bright space. About half of the linen-draped tables were filled with customers. A photograph of the café featuring a middle-aged couple and a younger woman posing in front of it to cut an opening-day ribbon hung near the door. The same young woman, a birthmark spreading across her pale skin, stood behind the counter, ringing up an order.

'Take a seat anywhere you like, love,' the woman said, gesturing to the room with a wave of her hand.

At least that was what Billie guessed the waitress said. She had thought she was prepared to decipher a Yorkshire accent since a few of the children evacuated to Barton St Giles had hailed from the county. But this was not like anything she had ever heard before. Missing aitches at the beginning of words were to be expected. What she hadn't bargained for was how all the words ran together as if there were no spaces between them. From the waitress's begrudging use of them, it seemed as though the government had figured out a way to ration consonants in Hull along with butter and eggs. She seemed to remember from her history lessons that much of Yorkshire had been inundated with Vikings in the distant past and Scandinavian trading partners more recently. Perhaps that accounted for the unfamiliar cadence to her speech.

Billie carried her valise to the table in the far corner of the café. She placed it beneath the table and pushed it underneath with her foot. She wondered whether or not she would need her ration book to order food at a restaurant. Was that how such things now worked? She rarely took meals in any sort of public establishment and certainly had not done so since ration books had been issued.

Not only that but the rules seemed to change about how they were to be used with alarming frequency. Billie had not had much appetite since her father and brother had left the village and none whatsoever since her mother had died. She couldn't remember the last time she had gone to the shops for any sort of foodstuffs. It was a wonder she had remembered to pack her ration book at all considering how little value she had placed on eating.

A woman with a small boy sat at a table nearby. She seemed to be scolding him for picking at his food and admonished him to clean his plate. Billie's heart gave a squeeze as she thought of all the times her mother had coaxed her not to waste food. In truth, the boy looked a bit like Frederick had done at that age with his dark eyes and wavy hair. She pulled her gaze away and allowed it to drift over the rest of the room.

A young man sat fidgeting at a table by a window overlooking the pavement. He repeatedly cracked his knuckles and jiggled his leg up and down so vigorously that the floorboards under Billie's chair rocked unsteadily in time to his movements. She watched as he lifted and lowered the menu several times, scarcely glancing at it as he did so. He started to raise it again when his attention was drawn to the entrance.

Billie watched with interest as all the people in the café turned to stare as a smartly dressed blonde sauntered to the young man's table. She waited as he stood and pulled out her chair before sitting and bestowing a dazzling smile upon him.

She felt herself shifting slightly forward in her seat as if magnetized towards the newcomer. She was just the sort of confident and self-possessed woman that belonged on the silver screen. Or, better yet, in recruitment films or printed advertisements for the women's auxiliary forces. Billie doubted the Territorials would have such difficulty attracting volunteers if they had a woman like the one seated opposite sporting their khaki-colored uniform.

Her glossy blonde hair swept back from her forehead into a perfect mound of tucks and swirls. Scarlet lipstick highlighted her mouth, and her severely cut navy-blue frock looked as though it had been designed just for her. She tugged off a pair of white gloves and laid them on the table. The café was small, and the voices of the other patrons carried easily.

'Please tell me you've already ordered. I'm absolutely famished,' the woman said in a clear, easy-to-understand voice. He shook his head, and she turned in search of a waitress. He started to raise his hand to hail the young woman from behind the counter, but before he could capture her attention, his companion had attracted her notice with the slightest waggle of her slim fingers.

'Good afternoon, Sally,' the blonde woman said to the waitress. 'If it's not too much trouble, we would like a pot of Darjeeling, a plate of scones and another of assorted sandwiches. And cakes to finish.' She waved away the proffered menu. 'That will suit, won't it?'

He nodded wordlessly and then shook his head slightly as if he felt off-kilter in her presence. The waitress nodded and smiled before hurrying away to do her bidding. Billie watched as the woman turned her attention to the table settings. She tweaked and rearranged the forks, knives and spoons, and adjusted the position of the jam pot and sugar bowl. She noticed the woman's lovely lips tighten slightly as she eyed a dispirited sprig of greenery stuck into a tumbler of water in an attempt to brighten up the center of the table.

The young man leaned forward and touched the back of his companion's hand. Something in the way her smile froze on her face made Wilhelmina lean forward a little more.

'Audrey, please tell me you have given some thought to my suggestion,' he said.

Billie felt the floor begin to bounce once more. The young man lay his free hand against his thigh to quell the jiggling.

The woman tilted her head to one side and languidly batted her long eyelashes.

'I am still mulling it over,' she said.

She attempted to pull her hand out from under his, but he clung to it tightly. Billie would have sworn Audrey winced before she left her hand clasped in his.

'Why is it such a difficult decision?' he asked.

Before she could answer, the waitress returned to the table and placed a pot of tea and a three-tiered rack filled with their order between them. Audrey slid her hand away and gently rubbed her wrist before selecting a tiny sandwich from the offerings before her.

Billie's view of the couple was abruptly cut off as the waitress stepped between her table and theirs.

'Now, what can I get for you, miss?' she asked.

Her voice was friendly, but her expression conveyed fatigue. At first glance, Billie wondered if she was one of the many people on the home front working countless hours for volunteer causes as well as a full-time job.

'Just a cup of tea, please,' Billie said. She was sure there was enough left in her purse to go as far as that, and felt certain that no matter the regulations governing restaurants and ration books, she was unlikely to set a foot wrong if she avoided purchasing any food.

'Here to work in one of the factories, are you?' the woman asked, pointing her notepad at Billie's valise peeking out from beneath the table. 'Or are you one of the many leaving the city?'

'Actually, I'm here to stay with my cousin. Are there lots of young women here seeking jobs?' she asked.

'We see a fair share. But I suppose most cities nowadays could say the same. There are any number of places looking to fill positions,' the woman said. 'Is this your first visit to Hull?'

'It is,' Billie admitted.

'You were lucky to get in, weren't you? I've heard they have soldiers stationed at the ports, the railway station and even on the roads leading into town, now that the defense area has been proclaimed.'

Just remembering the incident with the soldier brought a warmth to Billie's cheeks. She definitely didn't wish to discuss it in a small café.

'I was fortunate indeed. I wonder, do you know how much farther it is to Linden Crescent? I'm afraid I rather misjudged the distance from the railway station,' Billie said.

'Linden Crescent? It isn't much farther, even weighted down by baggage. It's not more than a ten-minute walk from here, even at a leisurely pace,' she said.

The woman with the small boy gestured to the waitress, and as she moved off to attend to her, Billie turned her attention back to the couple seated nearby. All the while as she sipped her tea, she covertly watched them. He made no further attempts to touch her, and she kept the full width of the table between them.

She glanced out of the window, past the bloom-filled boxes, and noticed the rain had tapered off. She drained her cup of the last drops of tea and slid her valise out from beneath the table. A wave of nervousness washed over her as she considered the recklessness of her voyage. What if Lydia had not really meant for her to come? Or at least not without some sort of notice. Still, there was nothing to be done about it now. She gripped the handle of her valise, consulted the directions and strode out of the door to discover if she had thrown herself headlong into a mistake.

TEN

Hull
Special Constable Upton's PNB

The streets were dark and filled with puddles left by the earlier downpour as Peter made his way between the police station and the neighborhood he had been assigned to patrol that evening. The hum of the city filled his ears much as the salty tang of the nearby tidal river filled his nostrils. Brick buildings, many constructed more than a hundred years earlier, towered and leaned on all sides of him as he strode down the pavement.

Hull had a long history of human occupation, and while some said its glory years were behind it, he felt a fierce glow of pride in his city. It had gained the formal name of Kingston upon Hull in the days of Edward I who acquired it during his quest to hammer the Scots. Ever since, it had served as an important port, both for overseas trade and for moving goods within the country. The severe economic decline since the Great War had left vast numbers of dockers and shipbuilders unemployed, but Peter refused to believe a place that had been a force to be reckoned with for much of its history could be kept down in the long run. After all, Hull had always been a stubborn and determined sort of city. Hadn't they been one of the first to declare for the Parliamentarians and to refuse entry to Charles I and his supporters? If a king's siege couldn't break them, he doubted empty wallets or Axis Powers would manage it.

But his purpose in being out at night had little to do with admiring the sights and sounds of the city. In addition to increased demands on the police through a rise in crime rates, the government had come to rely upon the constabulary to enforce all the new wartime regulations.

Chief among these was the vital enforcement of the blackout. All cities and towns in the United Kingdom, from great metropolises like London to the tiniest hamlets in the Highlands of Scotland, were required to completely obscure all signs of light. But for cities like Hull, where geographical features like the river Humber and the river Hull made identifying the city easy work for enemy bombers flying above them, it was all the more vital that such lighting restrictions be strictly observed.

Even after several months on the force, Peter was still surprised at the dust some of his fellow residents kicked up when confronted with a lighting violation. Almost nightly, he spotted light glowing beneath a householder's blackout curtains. Less frequently, but with disheartening regularity, were the citations he gave to those residents who made no effort to bother obscuring their lights at all. It was as if a small but dangerous segment of the populace did not believe that there was any real danger facing them.

Over and over, Peter had heard disgruntled chatter in buses and pubs railing against what they claimed was a phony war. That is, they did until Dunkirk. He couldn't say he had been relieved by the events that had ensued only a fortnight prior, but he did find there were fewer folks who gave him quite such a hard time about dousing the lights. Prior to that nightmare, when he rapped upon the door of a house where he had spotted chinks of light, more often than not he faced a hostile and defensive reaction from the householders.

He had even come to make a bit of a game of it, guessing what sort of an excuse would be offered when he knocked upon the door with his violation pad in hand. After Dunkirk, he had been met with at least as many sheepish apologies as scowls and insults. As he made his way along the alley behind a row of shops and office buildings, he spotted a faint glow emanating from a nearby building he recognized as a café that he had often passed on his rounds. He quickened his pace and reached into his uniform jacket pocket for his summons pad.

A set of stairs next to the offending window led up to a heavy wooden door. He took the steps two at a time, launched himself on to the top step and pounded on the door. When he received no immediate response, he rapped loudly upon it a second time, then tried the handle. Just as he was withdrawing his hand from the unyielding knob, the door cracked open and a blonde woman of approximately his own age poked her head through the crack.

'Good evening, Constable. Is there something the matter?' she asked.

Her posh accent rolled off her like a cloud of expensive perfume. Even from what little of her could be seen through the crack in the doorway, it was clear she was a beauty. Her blue eyes were curious rather than defensive, and he thought it likely she had not spent a great deal of time explaining herself to the police. She smiled at him and for a moment he lost his train of thought. His breath caught in his chest, and he wondered if he had seen her in the pages of a magazine or even on the silver screen. With an effort, he recalled himself to his duty.

'I'm afraid I'm going to have to cite you for a lighting

violation. The light streaming from this window can be seen all the way down the alley,' he said, pointing towards the offending window.

The woman opened the door a bit wider and stuck her head out to verify his claim. As she did so, he was struck anew by how lovely she was. Her accent had revealed her class, but the way she moved also spoke of her background. And, perhaps, her personality as well. Unlike so many others he had encountered, she showed no sign of prickliness concerning her responsibility in the matter. She simply nodded.

'I'm terribly sorry, Constable. I can't imagine how I could have been so careless. We all must do our bit, mustn't we?' she asked, once again giving him a dazzling smile.

Peter felt his heart give a little squeeze in his chest. It was an unexpected pleasure not to be harangued for doing his duty, and all the more so because she was lovely to look at while he did so. Despite his total conviction that the blackout regulations should be strictly enforced, he felt an unusual level of remorse at the notion she might feel criticized in some way.

Still, he prided himself on enforcing the regulations in an utterly even-handed manner, regardless of the violator in front of him. It would be far too easy to be swayed by sob stories from a confused elderly lady or an exhausted young mother with a baby balanced on her hip and a toddler tugging at her skirts. He had promised himself that he would write up a summons for every single blackout violation he encountered on his rounds, no matter who it was doing the violating.

He bent his head over his summons pad partly as a way to pull his attention from her face. He jotted down the date and the time as well as the address and tore off the summons neatly before handing it to her.

'The owner of this property will be required to appear in court to answer the charge. Please adjust your blackout curtains and don't let it happen again,' he said.

'I'm very sorry to have troubled you, Constable. I'll see that it won't happen again,' she said, reaching her hand out for the summons. 'Is there anything else?'

'No, miss, that'll be all,' he said.

And then, just like that, she slipped her arm back through

the gap in the doorway and closed it firmly in his face. He paused on the step, waiting and watching as a flickering form moved in the gap of light streaming through the window before twitching the blackout curtain in place and leaving him entirely alone in the dark once more.

ELEVEN

Kingston upon Hull
Dear Frederick,

How I wish you were with me as I head for Cousin Lydia's house. What fun it would be to share the first glance of her with you! As you are elsewhere, I shall make careful note of every detail so that should my letters ever find you, you will feel as though you had been there, too. I can almost feel your elbow in my ribs as I pen this, urging me not to take everything so seriously and to simply enjoy the moment as it unfolds. Even though I am rather ashamed of myself when I think of how brave I know you have had to be, I must confess that I am feeling ever so slightly nervous now that I have ventured from home. I shall do my very best impression of you as I navigate the unfamiliar terrain.

Please do write should this letter reach you. I am desperate for news from you. I've enclosed the mysterious Lydia's address.

Love,
Billie

Just as the waitress had said, even weighed down by her bag, in under ten minutes she found herself at the turn for Linden Crescent. The street curved away from the main thoroughfare and was clearly one that tended towards prosperity and respectability. In fact, the houses appeared quite new and undeniably modern. The detached and semi-detached brick buildings sat back from the bustle of the street sufficiently to provide small but tidy swathes of lawn punctuated by neat beds of brightly blooming plants. As she spotted a brass number indicating she had arrived at number seventeen, she stopped in her tracks as a wave of surprise washed over her.

The house in front of her looked nothing like its neighbors. In fact, it looked nothing like anything Billie had ever witnessed outside the pages of a glossy magazine in the village shop or on the silver screen. She had heard of art deco, of course, but it had not made an appearance in Barton St Giles. Smooth white stucco covered the exterior walls, gleaming against the deeply gray skies beyond. A two-story, curved bay window with black lead trim stretched towards the street, while a small second-floor balcony provided a sort of protective overhang for the front door. Square stone paving covered the small front garden with the exception of one small tree in its center.

Billie looked down at her sensible but unfashionable shoes, bespattered by the downpour and passing motorcars. She tightened and loosened her grip on her mother's fusty, dated valise. She was absolutely certain she would be hopelessly out of place in such a house. Still, she had come too far to turn back now.

She took a deep breath, then mounted the shallow front steps and grasped the black iron knocker to deliver a few quick raps that sounded to her ears more confident than she felt. She stood on the step feeling entirely conspicuous as a minute and then another passed. A feeling of unease crept over her as she considered the possibility that it would have been far wiser to inquire as to whether her cousin was in Hull before setting off without any confirmation there would be someone to greet her upon her arrival.

She felt rather foolish as she stood staring at the closed door in front of her. She had not the slightest idea what to do should her cousin not arrive before nightfall. She doubted she had sufficient funds to pay for a night at a hotel or some other sort of lodging, even if she could locate such an establishment.

As she retreated down the steps, she told herself something surely would work out. She could always retrace her steps to the train station and collect herself there. The woman at the café had said that people were flocking into the city day and night to begin jobs at the local factories. Perhaps she could apply for a position at one of them.

While she had never looked for a place to stay on her own before, that did not mean such things were not possible. After all, she had intended to join the services, and living away from the rectory would be part and parcel of that decision. She squared her shoulders and drew in a deep breath. There was no need for her to turn tail and run back to the rectory, hoping that Ronald's offer still stood. Surely, she could figure out a way to handle things on her own. She decided to leave a note for Lydia.

Certainly, she would return home at some point and would be just as happy to meet with her at some point in the future. She descended to the pavement and snapped open her handbag. Searching for the small notebook she always kept within its depths, she failed to notice the sound of footsteps approaching until they were almost upon her.

She had just located the notebook when she heard a voice calling insistently in her direction. She turned and faced the corner from which she had entered the street and spotted a striking woman striding purposefully towards her, arms outstretched with a decidedly foreign exuberance.

While it could not be said that the woman had broken into a run, she had moved swiftly enough to be ever so slightly out of breath. An enormous smile spread across her face as she came to a stop.

'My dearest Billie, I knew that must be you. You're simply the very image of Grandmother Phyllida when she was about your age, but I expect you know that already, don't you?' the woman said, reaching for Billie's hand and spinning her around. 'Let me get a good look at you.'

Billie had no idea what to say. She had no notion of any resemblance she had to a grandmother. Her father, being the one who would have been the keeper of such information, had never felt moved to remark upon it. Not only that but Lydia seemed to feel as though the two of them had already met and even had a rapport of sorts. From the easy way in which she swept an intelligent and lively gaze over her before nodding with satisfaction, to the proprietary way she tucked her arm through the crook of Billie's own, she presumed a connection that was utterly disconcerting and thoroughly beguiling.

Billie decided that the woman before her looked nothing like the person she had expected. For one thing, she was younger than Billie had assumed she would be. She had expected Lydia to be of her parents' generation, but unless she was remarkably well preserved, she appeared a good dozen years younger than them. For another, everything about her simply sparkled. Billie could in no way reconcile the creature who stood next to her with any member of her own family.

Admittedly, she could see traces of her own father's high forehead and strong nose reflected in her cousin's face, but that was where the resemblance ended. Her father never paid attention to whether or not his socks matched or his bedraggled and hopelessly decrepit jacket was covered with the previous day's meals. He certainly never looked as though he had stepped from the pages of a fashion magazine.

Her father and her mother both preferred serviceable garments in colors that allowed them to blend into a stand of beech trees or a newly plowed field. The most colorful attire she could remember her mother wearing was a summer frock she had made for herself from a length of dusty rose cotton.

From her waves of glossy dark hair, to her bold red lipstick, to the tottering height of her decidedly impractical court shoes, Lydia would not have blended in against any sort of background. Her severely cut suit in royal blue and the jaunty silk scarf that fluttered out behind her as she moved both spoke of a willingness to stand out in a crowd. Lydia tucked her gloved hand into the crook of Billie's arm and tugged her up the steps towards the door once more. Billie barely had time to hoist her valise before she found herself swept along in her cousin's exuberant wake.

Lydia fitted a key into the front lock, turned it and pressed open the front door, beckoning for Billie to follow. Another flash of lightning streaked across the sky and she gratefully hurried after her cousin who moved like a whirlwind along a black-and-white marble-laid hallway. Billie hurried after her as best she could.

She followed Lydia into a room off to the left, overwhelmed

by the sight before her. Her life at the rectory had been one of comfort and relative ease. There had always been plenty to eat, a soft bed in which to sleep and furniture aplenty. However, everything had been assembled from the castoffs of other households' clear-outs or brought home from a village jumble sale in support of some charitable cause or another. None of it had been chosen to suit any particular taste or because it would look well in the room for which it was intended. This room, however, had clearly been carefully designed by someone who knew what they were about.

Lydia crossed the room and drew the blackout curtains over the long windows. She pulled off her hat and gloves, and reached out a long, slim hand to snap on a lamp. Once again, Billie had the impression she had suddenly found herself on the Hollywood set of some big-budget production. All the furnishings in the room appeared exquisitely modern. Gleaming chrome and glass and lacquer made up the bulk of the arrangements.

'You must tell me everything. When did you arrive? How long can you stay? Are you hungry?' Lydia asked, gesturing towards a buff velvet-covered sofa.

Billie eased herself gently down on the edge of the sofa, hoping none of the dust and grime she had undoubtedly collected through the course of her journey would transfer itself on to the upholstery. Her cousin settled herself in a chaise opposite and kicked off her shoes before stretching luxuriously out on the furniture.

'I left on the early-morning train from Barton St Giles and only arrived in Hull this afternoon,' Billie said.

'I hope you didn't have any trouble entering the city. It wasn't until after I sent my letter that I gave any thought to the fact that you might not find it easy as someone who is not a permanent resident.'

'The soldier who stopped me at the station did take some convincing, but it turned out just fine in the end.'

'Good girl. As I said, you remind me very much of my grandmother.' Lydia smiled at her. 'Now, how long are you able to stay?'

Billie wondered how direct she ought to be. She thought

about her opportunities back in Barton St Giles and also about her eagerness to start an entirely new life. Perhaps she ought to take a cue from Lydia's own manner. After all, it was no time for excessive politeness.

'I am able to remain in Hull for just as long as you're willing to have me. With things as they are with my father, I have no idea when he would be able to return to the rectory and resume his duties in the village. And, truth be told, I am in no way eager to be on my own with my father's curate.'

Lydia leaned slightly forward and smiled. 'Do I detect a bit of a mystery there?' Lydia asked. 'Have you broken the poor young man's heart?'

'Ronald made me an offer of marriage but only in order to protect both of our reputations. It certainly was not a question of anyone ending up with a broken heart as he made it very clear it would be a matter of convenience, at least on his part,' Billie said.

'You don't seem particularly heartbroken yourself, so I can only conclude you were in no way eager to accept,' Lydia said.

'The only thing I was eager to accept was your invitation to put as much distance between myself and Ronald Kershaw as possible,' Billie said with a smile. Her cousin beamed back at her.

'That's the spirit. Then it appears I shall enjoy your company for some time to come. I couldn't be more pleased. While I'm very sorry about your mother's death and your father's internment, I'm a firm believer in salvaging what's worth saving. War may be raging all around us, but it has brought you to my doorstep, and for that I am very grateful. Which leads me to my last question. Have you eaten?'

'I stopped in at a café on my way from the station to wait out the rain,' Wilhelmina said, neglecting to mention her purse had only sensibly stretched to a cup of tea.

Lydia glanced over at a rounded chrome-cased clock on a nearby table. 'Your arrival calls for a celebration. I believe cocktails are in order. What do you say to a Gin and It?' she said, pushing up off the chaise and getting to her feet.

Billie felt out of place once more. She had no notion whatsoever of what 'It' might be and, truth be told, while she knew that gin was some sort of spirit, she had no idea if she would like it or not. Her parents had not held with imbibing alcohol and had not kept it in the house. And as they were known as teetotalers, such refreshments were not offered to them when dining in the homes of friends or parishioners.

She glanced down at her bedraggled shoes and then at the dainty pair Lydia had cast off so effortlessly on the floor between them. If she could be Billie rather than Wilhelmina with nothing more than the declaration that it was her preference, what was to keep her from changing anything else she decided to choose?

'I would say I would be delighted,' Billie said.

Lydia busied herself at a drinks cart tucked into a far corner of the room next to a spotless gas fireplace. Before Billie could change her mind, Lydia handed her a tall glass. Billie took a small sip and discovered she found the taste bracing but not unpleasant.

'Now, my dear, you must tell me everything. I know nothing whatsoever about you and am burning with curiosity.' Lydia took a sip of her drink, then smiled encouragingly over the rim of her glass.

'I am not sure that there is a great deal to tell. After all, I've lived the quiet life of a country rector's daughter.'

'But that's just it, you see; I have no idea what such a life must be like. I've spent all of mine in large, bustling cities. I imagine it quite idyllic, but I suppose it could be entirely different.'

Billie took another sip. Her head felt a bit light, and she wondered if it had been wise to accept the drink with no experience of such things and so little in her stomach. But it was not an entirely unpleasant feeling and she found it loosened her tongue.

'There were many things about life in Barton St Giles that I enjoyed very much, but life in such a small place can feel restrictive.'

'So, an eagerness to be rid of the curate was not the only thing that prompted you to accept my invitation?' Lydia asked.

'No. I had wanted to venture off elsewhere some weeks ago and had even attempted to join the ATF, but my mother vehemently opposed the idea.'

'There is nothing to stop you from joining now, is there?' Lydia asked. 'Not that I am eager to see you head off when you have only just arrived, but if you are still interested, it seems you could enlist.'

Billie's stomach squeezed at the memory of her mother's voice ringing in her ears as she fled the reading room with her hand pressed to her stinging cheek.

'Even though I would very much like to do my bit in some significant way, the last request my mother made of me before she died was that I not enlist in the services. The idea of ignoring her wishes is not one I feel I can entertain.'

Lydia placed her empty glass on the table beside her. 'I understand. There are plenty of ways that you could be of real use on the home front. Come to think of it, we could use more help at the central library in the information bureau.'

'You work at a library?' Billie couldn't believe her ears. She had read most of the books in the reading room in Barton St Giles at least once and some several times over. She couldn't imagine how glorious it would be to find herself surrounded day in and day out by a city library's worth of books.

'I've been one of the librarians there for the past four years.'

'And you think there may be an opening for me as well?' Billie's heart gave a little leap in her chest.

'The position is not as a member of the library staff per se but rather someone to help out at the information bureau.'

'Is that working with the card catalogue?' Billie was certain she wouldn't mind any sort of work that would place her in the library.

'No. It is actually a separate service that provides a sort of clearing house of information for city residents. People telephone or stop in to ask about wartime regulations or available assistance and even to leave forwarding addresses for themselves or loved ones if they decide to relocate further from the coast.'

'So you need someone to assist with those inquiries?' Billie asked.

'We do. One of the women who was volunteering decided to leave Hull once the coastal defense zone was announced. I'm sure if you are interested, the position could be yours.'

As much as the idea of working at the library appealed to

her, Billie couldn't help but consider the state of her finances. In the past, she would have felt uncomfortable turning the topic to money but somehow she felt emboldened to do so. Maybe it was the drink.

'You said she was a volunteer. I am afraid I find myself in the position of requiring an employer who pays a wage.'

Lydia waved her hand in the air as if to bat away any such suggestion.

'Nonsense. I have plenty of money and can think of nothing I would like more than to put your mind at ease on that subject.'

'I couldn't possibly accept. We've only just met.'

'Consider it my way of doing my bit for the war effort. Besides, it isn't as if I came by it through any effort of my own. An eccentric aunt on my mother's side left me pots of it. It would be a pleasure to share my good fortune with someone else.'

Billie didn't know what to say. She hadn't realized how much her concern about her finances had weighed on her until there was hope in sight. She sagged back against the cushions behind her as though her bones had dissolved.

'I'll take that as a yes,' Lydia said, an enormous smile spreading across her face. 'I propose we head out for a bite to eat at a restaurant. Afterwards, we could catch a film at one of the many cinemas. Your arrival calls for more of a celebration than a mere cocktail.'

Billie wanted to say yes. In fact, the cinema was one of her favorite pastimes, though not one she indulged in with any degree of frequency. Her mother had not entirely approved of the sorts of goings-on often featured on the silver screen and also thought that the expense of it was an unnecessary indulgence. Her hesitation sprang not from a lack of desire to see what might be on offer in the big city but rather the fact that in order to attend the cinema it would be necessary to go outside in the dark.

She had not found it easy to force herself out of doors once the sun had gone down ever since her mother's accident. She could not imagine she would be more inclined to do so with the preponderance of cars that prowled the streets. Still, her cousin looked at her with such eager anticipation that she could not find it in her heart to refuse. Instead, she nodded with more enthusiasm than she felt.

'That's settled, then. But first I'll show you to your room where you can freshen up.'

The room Lydia led her to on the second floor at the front of the house outstripped Billie's wildest imaginings. From the curtains to the satin bedspread to the plush, dove-gray fitted carpets, it was far grander than any room in which she had ever stayed before. As she gingerly set her valise on the floor, hoping it would not dirty the pale carpet, she was struck by the notion she had no idea what to wear for an evening out in a city restaurant. Or at the cinema, for that matter.

'What sort of attire would be appropriate for our outing?' she asked. 'I am afraid I may not have packed the sort of clothing that would be suitable for our plans.'

'Let's take a look at what you've brought,' Lydia said.

Billie knelt and unbuckled her valise. A piece at a time, she spread her clothing on the bed. Lydia looked it all over before arching a well-plucked eyebrow and leaving the room. She reappeared a moment later holding a red cotton dress and a pair of black low-heeled shoes.

'Why don't you give these a try? I think we are about the same size.' Lydia held out the garments and headed for the vanity table placed near a window while Billie tried them on.

'What do you think?' Billie asked as she slipped on the second shoe, delighted to discover that Lydia had been correct about the fit.

'Perfect. Now you just need to freshen your face. Have you a lipstick?'

'No. I've never owned any,' Billie said. Lydia's attractive face pinched into a puzzled frown as if not believing what she heard.

'Not even one tube?'

'Not even one tube,' Wilhelmina said.

'We can't have that, now can we?' Lydia said, patting the seat in front of the vanity table. 'It's your patriotic duty to keep yourself looking as though you're making an effort.'

She crossed the room and sat. Lydia reached down and lifted her chin. 'Now, open.'

Billie did as she was commanded and tried not to breathe as Lydia swiped a coat of lipstick across her lips. Lydia opened a drawer in the vanity table and dug through a jumble of brightly colored scarves, selecting one in a black-and-white polka dot pattern. She deftly knotted it round Billie's neck and turned the tails to spread out over her shoulder.

'There. Take a look,' Lydia said, pressing a silver-framed mirror into her hand.

Billie didn't recognize the person reflected there in the least. Between the scarf and the lipstick and the way Lydia had rearranged her hair, she hardly recognized herself. Her heart lifted in her chest and she felt as though she might just be able to try some of the things she had always wanted to experience. Things that would not have been deemed suitable for a rector's daughter in a small country village.

Her hopeful thoughts were tainted by a bit of guilt. None of this would have been possible had her mother not gone out searching for her in the dark that night. Lydia did not seem to notice any hint of remorse on her part, however. She popped open a small compact and dabbed a bit of powder on to Billie's nose and forehead.

'I don't look like the same person,' Billie said, gazing into the mirror again.

'Small changes can make a big difference. Now you need just one last thing to complete your ensemble.' Lydia left the room once more and returned with a white silk flower pinned in her hair. She fastened a second one to Billie's. 'You must always leave the house with a little something reflective on. Just because we're in a city doesn't mean it's not pitch-black on the streets at night.'

A knot drew tightly in Billie's stomach. She hadn't been out in the blackout since the night her mother died. Lydia seemed to have noticed her look of apprehension because she reached out and gave her hand a firm squeeze.

'Don't worry. I know how to find my way around in the dark.' Lydia tugged Billie to her feet, and before she could lose her nerve, she followed her cousin down the stairs and out of the door into the darkness.

TWELVE

Kingston upon Hull
Dear Mrs Hopkins,

I left the village on the spur of the moment and am ashamed to say I hurried off without returning the books I most recently borrowed from the reading room. I assure you they are in good order and can be located on the hall table at the rectory. I am so sorry if I have given any trouble over them.

I can only hope that the library in Kingston upon Hull will provide as many happy hours as the reading room has always done under your expert ministrations!

Love,
Wilhelmina

Even in the dark, the street leading to the cinema looked familiar. Billie recognized a bakery, a bank and the teashop with its window boxes filled with pink and white blooms flanking the door where she had stopped to shelter from the rain. Her pulse raced and her mouth went dry every time a motorcar approached them with its headlights shielded to dim their glow.

A truck filled with soldiers honked at them just as they turned a corner and down a street that veered off the familiar road and on to one that opened out into a wide avenue filled with far more hustle and bustle than anything she had ever seen in an evening in Barton St Giles. Everywhere she looked, there were throngs of people going about their business.

It was nearly impossible to make out the details of them in the dark, but Billie had a clear sense of their presence. Time and again, movements – the swishing of a skirt hem or a hand raised in greeting – caught the corner of her eye. Whistling, laughing and footfalls filled her ears and made the nearness of strangers all the more real. Lydia stepped closer to her as the noise of the crowd washed over them and tucked her arm through Billie's. With her free hand, she pointed towards a large building with a queue spread along the pavement in front of it.

'That's the Royale Cinema. It's always filled to the gunwales,' Lydia said.

'What's playing?'

'Does it matter?' Lydia asked.

Billie shook her head. The film was hardly the point. Just having something to take one's mind off the troubles of the present was all most people were hoping for. If the film was a good one, so much the better. Not that even a trip to the cinema was entirely devoid of thoughts of the war. After all, there were always newsreels and advisory segments to yank viewers back into reality if the magic of the silver screen had managed to help folks forget their worries for an hour or two.

They took their places at the back of the queue, and Billie was surprised at how quickly they reached the front of it. There was something unnerving about standing in the dark surrounded by the chatter of strangers. As much as she had craved the chance to spend time in the wider world beyond the confining borders of the village, she realized she had not appreciated the comfort of never being amidst a group of people she didn't know.

Now and again the sound of unfamiliar accents filled her ears. Billie noticed that many of the people in the city, like the waitress at the café, had a pattern of speech unlike any she had heard in the south. But many of the people she encountered, like Lydia, or the soldier who had stopped her at the station, sounded much like the villagers in Barton St Giles. The waitress had remarked on how many newcomers had flooded the city, and Billie supposed that would explain it. She hoped in time she would find it as easy to understand what was being said as Lydia seemed to do.

As they stepped through the doors into the cinema, Billie's eyes smarted from the sudden suffusion of light. She blinked and looked around, taking in the soaring ceiling, the plush carpeting underfoot and the gleaming brass of the velvet rope holders. Motion picture posters featuring glamorous starlets and craggily handsome leading men lined the walls of the corridor they made their way along, buffeted by the crowd.

They slid into two seats towards the back, near the center. Billie worried for a moment that they wouldn't be able to see a thing when a tall man in a broad-brimmed hat took the seat directly in front of them. But as soon as he settled himself, he removed his hat and she found she could just see over the top of him.

With more ease than she would have imagined, Billie found herself pulled into the story unfolding on the screen in front of her. The hero had just come to realize how much he cared about the girl he had taken for granted back home when the film sputtered to a stop. The sound of the film cut out abruptly and a noise that she recognized only from newsreels reached her ears. But the sound wasn't coming from any recording.

Even from the cushy depths of the cinema, it was possible to recognize the sound of the air-raid sirens. Barton St Giles had not yet had reason to use the siren the WI had raised funds to install; Billie had never even heard it tested. Her village had been too inconsequential and too far from the coast to be of much interest to enemy bombers.

Still, the villagers had practiced drills and Billie had thought she had been certain of what to do in case the alarm had been raised. The local air-raid warden had mustered a group to build a public shelter next to the church, as well as several others about the village. Mildred Dawes had made a point of dragging both Billie and her mother along with her to assess them on behalf of the community when they had first been installed.

Billie's heart thudded wildly in her chest as she realized that she had not the least idea of where to take shelter in Hull. She turned to Lydia to ask. Her cousin's face had drained of color. All around them, people dropped their voices into whispers, as if the pilots of the enemy planes might somehow be able to find them if they spoke any louder.

'Please remain seated,' a voice called out from the front of the theater. A man wearing an Air Raid Precautions band on his arm stood illuminated by the glow of the blank screen behind him. 'It is safer to remain in the cinema than to take your chances in the street trying to reach the public shelter.'

'Do you think he's right?' she asked Lydia. Her cousin lifted her shoulders wordlessly. The tall man seated in front of them turned around and provided an opinion.

'I wouldn't bet on it if I were you. I'm not going to sit here and wait for a bomb to drop the roof in on me. If it catches alight, we'll all be burned to death if we aren't crushed by falling debris.'

With that, he crammed his hat back on his head and shot to his feet. The people on the outside end of his row stood to allow him to pass but no one followed him up the aisle.

'I entreat you not to leave the building. It is far more dangerous to take your chances in the open streets,' the warden called out once more.

The man in the hat raised a hand in a silent retort and strode to the door. Billie turned and watched him as he passed out of the cinema and out of sight. Lydia turned in her seat to face Billie.

'What do you think?' she asked. 'Shall we take our chances or remain here?'

'Where is the nearest public shelter?' Billie said.

'We passed it as we entered the avenue. It's right near that large bank near the center of the square. I'd say it is only a few hundred yards away. Maybe we should go into the lobby at least to see how things look on the street.'

'If a member of the ARP advises us to remain here, it might be better advice than the recommendation of some passing stranger,' Billie said.

Once again, it felt odd to have no knowledge of those around her and whether or not they were the sort whose advice she would be inclined to heed. The man in the hat seemed so sure of his decision, but it was impossible to say that he was not the sort of man who took wild chances simply for the pleasure of doing so.

Lydia had just opened her mouth as if to reply when a deep shudder rumbled through the walls and along the floor. The lights on the walls and the ceiling flickered and then blinked out. Another shudder and then another rolled through the cinema like some sort of tidal wave made of vibration and fear. Lydia reached for Billie's hand just as a pebble-sized chunk of plaster dislodged from the ceiling and landed in her lap.

'I think that decides it, don't you?' Lydia asked.

THIRTEEN

Kingston upon Hull
Dear Mr Carston,
 I wanted to thank you for the countless hours you spent preparing the rest of the villagers for the possibility of an air raid. I know it must often have seemed a thankless task, but I wish to show my appreciation and to let you know that your advice came in very handy during a recent raid here in Kingston upon Hull . . .

Her back was stiff and her shoulders and neck ached when the sirens finally stopped six hours later. Although it was still just past four in the morning, the city was no longer shrouded in darkness. Building after building appeared to be lit up as if the blackout was not in force. Billie squinted, trying to make sense of the scene before her. With a jolt, she realized that the street was lit by a series of fires glowing all along its length. She rushed out into the street, with Lydia following closely on her heels.

Clanging and honking and the howling of dogs filled the air. As Billie raced on to the pavement, a hand reached out and clutched at her leg. She stopped and looked down, recognizing the man from the cinema who had decided to try to reach the shelter.

'You were wise not to leave,' he said, releasing his grip. He sat slumped against what remained of the front of a building, pieces of it strewn about him. Blood streaked down his face from a wound to his head. His hat was nowhere in sight.

Lydia bent down, removed her scarf and deftly wrapped it

around his injury. She turned to Billie. 'I'll stay with him. Why don't you go along and see how bad things are?'

Billie nodded and started up the street. After only a few yards, she stopped to try to get her bearings. Many of the buildings that had stood shrouded in darkness when she had entered the cinema were now no more than heaps of brick and stone and smoldering beams. Even the towering bank that had taken up such a prominent spot on the square was reduced to a mound of debris. In fact, she would not have recognized it if she had not noticed two enormous safes standing alone in the center of the rubble.

A gang of young men stood around them, pulling at the door handle of one of the safes. She was about to take a step towards them when a man appeared in front of them and shooed them away.

Billie turned her attention further up the street. Fires sputtered and glowed in piles of debris heaped up on both sides of the street. Men worked together to move large chunks of masonry and wooden beams blocking the road and preventing emergency vehicles from passing. The avenue filled slowly with people emerging from wherever they had sheltered during the raid, and she could see in their faces the same sense of shock she felt at the sight of it all.

She spotted the café where she had stopped earlier in the day. The front of it smoldered and smoked. The cheerful window boxes that had graced the front of the building were charred, and the plants that only a few hours before had burst with bloom were singed and withered. The glass from the front windows crunched under her feet as she approached the building and peered in through a jagged opening.

Despite the damage to the exterior, the inside closely resembled the establishment she had visited only that afternoon. The tables, draped with white cloths and ringed by painted wooden chairs, all remained in their original places. The framed photograph that had held pride of place near the entrance had somehow been knocked to the ground.

Even from a distance, she could see a jagged crack marring the glass protecting the smiling faces beneath. Her gaze moved along the room until it reached the long counter where the brass till sat as if waiting to ring up a customer's bill. Even from a distance, it was clear to see that the cash drawer had shot open, perhaps in the blast. More worryingly, on the floor, sticking out just past the edge of the counter, was the toe of a woman's shoe.

FOURTEEN

Hull
Special Constable Upton's PNB

No matter how many hours he had trained or how often he had run possible emergency scenarios through his mind, nothing could have prepared him for the reality. He had just passed one of the city's cinemas when the air-raid siren sounded. Pedestrians filled the street, either on their way to or from evenings out to see a show or attend a concert. Peter watched in horror as the smiles of passersby and the murmur of jovial banter turned to looks of shock and cries of panic.

Incendiaries blazed down from the sky, and suddenly the crowds began to scatter in every direction. Peter looked for someone wearing an armband that proclaimed him to be an air-raid warden. Spotting no one fitting that description, he yanked his whistle from his jacket pocket and raised it to his lips. Despite the clamor, its shrill notes caught the attention of those nearest to him.

As quickly and efficiently as he could manage, he shepherded terrified people to the shelter the city had constructed in the center of the square only weeks earlier. Couples, some with a few children in tow, and even an elderly man caught off guard while walking his dog all raced into the shelter at his urging. After sweeping his glance over the square for a final time to assure himself no one had been left without cover, he yielded to the urging of the anxious people calling to him from inside the shelter.

Throughout the long hours pressed into the shelter alongside the others, he had been able to convince himself that surely the sound of the bombing must be worse than the reality. But when the sirens ceased their blaring and he emerged ahead of the others, the truth was far different. From his vantage point at the center of the square, he could see severe damage to buildings and multiple fires burning with varying degrees of vigor. In the distance, fire engines rang their bells, and with each passing second, the sound of approaching help grew louder. Light punctured the night sky above the neighboring streets as well, and Peter wondered at the damage to the entire neighborhood.

At first glance, the people he spotted were mostly unscathed. A crowd spilled out of the cinema nearby. One man sat pressed against a damaged brick wall, a few buildings up from the remarkably intact cinema. A woman crouched over him, pressing something to his head.

The first order of business was fire. He raced towards a tall building with flames reaching skyward from the roof. As he approached it, two men with hand pumps and a ladder appeared from an alley and began the work of dousing the flames. A fire engine pulled up at the top of the street, and Peter raced towards it to identify himself. As the fire crew set to work with the pumper truck, Peter helped to rally volunteers from capable-looking passersby.

One of the firefighters called his attention to the opposite side of the street. He blinked his eyes in an effort to clear an illusion from his field of vision. Where the National Provincial Bank had stood throughout all of his life, there was now nothing more than a pile of strewn rubble. Nothing except for two large safes sitting amid a smoldering pile of debris.

Peter quickened his pace in the direction of what was left of the bank. Several men, a few years younger than him, were making their way to the safes as quickly as they possibly could navigate the litter-strewn street. As he hurried towards them, a movement to his right caught his attention. A young woman moved from the pavement in front of a damaged building and stepped towards the doorway. Before he could shout to her to remain outside the building, she had disappeared within it. A shout from the vicinity of the safes drew his attention back to the bank site.

'Leave that alone now, lads,' he heard someone call out. A large man stood, his arm outstretched and pointing at the pair of safes. The young men paid little heed to the admonishment, and one of the taller of them laid his hand upon one safe's door handle and commenced to try his chances. Peter called out to them and closed the gap between them.

'Police,' he said. The ringleader of the young men released the safe handle, and all the lads slipped off into the anonymous crowds. The large man turned to him, shaking his head.

Peter stepped towards the safes and tried both handles himself. Each of them held fast.

'Can you believe that? The whole bank reduced to a pile of dust, but the safes are completely intact,' the man said. 'If I ever need a safe, I'll know which sort to buy.'

Peter was about to agree when a fiery chunk of debris dropped from a tall building on to the roof of the shop he had seen the young woman enter. A row of slates loosened and tumbled to the ground, exposing the flammable surface beneath. The flaming debris grew brighter as it settled on the wooden sub-roof. He looked for available firefighters, but everyone was already hard at work battling other blazes.

He could not remember noticing the young woman leaving the building. It was just the sort of foolish behavior from the public that added an unnecessary load in an emergency. Anyone with any sense at all would not have taken that sort of risk. What could have prompted her to launch herself into such danger? He turned his back on the safes and broke into a run.

The door to the shop stood open, and at first glance he saw no one. The only thing that called his attention was the open drawer of the till. So that was it. He knew it wasn't reasonable, but he couldn't help feeling even more outraged by female thieves than the males of that particular subset of the criminal class. A cracking noise sounded above him, and he glanced up at the ceiling. He felt a wave of fury wash over him as he considered that someone's criminal act was distracting him from helping those far more deserving.

She must have slipped out through a door at the back of the shop. There had to be one. All at once, a shower of sparks landed on the floor at the far side of the room. Another noise caught his attention, one from behind the counter where the ornate brass till sat. The young thief appeared from where she had been crouching behind the counter. Counting her ill-gotten gains, he supposed.

She didn't appear to be a hardened criminal. Rather, she looked to be in shock. Her dark eyes were wide, and her red lips parted slightly as if he had surprised her. He stepped closer with the intention of guiding her out of the building and bundling her off somewhere for safekeeping until he could arrest her for looting. Perhaps it was the first time she had attempted such a brazen act.

'Look here, miss, I'm a police constable and I need you to come with me,' he said, hoping he sounded convincing. 'The roof of this building has caught alight, and in case you hadn't noticed, cinders are falling in through the ceiling. You must leave immediately.'

She shook her head and took a step backwards.

'You seem like a nice sort of a girl. Why don't you put the money back in the till and we'll forget all about the theft? That way we can get out of here before anyone gets hurt.'

Peter ignored the sound from the ceiling and the heat pulsing above him and instead moved towards her. He stepped over a framed photograph that had fallen to the floor. She took another step away from him and he wondered if she was going to attempt to make a run for it. Considering the circumstances, they might both be better off if she did, even if it meant letting her get away with whatever she had helped herself to from the till.

'You're a constable?' she asked.

'That's right, and I am ordering you to come out from behind there. We have to leave at once, no matter what you've done. You're putting us both in danger messing about like this.' He felt his patience evaporating as a wave of heat pulsed towards him from above.

'If you're really a police officer, you will want to see this,' she said, looking down at the floor.

There was something in her voice that drew him towards her, despite the ominous crackling coming from the ceiling. Most of her small figure was blocked from view by the counter, and he instinctively placed his hand on his truncheon as he crossed the room. He rounded the corner of the counter and stopped short.

'She's dead,' the young woman said. 'They taught us how to check for signs of life at the Women's Institute meetings, and there aren't any.'

Peter squatted down to look at the woman sprawled on the floor at his feet. He wrapped his fingers around her wrist to feel for a pulse and realized with a shock that not only was there none but her skin felt cool to the touch. It was only then he noticed that the hair on the back of her head was matted with something sticky. His stomach roiled as the metallic tang of blood filled his nostrils.

He moved the curtain of pale blonde hair away from her face and felt his heart squeeze in his chest as he recognized her as the woman he had cited for a lighting violation. He knew the war was claiming young lives every day, but there was something about seeing such a vivacious creature snuffed out in her own city that made the threat feel more real to him than anything else had up until that point.

He rose slowly and looked around for signs of debris that would indicate that her death was a result of the bombing. The area around her body was free of rubble. Not a thing seemed out of place besides the body. He simply could not see anything to which to attribute her death. He stood and faced the young thief. Was she a murderer, too?

'Did you kill her?' he asked.

The young woman locked her gaze upon his own. 'Of course not. But someone obviously did. She wasn't killed by the air raid, that's for sure.'

Peter turned his head as another scattering of cinders crashed to the floor behind him. The young woman seemed to pay no heed as she leaned over the body again.

'She was struck on the head, but there isn't a weapon anywhere in sight,' she said. 'See what I mean?' She pointed at the area surrounding the body. The floor was entirely clean, and a broom leaned against a nearby corner.

This was not the sort of conversation he ever expected to have with any woman and certainly not in the aftermath of an air raid. Even if she was right about the victim's death, there was no time to stand about chatting.

'We have to get out of here,' Peter said again.

'Aren't you going to look for clues? Gather evidence of some kind?' she asked, her voice beginning to rise.

'There's one dead woman in here already,' he said, looking over his shoulder as a groan from the ceiling joists met his ears. 'Neither of us wants there to be another one.' He reached out and gripped her by the arm. 'If I have to arrest you to get you out of here, I will.'

'On what charge?' she asked as she yanked her arm away from him. He was relieved to see her glance towards the door as another shower of flaming debris fell from above. This time it landed in the center of one of the tables, and the tablecloth gave off a singed smell as though someone had become careless with the ironing.

Before he could answer, an overhead beam let out a tremendous crack. Out of the corner of his eye, he noticed something tumbling towards him. Something hot and heavy skimmed his shoulder. Without another word, he darted towards the startled thief, tossed her over his shoulder like a sailor hoisting his ditty bag and raced for the door.

The heat and noise were so intense that he barely noticed the weight of her body until he lowered her to the safety of the pavement opposite the burning building. As he turned to look at the danger they had just escaped, he felt a wave of relief wash over him. Flames fully engulfed the roof, and tendrils of fire greedily licked the wooden window sashes. He felt a tug on his arm and looked down at the thief.

'What were you thinking? We can't just leave her body in there,' she said.

'I was thinking we would be lucky to make it out of there alive,' he said.

'What about the evidence that needs to be collected?' she said, pointing at the café and stepping off the pavement as if to head towards it.

He reached out a restraining arm, but there was no need to hold her back. She stopped dead in her tracks as a cracking, groaning sound thundered from the café. With a tremendous rush of noise and heat, the entire roof folded in on itself and careened to the ground. She staggered back as a cloud of smoke barreled through the broken windows and the gaping door.

'There's not much anyone can do about evidence now,' he said.

She turned to him and placed her hands on her hips. 'What about a report? Surely you should at least take a statement from me about what I saw and also make an official note that mentions there was no debris around her body?'

He hadn't expected any thanks for saving her life. That wasn't why he volunteered for the constabulary. But he also didn't expect to be lectured on priorities by a member of the public with as little common sense as she seemed to possess. As much as he was inclined to give pretty girls the benefit of the doubt, she was plucking his last nerve.

Still, he told himself, she had suffered a series of shocks in short order. Between the bombing raid, discovering a dead body, being caught while looting and then narrowly escaping being burned alive, she had spent an eventful night. Women couldn't be expected to hold up under that amount of strain, could they? So rather than giving her a well-deserved scolding, he merely pointed at the blazing street.

'There are far more pressing matters to attend to than filling out forms about those who were beyond help. You should be grateful I have decided not to file a report accusing you of looting,' he said.

As the girl opened her mouth to speak, an older woman rushed to her side and wrapped her arm around her. Seeing his opportunity to leave her in someone else's hands, he tipped his uniform cap and sprinted up the street.

FIFTEEN

Kingston upon Hull
Dear Candace,
   I do hope your base has not been the target of any air raids! My arrival in Hull coincided with the first one of

any significance here. My cousin and I spent a long and, truth be told, terrifying night in the cinema waiting out the bombing. When it was all over, that block of the city had been so severely damaged by fire that it looked like something that should have been on the cinema screen rather than real life.

Even more unnervingly, soon after the sirens stopped, I discovered a dead woman on the floor of a café. She couldn't have been much older than either of us, and it made the war seem so much more real somehow. I know we've been expecting raids for months, but nothing prepares one for the reality of it. The smoke and the heat and the stunned looks on the faces of passersby were beyond my worst imaginings.

But let me not only speak of troubles. My cousin is completely charming and her home is like something straight out of a glossy magazine. She is quite glamorous and sophisticated, and she insists it's a patriotic duty to wear red lipstick. Did you know Hitler hates red lipstick? I shan't be without it from now on!

Do write when you have a chance and let me know you are well and safe. I miss you.

Love,

Wilhelmina

D espite the comfort of the bed in Lydia's guest room, Billie had not managed to rest in the hours since their return from what had promised to be a pleasant evening. The sound of the roof of the café as it collapsed in on itself filled her ears long after they had made their way from the square near the cinema and into the quiet depths of Lydia's tranquil home. Lydia had made them each a steaming cup of Horlicks laced with heavy-handed splashes of whisky to lull them to sleep, before tucking Billie into bed beneath the smooth, satin covers of the inviting guest bed. She had left the door to the room open, assuring Billie that she was just across the hall and to call out if she needed anything.

Billie had lain awake until she heard Lydia moving about and had slipped immediately out of bed, eager to find a way to be of help. Surely there would be much to be done. She dressed quickly in a serviceable gabardine skirt and cotton jumper. She sat at the vanity table to arrange her hair. Lydia had left the tube of lipstick from the evening before lying next to the hand mirror. She picked them up and, after fewer tries than she expected, was pleased by her efforts to apply the scarlet color to her lips.

She found Lydia standing over a percolator in a sparklingly clean and startlingly modern kitchen. Her cousin looked her over as if searching for signs of distress or illness.

'It looks as though you are still planning on joining me at the library today. Between the air raid and finding that poor young woman, I wouldn't blame you if you wished to have a day to collect yourself instead,' Lydia said.

'I should prefer the distraction of keeping busy. Besides, I cannot imagine sitting around loafing when there must be so much that needs to be done.'

A distraction was truly what she needed most. She couldn't get the image of that poor young woman from her mind. She had been so vivacious and lovely when Billie had first seen her sweeping gracefully into the café and drawing the admiring glances of all the other patrons. It seemed utterly incredible that only hours later she would be lying lifeless in that same room.

Even more disturbing was Billie's conviction that the young woman had not met her sudden death by dint of an enemy bomb. What were the chances anyone would believe her with all the evidence buried under so much rubble? If the constable who had seen the same scene with his own eyes had not felt it worthy of further investigation, would anyone else?

'That's the spirit. Your attitude is one more reason I am so delighted to have you here with me,' Lydia said.

Billie's heart gave a little leap in her chest. After the scene at the café, she had worried that Lydia would hand her a ticket back to Barton St Giles with an admonition not to darken her doorstep again. Even hours after the high-handed constable had carted her out of the building, slung over his back like a sack of laundry, her temper still flared when she called to mind how he had dragged her from the scene and deposited her on the pavement with an obstinate refusal to concern himself with the body still sprawled in the café.

As soon as they had breakfasted, they made their way along the streets between Linden Crescent and the Central Library. Billie was struck by how many people had flooded the streets to see what exactly had suffered damage and what remained unscathed. The destruction increased as they moved closer to the center of the city. What had felt overwhelming and numbing in the wee hours of the morning seemed all the grimmer in the bright light of day. The sense of unreality she had felt upon emerging from the cinema only hours before had not lessened. They came across the remains of what had been a towering brick building, and Billie heard Lydia give a slight gasp.

'I have patronized Huntington's department store ever since I first arrived in Hull. What a very great pity it is to see it so badly damaged,' Lydia said, reaching for Billie's arm and tucking her hand protectively through the crook of it. Billie felt her cousin stretch herself to her full height and stride along with a little more spring in her step.

'It is a good thing the nation has been preparing for this sort of attack for months,' Billie said.

Lydia nodded, and they walked on in silence until they turned down Albion Street and stopped in front of a handsome brick and buff-colored stone building. Figures carved into the stone face of the building curved around either side of the words *Central Public Library*. They mounted the shallow steps and passed between a pair of columns, and Billie noticed Lydia hesitate before pulling open the front door. As they stepped into the high-ceilinged foyer, she heard her cousin exhaling slowly.

'Is there something wrong?' she asked.

'I must confess that I had wondered if the library had suffered any damage. Just the idea of an incendiary bomb falling on all the books was enough to break my heart,' Lydia said.

Billie had not even considered the possibility of a library going up in flames. As she stood there in the center of the entrance hall, her heart turned over in her chest. The foyer was larger than the entire reading room back in Barton St Giles. As a lifelong, enthusiastic reader, the notion that books could be among the casualties of war was peculiarly grieving. It wasn't that she felt that things counted for more than human life, but there was something so poignant about the value of the library and the loss that would be felt should it be damaged.

Lydia gave herself a little shake and then strode on ahead towards an enormous circulation desk positioned at the end of the foyer. Billie quickened her pace to catch up. After her cousin had shown her where to store her handbag in the employee cloakroom, she was set to work directing people who entered the building looking dazed and concerned towards the section of the library carved out to serve as the information bureau.

About halfway through the morning, a woman appeared looking more frazzled and agitated than had anyone else she had encountered so far. All the people Billie had seen staggering about the streets when the air-raid sirens had silenced had looked haggard and agitated, but none of them seemed as overwrought as the woman standing before her. While her clothing appeared to be of high quality and well cut, it could not be said that she had dressed with care.

Her hat sat slightly askew on a head of ash-blonde hair which might have benefited from more attention from a comb. Even though her blouse appeared to be constructed of real silk instead of the more common rayon or even cotton, the placket was mis-buttoned. She stood in the center of the foyer looking as though she wasn't sure if she should proceed. Billie gave the woman an encouraging smile and took a step towards her.

Many a time she had seen her mother do exactly the same thing. Martha Harkness had been an expert at putting people at their ease so that they might feel comfortable asking for help or opening up about painful or embarrassing topics. Billie had not realized how much she had learned from her mother about making herself of use to strangers in need until she had fielded so many requests in the library that morning.

'Are you looking for the information bureau?' Billie asked.

The woman nodded slowly, a mixture of fear and relief flooding her face. 'Yes, I am. Is this the place where you go to find out if someone has been sent to the hospital . . . or worse?' the woman asked.

'Yes, it is. Is there someone you are looking for?' Billie asked.

'I'm looking for my daughter,' she said. 'She never came home last night, and I haven't been able to find her at any of her friends' houses either.'

'May I have your name, please?' Billie asked. Once again, she was struck by the unfamiliar experience of being in the company of a total stranger.

'Mrs Chetwell,' she said.

'Why don't you follow me, and we can take a look at the lists. We received an update a couple of hours ago, so it has the most recent information available,' Billie said.

She did not feel she could simply send the woman off on her own. Billie nodded to her cousin to indicate that she was accompanying the woman and that no one was in the foyer to greet newcomers looking for help. Lydia nodded back as if to acknowledge her silent statement and bustled out from behind the circulation desk to staff the position herself.

'Do you have any reason to suspect that your daughter would be among those who were troubled by the bombing last night?' Billie asked. 'Troubled by' seemed to be such a benign way to describe what had happened, but she didn't think that it would be in anyone's best interest to agitate the poor woman further.

'No, I suppose I don't have a particular reason to be worried about her, other than the fact that she never came home, and I have not been able to locate her today,' the woman said.

'Does your daughter often spend the night away from home?' Billie asked.

'She has been staying out more often lately, especially if she will be out late at a dance or the cinema or even a party. She also attends the local art college, and they often have exhibitions or even late nights at the studios working on projects outside of class time,' the woman said.

Billie noticed that as the woman spoke, her face lost a little of its pallor. So far, the number of casualties and injuries had not been all that great, and Billie thought it likely that the woman was simply a concerned mother who found the occasion of the bombing awakening all of her maternal instincts. Billie stopped at the bulletin board set aside for posting lists of address changes, injuries and hospitalizations. She turned towards the woman.

'Here you go. Why don't you take a look at the names on the list and see if your daughter's is among them?'

She gestured towards the board, and the woman stepped closer and painstakingly ran her finger over the column of names. She shook her head and turned back towards Billie.

'Is this a complete list of all the people injured in last night's raid?' she asked.

'It's the most complete list so far. The police are supposed to be sending someone with more information in an hour or so. They liaise with us throughout the day in order to keep the information current. Did you not see your daughter's name on the list?' Billie asked.

'No, she wasn't there,' the woman said.

'That's a good thing, isn't it?' Billie asked.

'I suppose it is. But where can she possibly be?'

'Perhaps she's just having a lie-in after all of the excitement last night. I know it was difficult for me to get out of bed this morning when it was time to come into the library,' Billie said.

That wasn't entirely true. Billie had never even gone to bed in the first place. Between the hours spent at the cinema and then the incident at the café, she had barely made it back to Lydia's house before they turned around and headed to the library.

Besides, she was certain she would not have been able to sleep anyway with her thoughts swirling with all that had happened. She couldn't imagine anyone would have found it easy to sleep, but she guessed it was conceivable that the woman's daughter had done so. And it certainly wouldn't have done her any good to encourage her to lose hope.

'I suppose that's possible. I mean, that's what her father suggested was likely. He didn't think I should've troubled officials with my concerns. He always says that I'm far too inclined to worry,' she said.

'I think most mothers would do what you have done. I'm sure your daughter feels very lucky to have you,' Billie said, thinking of her own mother and how many times she had fretted over Billie's exploits.

Seeing the worried look on the woman's face, she felt anew her remorse for worrying her mother on the night she died. She wondered if she sought to comfort the woman to soothe her own conscience.

'Thank you very much for saying that, my dear,' the woman said. 'If I don't hear from Audrey by the afternoon, I'll be sure to come back.' With that, she raised a hand and hurried off.

Billie felt a knot gathering in her stomach. All the assurances she had given to the woman seemed to evaporate with a single word. The woman's daughter's name was Audrey.

SIXTEEN

Kingston upon Hull
Dear Mrs Palmer,

Please don't fret about Candace any more than you can possibly help. I understand that it must be difficult for you to have your daughter so far from home and for you not to have a chance to see her with your own eyes. I can tell you that her letters to me are also filled with cheery bits of news and mention of friends she has made and things she has learned. I do not think for a minute she is keeping things from you, nor do I believe she is suffering through particularly dire conditions. Perhaps you could send her a care package filled with those fig bars you are so famous for baking. Even if she is feeling blue, I am certain they will buck her right up!

Love,
Wilhelmina

It felt like hours before she had time to do anything about her suspicions. A steady stream of people seeking information arrived at the library with other concerns. At midday, Lydia provided someone to relieve her.

'You must be in need of a bite to eat and a cup of tea by now,' Lydia said.

'I haven't any appetite, but I do have a question about the

information bureau. What do you do if you think you have some information that should be added to the list?' Billie asked.

'What sort of information do you mean?' Lydia asked, leading her to the small staffroom in the rear of the building and pouring out a cup of tea for Billie.

She described the encounter she had with Mrs Chetwell and her concerns that the dead woman was her daughter.

Lydia lowered her teacup and gave Billie a long look. 'Mrs Chetwell, did you say?'

'That's right.'

'We are in contact with the police department daily to keep the information up to date. Why don't you take our list to the station straightaway? You can tell them that Mrs Chetwell was in looking for her daughter.'

There was an urgency to Lydia's voice that made the knot in Billie's stomach return. Her previous interactions with the constabulary had been fraught with difficulty, and she was not eager to go to the station. But as she recalled the young woman at the café and the anguished look on Mrs Chetwell's face, she knew she must report her concerns.

'Do you know with whom I should speak?' Billie asked.

'Go to the front desk and ask for Avis Crane. She is the library contact at the station.'

'Where exactly is the station?' Billie asked.

'Just take King Edward Street to Victoria Square. Then turn east on Alfred Gelder Street and it will be just ahead on the right. At least that should be the way to go so long as the streets aren't blocked off by rubble.' Lydia worked a key off a ring she retrieved from her skirt pocket and handed it to Billie. 'After that, you'll have done enough for one day. Take my key and head on home after you've spoken with Avis. I'll see you this evening.'

The path was clear all the way along her journey, but now and then there were signs of the air raid the night before. Piles of debris sat on empty patches of ground, and a hovering smell of smoke drifted in the air. Knots of people chatted in front of some of the more spectacularly damaged buildings, pointing and shaking their heads.

She passed the Royal Infirmary, the City Hall and the

Wilberforce monument before spotting the final turn for the police station. The lobby of the station buzzed with activity. Along a wall opposite a long counter, people sat crowded on to wooden benches. Billie looked around for any sign there was a queue or system for being assisted. The people on the bench paid her no mind as she approached the counter and asked after the whereabouts of Avis Crane.

The man behind the counter pointed to a long corridor and said she would find WPC Crane in the room at the end of it. Without another word, he beckoned to the person behind her. Billie hurried down the hallway and knocked on the door at the end.

A voice bid her enter, and she stepped into a room barely larger than a broom closet. It just managed to fit a desk, two chairs and a coat rack suffering from bad posture. A bare bulb hung from the ceiling in the center of the room. High up on one wall, a single, tiny window allowed a bit more light to penetrate the space. A gray-haired woman with an unlined face sat behind the desk and gestured towards the chair Billie assumed was for visitors.

'May I help you?' she asked.

'Are you Avis Crane?' Billie asked, taking the offered seat.

The woman behind the desk nodded. 'Yes, I'm WPC Crane. What can I do for you?'

'My cousin, Lydia Harkness, sent me on business from the information bureau,' Billie said.

'You're Lydia's cousin? You know, I can see a family resemblance now that you come to mention it,' the woman said, scrutinizing Billie even more closely. 'I had no idea she had relatives in the area.'

'That's just it; I haven't been in the area. I arrived from Wiltshire by train yesterday. I had found myself at a loose end recently, and my cousin was gracious enough to invite me for a visit. We had set no fixed arrival date, so I'm not surprised she had not mentioned me,' Billie said.

'You must have been at a very loose end to make the journey from the relative safety of Wiltshire to the northeast coast,' Avis said, squinting at Billie and searching her face with a piercing gaze. 'Did you also have a job lined up here?'

'My mother was recently killed in an accident, and my father and brother are both serving overseas. I found myself rattling around a large rectory with my father's curate, which was causing a great deal of gossip. I felt it would be better to take my chances with enemy activity than to endure the small-minded remarks of the local church women,' Billie said.

'You have my condolences. Both on the loss of your mother and the unwanted attention of small-town residents,' Avis said. 'Now, what is it you wished to discuss?'

'How do you determine which names go on the list for the information bureau?' Billie asked.

'Sometimes the information is given to us by people who wish to announce a change of address. After a bombing, many people are eager to relocate to safer locations like your own Wiltshire. In other cases, someone is injured, and their names are listed along with the hospital where they can be found.'

'What does someone do if they are concerned that a loved one is missing but has not been listed?' Billie asked.

'Usually, we would expect such a person to come into the police station and report that person missing. Has someone reported a missing person at the information bureau?' Avis asked. The crinkle appeared between her eyebrows, and Billie felt a knot gather in her stomach once more.

'Yes. A woman came in to check the lists for her daughter's name. She never came home last night, and the woman wasn't able to contact her at any of her friends' residences either,' Billie said.

'Often, young people are looking for any excuse to have a taste of adventure. Perhaps you even felt that way yourself when you set off for Hull, despite the fact that you would be placing yourself in greater danger coming to the coast,' Avis said, raising an eyebrow at her. 'More often than not, these young people return home with a bit of a hangover and possibly a broken heart.'

'I'm concerned there might be more to it than that,' Billie said. 'I don't want to raise any unnecessary alarm, but I suspect I know what happened to her daughter.'

'I think you had better tell me exactly what's on your mind,' Avis said. She looked at her watch and then back at Billie.

'Last night, after the bombing, I found a woman's body in a café,' Billie said.

'I did hear mention that a young woman was killed during the air raid last night. But what makes you think that she is that woman's daughter?' Avis asked.

'I had been in the café earlier that day and had seen the same young woman there. She was also a customer, and I overheard her speaking with a companion who called her Audrey,' Billie explained.

Avis leaned forward slightly. 'And the woman's daughter is named Audrey?'

Billie nodded slowly. 'I know that Audrey isn't the most uncommon of names, but it did seem to be worth checking into further.'

'How did you come to find her body?' Avis said.

'I noticed a leg sprawled across the floor of the café and thought that someone was injured and needed help getting out of the building. Perhaps it was foolhardy of me, but I didn't know she was dead until I checked for a pulse.'

'And you didn't find one?'

'No. In fact, the blood on the back of her head had dried and her skin was cool to the touch.'

'I don't suppose that you would be interested in a job with the constabulary, would you?' Avis asked. 'We are actively trying to recruit women for the department in order to replace the men who are serving in the forces. We could use young ladies like you who seem bright, capable and alert.'

Billie couldn't believe her ears. She had never remotely considered working as a police constable. She had heard of such things, of course – who hadn't? Still, female constables were exceedingly rare. She knew that there had been a quantity of them during the Great War, but since then their numbers had dwindled as to be almost non-existent. In fact, the woman seated across from her was the very first female officer Billie had ever encountered.

The idea of joining one of the auxiliary services had seemed to be daring and entirely outside the normal realm of women's experience. The notion of joining the police force was astonishing. Her stomach fluttered with excitement at the possibility.

Unbidden, an image of her mother's face rose in her mind's eye, and the sound of her voice begging her to promise not to join the services rang in Billie's ears.

Billie didn't know what to say. She was not accustomed to receiving praise for launching herself into situations without thinking them through.

'I am sure anyone would do the same,' she said.

'Sadly, you are quite wrong about that. There are many people who could assist people at the information bureau but far fewer who would be as well suited for the constabulary,' Avis said.

'You're offering me a job?' Billie asked.

'I most certainly am. The department has authorization from the city council to hire four female officers. I'm the first and you would be the second. Two women are being hired for clerical roles within the station in order to free up men to be out patrolling, but two of the new officers are destined to be on patrol themselves. Which do you think you would prefer?' Avis asked.

Billie's heart soared, and she replied without a thought. 'A patrol officer. I have no interest in sitting behind a desk typing up reports and memos. If that was the job on offer, I would be happier working in an armaments factory,' Billie said.

She wondered if she had said too much as a look of concern slid across Avis's face. Upon reconsideration, any position in the station seemed that it could be exciting and useful in a meaningful way. She instantly regretted her hot-headed response. She could hear her mother's voice in her head cautioning her about thinking before she spoke.

'You should know that although you would prefer to patrol, there may be times when you would be required to perform clerical duties. Those jobs are invaluable and the station cannot function properly without them. Can you imagine how difficult it would be to bring people to justice if no one knew where the evidence should be stored or how reports should be filled out to document what had occurred?' Avis asked.

Billie felt chagrined. She had spoken out of turn and without due consideration. Of course, clerical duties were important and just as valuable as being out on the street and apprehending criminals.

'I've allowed my enthusiasm to run away with me. I simply meant that I do not want to be one of those women who sits idly by while others get on with difficult tasks. I am perfectly capable of typing or filing or even making the tea, should it come to that. The events of last night are still fresh in my mind, and I am sure that I was influenced by my reaction to finding Audrey's body in the café,' Billie said.

Avis leaned back in her chair and gazed solemnly at Billie. Her clear gray eyes sat unwaveringly beneath her level sandy-colored brows. Just as Billie was wondering if Avis was about to withdraw her offer of a job, Avis broke into a wide smile and leaned across the table with her hand outstretched. Billie stuck out her own and grasped it. Avis gave her a firm shake and then withdrew her hand and picked up a folder lying on the top of her uncluttered desk.

'That's just the spirit we are looking for in our WPCs. But I shouldn't wish for you to imagine that your duties would often involve discovering dead bodies littered about the city,' Avis said.

'I am sure every constable hopes not to encounter such things,' Billie said.

'Just so. If suspicious deaths are rampant in our city, it means we are not doing our job of maintaining law and order,' Avis said. 'For the most part, you would be asked to assist with matters pertaining to women and children. These are among our most vulnerable citizens by and large, and I find that the male officers often are not as sensitive to their particular situations as they might be.'

'I see,' Billie said, feeling a slight shadow of disappointment pass over her.

'Not only do they tend to be insensitive towards the types of situations women might find themselves in as victims, but they seem to be blinded to the idea of women as criminals and thus have allowed more women to perpetrate crimes than is at all reasonable. A police force that includes women as officers will help to balance out both of those failings.'

Billie's spirits rose once more as Avis slid a piece of paper across the desk towards her and tapped at the top of it.

'I'd like you to fill this out so that we can place you on the roll as soon as possible.'

Billie looked down at the form and felt her heart race. It looked so official and made it seem real. She really was going to be a police constable.

'How soon would I take up my post?' Billie asked.

'Be at the police court tomorrow morning at nine and report here as soon as you are sworn in. Is that soon enough for you?' Avis asked.

'Absolutely,' Billie said.

'Do make sure to be on time. As a woman police constable, you will face enormous scrutiny of your every action. Can I count on you to be there?' Avis asked.

'Unless we are bombed again tonight and I don't make it out alive, I will absolutely be there,' Billie said.

SEVENTEEN

Kingston upon Hull
Dear Mr Roberts,

I am writing to ask if there is something that ought to be done to keep my father's motorcar in good order during my extended absence. Perhaps it might be used for the war effort in some way. I have left it at the rectory but as Ronald does not drive, I thought it best to make inquiries with a professional, such as yourself . . .

Billie had thought she would have little trouble finding her way back to Linden Crescent after traversing the nearby roads on four previous occasions. Nevertheless, she found herself reduced to asking a passerby and then a police constable for directions. Perhaps the streets looked quite different in the light of a sunny day. Maybe it was the disorienting effect of the bomb damage. Even more likely was the agitation she felt at the turn of events.

She had never expected to be made an offer to join the constabulary when she had taken leave of Lydia that afternoon. As she picked her way over piles of broken bricks and around mounds of smoldering rubble, she still could not quite believe all that had occurred since her arrival in Hull. She had met a long-lost cousin, survived her first air raid, discovered a body, confronted a constable and accepted a position only recently opened to women. And now she had to tell Lydia that the information bureau would not be able to count on her help.

With a start, she realized she had not given any thought to refusing Avis's offer in order to avoid disappointing Lydia. She could only hope that Lydia would be as pleased with her independent spirit as she was herself. As she turned on to Linden Crescent and approached number seventeen, her footsteps slowed, and she ran a list of possible reactions to the news from Lydia through her mind.

She mounted the steps and tried the lock before remembering Lydia had given her the key. She let herself into the empty house and called for her cousin, just to be sure she was indeed the first to arrive. Her nerves jangled, and she was struck by a desire for some sort of task to take her mind off the wait for Lydia's return.

Billie made her way into the kitchen and took stock of the larder. Breakfast had been a haphazard affair, and Billie had thought at the time that Lydia had bothered only on her new housemate's account. An examination of the cupboards and fitted cabinets only served to strengthen that impression.

To distract herself, as well as to do something to thank Lydia for her hospitality, she determined to prepare some sort of meal while she waited to deliver her news. She found half a loaf of slightly stale wholemeal bread, a dusty tin of sardines, a pat of butter and a pint of milk. After a bit of trial and error, she managed to operate the cooker with enough skill to prepare two plates of sardines on toast before she heard the front door open and Lydia's voice calling her name.

Billie had meant to deliver the news about her job as soon as Lydia arrived but found herself reluctant to wipe the smile from her cousin's face. Lydia had declared the meal a complete triumph and had marveled at the way Billie had managed to make anything the least bit appealing from what little there was to be had in the pantry.

'What an enormous treat,' Lydia said as she carried her plate to the dining room. 'I cannot seem to be bothered about meals with just myself to feed. And besides, I've never excelled in the kitchen under any circumstances, and with the rationing and the queues it all seems like too much trouble.'

'It seemed the least I could do,' Billie said, following her to the table. But once there, she had no appetite. Concern for how Lydia might take her news drove all desire for food from her.

'Are you feeling quite all right, my dear? Last night's events haven't got you down too badly, have they?' Lydia asked, inclining her head towards Billie's untouched plate.

'No, it's nothing like that exactly. Well, I suppose, in a way it is,' Billie said.

'Are you wondering how to ask me if I will put you on the next train back to Wiltshire?' Lydia asked.

Billie turned to her with a jolt of surprise. She looked at her cousin, carefully examining her face for any signs of encouragement to leave. Although Lydia was doing a valiant job of keeping her features in check, Billie was touched to see clear signs of sadness in a downward turn of her mouth and the slight crinkle between her eyes.

'No, quite the opposite, actually – although it would include me taking my leave of you in a way, I suppose,' Billie said.

'What is it, then?' Lydia said, lowering her fork and giving Billie her complete attention.

'While I was at the police station, your friend Avis Crane made a most extraordinary suggestion.' Billie swallowed and gathered up her courage. 'I'm shocked to say she offered me a job. But I shan't consider taking it if you don't approve.'

'I would be quite shocked if she hadn't,' Lydia said.

'You would?'

'Certainly. When I sent you to see her, it was for the express purpose of allowing her to get a good look at you,' Lydia said. 'I thought it far better for her to see for herself what you would be capable of than for me to simply recommend you as a WPC.'

Billie felt a wave of relief flood over her at Lydia's response. The look on Lydia's face told her that she was more than welcome to pursue the possibility and would have all the support she might want in doing so.

'So, you don't mind that I accepted on the spot? After all, I agreed to help out at the information bureau, and it will be short-staffed again.'

'Of course not. There are any number of people who would do a remarkable job assisting at the information bureau. I never meant for you to feel as though you had no choice in the matter.'

Relief flooded through her as Lydia picked up her fork once more.

'You are absolutely sure?'

'Avis is quite a particular sort of person. If she offered you a position, I would not dream of trying to dissuade you. When do you start?'

'I am to appear at the police court in the morning to be sworn in,' Billie said, raising her fork.

'Grandmother Phyllida made something of a habit of appearing in the police court herself. I am sure she would be absolutely delighted if she knew that one of her descendants was entering that same sphere,' Lydia said with a smile.

'Your grandmother was a woman police constable?' Billie said, once again wishing her father had been more willing to share family history with his children.

Lydia smiled and shook her head. 'Quite the contrary. I'm delighted to say that she was repeatedly arrested for her activities as a suffragette. The notion that in just a few hours' time her great-granddaughter will be in a government-sanctioned position to be the one doing the arresting would have pleased her no end.'

'I wish I could have known her,' Billie said.

'I tell you what. Let's finish up and I'll dig out a family album or two for you to take a look at while I do the dishes. And then it's off to bed for the both of us, I think. You have a big day tomorrow,' Lydia said, reaching across the table and giving Billie's free hand a squeeze.

EIGHTEEN

Hull
Special Constable Upton's PNB

Peter paused and took a glimpse of himself in the reflection of the glass as he pushed open the door to the police court. It had taken some doing to remove the soot and dust from his uniform after the events of the night of the bombing, but his landlady had valiantly applied her efforts towards sponging off the greater part of the filth. There hadn't been time to launder it properly before he was due to appear in court, and so it would have to do.

The magistrate sat behind the high wooden bench, leaning sideways and speaking in a low tone with the detective who served as a prosecutor. Throughout the large room, Peter spotted familiar faces. Many of those hauled up before the court were repeat offenders. The Hull police court was the first stop for all crimes committed in the city and it dealt with the vast majority of those entirely within its own system. Public drunkenness, vagrancy, petty thefts and even blackout violations, like the one that brought Peter to testify that day, were all handled at the local level. Only occasionally were crimes committed that were deemed sufficiently serious to be passed on up the chain to the assizes at York.

In fact, Peter had only seen one such case in his time with the department, and it had not been something he wished to witness again anytime soon. That case involved an abusive father and the death of a child, and it had turned Peter's stomach inside out when the evidence had been presented on the same morning he was due to testify concerning motor vehicle violations involving soldiers from a local base.

He couldn't say he was particularly looking forward to his involvement with the court that morning either. It was always tedious to find himself recounting the violations of others. He certainly was not looking forward to besmirching the character of a dead young woman by pointing out her flouting of local ordinances just prior to her death. It didn't help matters that the young woman in question was the daughter of a city councilor. Sergeant Skelton had given him a telling off for not having recognized her from photographs in the papers. But as far as he was concerned, the society pages weren't for the likes of him.

As he looked around the room, his gaze lingered on an attractive young woman seated on one of the front benches. A demure navy-blue hat sat perched neatly upon her head, and her dark suit and gloves gave her an air of self-assurance despite her obvious youth. As the bailiff called his name, he realized with a jolt she was the maddening young woman he had hauled from the café. Just what the devil was she doing there?

Kingston upon Hull
Dear Candace,
    You will never believe the job I have been offered . . .

Billie tugged at the base of her gloves nervously. She smoothed her hands down over her skirt and checked her hat to be sure it was fixed firmly upon her head. Out of the corner of her eye, she saw the door to the courtroom crack open, and a figure that struck her as somewhat familiar strode in. Her breath caught in her throat as she recognized the police constable from the café. She wondered what on earth he could possibly be doing at the police court that morning. She was already nervous enough about appearing before the magistrate without encountering someone who had been so dismissive of her investigatory prowess. She could only hope he would be done with whatever brought him to the court before he spotted her.

As the constable approached the bench, she wished she had chosen a less conspicuous seat further back in the courtroom. Apparently, his name was Peter Upton, and from the way the magistrate addressed him, he was someone who had appeared in the court on more than one occasion. As he took his place before the bench, his gaze landed upon her and she was chagrined to realize that he recognized her, too.

From the scowl on his face, it was clear he had not forgotten who she was. His eyes widened slightly, and it took the bailiff two attempts to attract his attention to the matter at hand. She hoped that he would be needed elsewhere before it was her turn to be sworn in.

The bailiff announced the case number and stated the purpose of Constable Upton's appearance in court that day. He was there to provide a statement concerning a lighting violation. The magistrate turned and addressed him.

'Go ahead and tell us what you saw on the night in question, Constable Upton,' he said.

Billie watched Constable Upton's profile as he leaned slightly forward in his chair and began to speak. 'I approached the café at a quarter past ten on the night of the twenty-fifth of June. I had been on patrol along the alley behind the row of shops in which the café sat and happened to notice a patch of light showing through the window of the café. When I approached the rear entrance to the building and knocked upon the door, a young woman answered and expressed surprise that she was in violation of the blackout ordinance. While she was eager to make amends by adjusting the blackout curtains, I assured her that it was also necessary for me to cite the property and to summon the owner to court. She made every appearance of understanding the severity of the situation and, frankly, considering what happened within twenty-four hours, I'm afraid she was right to do so,' Constable Upton said.

'And what exactly do you mean by "considering what happened"?' the magistrate asked, leaning forward across the bench.

His glasses slid down his large nose and he peered over the top of them, taking in all the faces in the court as he did so. Billie had the impression he knew exactly what the constable was about to say and was simply trying to make a point for those assembled in the courtroom.

'Audrey Chetwell, the young woman who answered the door, was sadly killed in the café during the air raid the next night,' Constable Upton said.

Billie's heart thudded in her chest. Hearing Constable Upton mentioning Audrey's death out loud brought the whole scene back to her.

'A sad commentary, but a lesson to us all, is it not?' the magistrate asked. 'Do you think that the lighting violation had any bearing upon the Germans choosing to target the section of the city where she was killed in an air raid?'

'I'm sure that's not for me to say, sir. What I can tell you is that the blackout regulations are in place for everyone's safety. I should not wish for anyone to think that the unfortunate victim had any hand in what happened to her, but I'm afraid we should all take to heart the gravity of lighting violations. In my experience, there are any number of citizens of the city who do not take the blackout regulations seriously. A night on patrol does not go by when I don't hand out two or three such summonses, more often than not to those who feel such rules are an unnecessary nuisance,' Constable Upton said.

'I understand that the young woman found dead in the building was not the owner of the property. Was the owner notified of the lighting violation?' the magistrate asked.

'A copy of the violation was sent to the property owner's address as per regulations,' Constable Upton said. 'Mrs Jean Nichols.'

'Is the owner here in court today?' the magistrate asked as he looked out across the courtroom.

An older woman, who looked remarkably like the waitress who had served Billie when she had stopped at the café, got to her feet. The magistrate dismissed the constable and called Jean Nichols to the witness stand.

'Do you understand the seriousness of the summons here today?' the magistrate asked.

'I most certainly do understand the seriousness of the violation. My place of business has been destroyed in an air raid. What I don't understand is why it's my fault. How can it be my fault if I had no idea there was anyone there after hours?' she said, two bright spots of color flooding to her cheeks.

Her voice, heavy with the local accent, was shrill, and Billie thought she detected a note of hysteria creeping in.

'Are you denying that you are the owner of the property?' the magistrate asked.

'No. What I am denying is that I'm responsible for the lights being left on or the blackout curtains not being properly held in place. Every night before I close up the shop, I make certain to turn off all the lights and check that the curtains are firmly in position as an extra safeguard. I stood to lose a great deal if the city was bombed . . . and now I have,' the woman said.

'Not as much as the young woman who was given the summons, though, now have you?' the magistrate said.

'I am very sorry that such a thing happened, but I don't see why I should be made to pay. After all, I don't even have a café left to earn back any of the fine because of other people's actions,' she said, crossing her arms over her pillowy chest.

'I'm afraid that's the law, and there is nothing any of us can do about it. You can make arrangements for payment with the bailiffs. I wish you good luck with the restoration of your property and the reopening of your business. Next,' the magistrate said, waving his hand as if to dismiss her and looking out across the court.

Hull
Special Constable Upton's PNB

The witness stepped down from her spot beside the magistrate and huffed her way out through the door of the courtroom. Peter could not disagree that it seemed unfair not only that should she be fined but that she should lose her livelihood through the actions of another, but there was nothing he could do about any of it. Nothing about the war was fair, and there needed to be some way to hold people accountable for what happened on their properties. While she might not have known exactly what was going on in her place of business, she ought to have done. It was up to every citizen to be vigilant about their part in the war effort, and while he sympathized with her plight, he could not entirely respect her attitude about taking responsibility for what was happening on her premises.

His attention returned once more to the distractingly irritating young woman he had carried from the café. What was it about that place? It seemed to be almost magically capable of making women behave in ways that were unsafe or irresponsible. The magistrate called for the next item of business, and Peter found himself wondering once more what had brought his acquaintance from the night of the air raid to the court. Had she done something to cause another constable to arrest her? Or was she there for something smaller like a blackout violation or motoring summons?

As she stood and smoothed her gloved hands down over the front of her neat jacket and matching navy skirt, Peter could not help but feel she looked surprisingly respectable. In fact, he could not think of a young woman who looked less like the sort of person to stand belligerently in a burning building, berating him for his lack of prowess as an investigator. He was wholly unprepared for the magistrate's next statement.

'Are you Miss Wilhelmina Harkness?' he asked.

The young woman nodded.

'I am.'

He peered over his glasses once more and then shook his head slowly.

'Are you quite sure you wish to do this?' he asked. 'It isn't too late to change your mind, you know.'

Peter watched her posture stiffen and her shoulders square. A hush fell over the whole courtroom, and Peter felt the eyes of every person straining forward, just as his own seemed to do. Wilhelmina Harkness cleared her throat and took a step towards the bench.

'I am entirely certain I wish to do this,' she said in the same tone that she had used on him in the café.

'Well, then, if you're absolutely determined, please raise your right hand and place your left upon the Bible outstretched by the bailiff here,' the magistrate said, indicating the man approaching, a black-bound volume in his outstretched hands.

Peter held his breath as he watched her place her hand upon it and raise her right in the air.

'Do you swear to faithfully accept and execute the duties assigned to you as a constable of the Kingston upon Hull Constabulary?' he asked.

'I solemnly do swear,' the woman said.

'And do you swear that you are one Wilhelmina Harkness of seventeen Linden Crescent, Kingston upon Hull, formerly a resident of Barton St Giles, Wiltshire?'

'I do so swear,' the young woman said.

'You know you are the first WPC I have had the duty of swearing in. I understand there's only one other on the force at present, and one of my colleagues performed that particular duty. I wish you the best of luck in your new role and hope that you will not find it too distressing, my dear,' the magistrate said paternally.

Peter had often encountered WPC Avis Crane at the police station but had given no real thought to how the ranks of women on the force might swell. He certainly had no notion whatsoever that the girl he had hoisted to his shoulder and extracted from the café would be deemed the sort of person to fill such a role once the opportunity arose for someone to do so. He was simply flabbergasted.

When the rumors about women on the force had started to fly about, he had understood that they would be relegated to desk duties such as filing and typing. Perhaps they would be allowed to occasionally operate the switchboard when the police messenger boys were on their tea break. Everyone had assumed that the sort of woman who would be appointed to such a role would be an entirely benign, accommodating and compliant person who faded in the background, much like a desk lamp or a filing cabinet. She would be the sort of woman who would cheerfully make pots of tea and offer round plates of biscuits when the troops seemed to be flagging.

She would certainly not be the type who boldly confronted one with wild imaginings in the midst of a crisis. How on earth did a newcomer from some backwater in Wiltshire end up as one of only two women on the constabulary of an important port city like Hull? The mind boggled. In fact, it was all so surprising that Peter barely heard any of the rest of the proceedings after Wilhelmina Harkness took her seat once more.

He came to his senses as he heard the gavel bang down and the bailiff call for the court to recess. All around him people shuffled to their feet and filtered out of the room. His eye landed once more on the newly minted WPC. He felt his hopes for avoiding her evaporate as she turned and faced him.

She lifted a gloved hand in greeting and strode purposefully in his direction. After their last encounter, he had no wish to ever need to speak with her again. Unfortunately, she seemed not to feel the same.

'Why didn't you mention during your testimony that Audrey was murdered?' she said in a hushed tone.

Peter looked over her shoulder towards the magistrate's bench where even her lowered voice had attracted attention. The word 'murder' was not one to be bandied about lightly. He tucked his hand under her elbow which she jerked back.

'Please keep your hands to yourself. The last time you touched me, I ended up slung over your shoulder in a most undignified way.'

Peter found himself smiling. 'Is there a dignified way to be flung over a shoulder?'

'You know what I meant. And you haven't answered my question. Why didn't you tell the magistrate that Audrey might not have been killed during the air raid?' she asked.

'Because I wasn't here to give testimony as to how she died. I was only here about the lighting violation,' he said.

'You cannot be serious. We were both there and we both saw there was no debris around the body. In my opinion, it's a disservice to the victim not to investigate further,' she said.

Her dark eyes sparkled with fury, and a spot of bright color dotted each of her cheeks. He was not entirely sure it was a good idea to have given such a passionate person a badge.

'If you are going to be a constable, there is a lot you have to learn,' he said. 'It isn't your place to have opinions, at least not at the court. You answer the questions you are asked using facts.'

'Your testimony seemed pretty opinionated to me. You gave the impression that Audrey was responsible for her own death,' she said.

'It was not my intention to blame her, but if someone else takes her death to heart and adheres more vigilantly to the blackout ordinances, then I cannot see there was any harm done.'

'I suppose that means you don't intend to investigate what really happened to her, then,' she said.

His eyes were drawn to the clenched fists placed on each of her slim hips.

'I filed a report in which I described the scene as it appeared to me when I entered the café. It isn't up to a mere constable to decide whether or not there should be any further inquiry.'

'Did your report make mention of the possibility that she might have been murdered?' she asked.

'As a matter of fact, it didn't,' he said.

'I suppose you didn't mention the lack of debris surrounding her body either,' she said. 'I would have thought you were required to make an accurate and thorough job of your reports.'

'I did mention the absence of debris surrounding the body. And I'll have you know that you might be more grateful for anything I chose not to include in the report,' he said.

'Why would I be grateful that an officer of the law deliberately omitted details from a report?'

'Because if I had included everything, your name would have appeared in the report along with comments describing you as foolhardy and heavier than you look,' he said.

Without a backward glance, he left her standing there with much to think over. While she might have been entirely right about what she saw, and he thought that she probably was, she was going about it in completely the wrong way. And he wasn't about to be a part of it. After all, it was his intention to stay on the police force himself and to make whatever kind of contribution he was able to do. That would not be possible if he found himself kicked off for riling up a powerful family like Audrey Chetwell's.

NINETEEN

Kingston upon Hull
Dear Ronald,

As it appears I will be staying with my cousin indefinitely, I would be very grateful if you would send along

*the remainder of my clothing to the address at Linden
Crescent . . .*

A vis had given her a brief congratulatory smile and handed
her a stack of clothing items to slip into upon her return
from the police court. Billie entered the women's cloakroom, a space that, while a begrudging afterthought to the needs
of women in the police station, nevertheless provided a private
space to change into one's uniform. There were no mirrors in
the cloakroom, just as there were no other concessions to
comfort besides two hooks attached to the wall opposite the
door. Billie had no notion of whether or not she looked as smart
as she felt in her new uniform.

As she stepped out of the cloakroom, a man she had not yet
met, dressed in a police uniform of his own, stood nearby,
speaking with Avis. They turned and looked Billie up and down
as she approached. While Avis appeared to be looking on with
approval, Billie found herself disconcerted by the directness of
the man's gaze. A moment of panic swelled up in her chest and
worked its way towards her throat. Had she forgotten to button
something important? Or was he one of the men who had not
approved of WPCs joining the constabulary? Constable Upton's
warning rang in her ears as she approached the pair.

'Sir, please allow me to present Billie Harkness, our newest
recruit. She's the one I was telling you about,' Avis said with
an encouraging nod in Billie's direction.

'WPC Crane tells me you were sworn in just this very
morning, young lady,' the man said, taking a step towards her.

'That's correct. In fact, I just donned my uniform for the first
time,' she said.

'Then you are all present and correct for an assignment I
have in mind for you,' he said.

Billie looked up expectantly and moved her glance between
the man and Avis. She had no notion as to who he was and
wondered if his direction superseded Avis's own. As if she had
understood the implied question, Avis made an introduction.

'Billie this is Chief Constable Willis. He has the heavy responsibility of making an official visit to the family of the young
woman you discovered in the café. He felt it would be of use

to Mrs Chetwell for a WPC to accompany him on his task. I suggested you would be ideal for the role,' Avis said.

Billie could hardly believe her ears. She had hoped to be of real use to the constabulary as soon as possible but she scarcely dared hope she would be asked to participate in something so important so quickly. And to be able to be involved from the beginning in the investigation of Audrey's death was more than she could have hoped for.

'I appreciate your confidence in me, WPC Crane,' Billie said.

'I assured the chief constable that you would be just the right person for the job as you had met Mrs Chetwell previously and had so bravely tried to assist her daughter,' Avis said.

'Just so. Now, WPC Harkness, if you will follow me, I have a car waiting to take us to the Chetwells' home on the other side of the city,' he said, turning on his heel and striding down the corridor without waiting to see if she would follow.

Billie threw a glance at Avis once more as if to ask if there was anything else she ought to know, but Avis simply gave her a reassuring smile and turned towards her office, leaving Billie to hurry after the chief constable. She caught up with him just as he was reaching the door and wondered briefly what the protocol was for senior and junior officers. He answered the question for her by holding the door open and motioning that she should precede him across the threshold.

It seemed as though the world was becoming more and more complicated all the time. As the chief constable of the city, he ought to have first crack at entering and exiting any spaces when accompanied by his officers. But old habits die hard, and even though she was dressed in the uniform of the constabulary, first and foremost in everyone's mind, Billie was still female. The W in WPC seemed to outshine the rest of her role. The point was reinforced when they reached the motorcar and the chief constable held open the door to the vehicle and waited for her to settle herself inside it before he took his place behind the wheel.

'WPC Crane tells me that you hail from the south and have only recently arrived in our fair city,' he said.

'I've only been here for a few days, but I must confess I'm

growing to like it more and more all the time,' Billie said, looking out of the window as tall buildings and throngs of pedestrians streaked past her window.

She had not yet ridden in a motorcar in the city and was finding the experience both exhilarating and novel. On foot, so many of the details of the city filled her senses. The sounds and the smells and even the textures of the roadways and buildings caught her attention. But as they sailed past in the automobile, the individual details ran together and formed more of a streaming pulse. As they wended their way through the city, Chief Constable Willis pointed out building after building, which Billie attempted to commit to memory. Hospitals, schools, large department stores and equipment depots were all on the list of places he singled out for her attention.

The further from the police station they went, the lighter and lighter the damage to buildings from the air raid became. It seemed that the enemy pilots had a good sense of where their attack would create havoc for the greatest concentration of people. That thought sent a new one spinning through Billie's brain. It wasn't as though she had never considered the notion that there were enemy agents abroad in the country, but the idea that the Germans would have such a clear sense of where the population was concentrated in a single city that was nowhere near the largest in the United Kingdom sent a shiver up her spine.

She supposed with a thriving port such as the one found in Hull, there would be a great many visitors who could provide information about the city itself, whether through deliberate malice or from ill-considered comments. In fact, long before the war had broken out, the layout of cities could have been common knowledge to the enemy. After all, weren't many British subjects familiar with foreign parts themselves? How many of her fellow British subjects had experience of Berlin or Munich or Dresden? Just because such knowledge existed did not mean that there was anything particularly nefarious in its acquisition. She gave herself a slight shake and tried to focus once more on what the chief constable had to say about their surroundings.

She took the opportunity while he drove to observe him

surreptitiously. He was a man of average height and build. In fact, there was nothing particularly remarkable about his appearance. His face had the suntanned and slightly weathered appearance of a man who enjoyed spending time out of doors, although it was not perhaps so etched upon his face as to indicate that he was some sort of outdoor laborer. He looked the sort who enjoyed rambling on a weekend or perhaps fishing or gardening. She could even see him dressed in protective clothing moving dripping racks of honeycomb from an active beehive.

With his salt-and-pepper hair, blue eyes and clean-shaven face, he appeared to be a thoroughly ordinary Englishman. Without his uniform, she doubted very much that she would have picked him out of a crowd. Take away his authoritative bearing and he could have been just about anyone. He was the sort of man who might melt into a background without further notice. While that was not the sort of commentary one would make about the romantic hero in a melodramatic novel on windswept moors, Billie could see how it might prove a very handy attribute in a police officer, especially one who might wish to go about investigations out of uniform.

She found herself feeling quite curious about his past and how he had moved up through the ranks of officers to reach the position he now held. She suspected that asking him directly was probably not the best route to take. He had constrained his comments to pointing out local landmarks rather than to sharing personal pleasantries. Perhaps Avis would be willing to provide some information about him at some point in the future.

One thing was clear, however: he was a highly experienced driver. Although the damage from the air raid was far less severe in the section of the city they had entered, there were still considerable obstructions in the roadway. As he steered around piles of rubble and avoided gaping potholes, he gave no indication that their ride was anything out of the ordinary. Billie wondered briefly if he had served as a driver in the last war. Before she could create an imagined history for her boss, he lifted a hand off the wheel and gestured towards an enormous and ostentatious brick house.

'That's the Chetwells' home. Before we go in, let me apprise you of the situation. Councilor Chetwell has served the city in some capacity or other for years and is a man who holds a great deal of power in the community,' he said. 'In general, it is not procedure for a chief constable to pay these sorts of calls upon families who have suffered the loss of a loved one to crime. Generally, that is the role of a lower-ranking officer who is involved directly in the investigation,' he said.

'Do you intend to be a part of the investigation?' Billie asked.

'No, I do not. My job requires me to manage affairs from a higher altitude. The day-to-day operations of the constabulary fall squarely on the shoulders of others.'

'Then why are we here, sir?' Billie asked.

'The councilor has asked to see me personally. I imagine he has some questions about the role of the police and what to expect over the coming days,' Chief Constable Willis said.

'Please don't think I am ungrateful for the opportunity to be in the field, sir, but I am not sure exactly what it is that you would have me do,' Billie said.

'As I told Constable Crane, Mrs Chetwell will likely benefit from the comforting presence of another woman at such a difficult time. I understand that you have been recently and tragically bereaved yourself and can likely be relied upon to comport yourself with particular sensitivity in an instance such as this,' he said, turning to face her. 'I must caution you that such encounters are often fraught with emotion and that it may be unpleasant.'

The memory of Mildred Dawes's face as she swooped in with the news of her mother's accident raced through her mind. After her own experience, she doubted that Mrs Chetwell would likely be comforted by anything, but she was eager to help soften the experience in any way she could.

'I shall do my best, sir.'

'Good girl,' he said with a curt nod. 'I understand that your cousin is Lydia Harkness. If you are anything like her, you will be a great asset to the constabulary. A very admirable woman is your cousin,' he said as he reached for the handle and pushed open the driver's side door.

Before she could decide how the chief constable might have come to form his high regard for Lydia, he appeared at the passenger's side of the motorcar and held the door open for her. As she reached the path leading up to the Chetwells' house, however, Chief Constable Willis stepped briskly in front of her, mounted the steps, tucked his uniform cap under his arm and rapped upon the door. He seemed to give no thought to the fact that she hovered like a child behind its mother's skirts when a salesman appeared at the door.

In truth, she was quite grateful for him taking the lead. She was unsure of how to comfort a pair of grieving parents, at least as a police officer. At the rectory, there had indeed been a steady stream of people burdened with life's many troubles who made their way to the front parlor where her mother poured them endless cups of tea or who were invited to her father's study to pray or to rail against the Almighty. Surely this would not be entirely different, she reassured herself as the door opened slowly and an old-fashioned sort of servant stood on the threshold peering at them.

'Chief Constable Willis to see Councilor and Mrs Chetwell,' he said in a tone that brooked no resistance.

'Please follow me, Chief Constable. You are expected.'

He gave Billie a startled glance as he caught sight of her following in the chief constable's wake. Billie wondered how many of the people she would encounter in Hull would have the same reaction to a woman in a police uniform. She wondered if the hiring of female constables was common knowledge in the city or if she would be not only a novelty but also a surprise. Surely a city councilor would not be unaware of her existence as a possibility. After all, the city council voted in the hiring of women to the force, didn't it?

The elderly servant led them down a wide hallway with oversized oil paintings hanging on the walls. In some ways, the space was not unlike several large country manor houses Billie had visited in Barton St Giles, but there was something about it that did not come off the same way. The homes of the prominent families she had encountered in Wiltshire had been understated, even when displaying items that she later came to understand were of enormous value. Everything about the councilor's home seemed chosen to impress visitors and to announce the Chetwells' social standing. The uncharitable thought flitted through her mind that perhaps the councilor hailed from a less moneyed background than he attempted to project. It was almost as though everything in the space had been chosen to present his bona fides.

Billie felt ashamed of her musings as the servant opened a door at the end of the hallway and announced the chief constable. The woman seated on a chair next to an elaborately tiled fireplace was a husk of the woman who had appeared at the information bureau. Blue-black crescents hung beneath her eyes, and her body slumped as though every bit of hope that had held her upright had leaked from her slight frame.

Pacing the hearthrug was a large, florid man who looked to be barely containing a pulsing energetic vigor. He reminded her of a man who had served as a deacon in her father's parish for many years. The deacon had often been genial and generous, but as soon as he felt he was being challenged, he became aggressive towards those who questioned his authority or even his opinions. He stopped his pacing, but before he could speak, his wife welcomed them.

'It was good of you to come in person, Chief Constable,' Mrs Chetwell said.

Chief Willis crossed the room and bent over the grieving woman. He lay a hand on her bony shoulder and then covered her clasped hands with his own.

'I'm only sorry our visit is occasioned by a tragedy such as this. Please accept my condolences on behalf of the entire Hull Constabulary. Truly, the loss of your daughter is one the whole city feels along with you,' he said, inclining his head towards Billie as if to include her in his offer of condolence.

Mrs Chetwell flicked her gaze up towards his face and a tear streaked down her pale cheek. Councilor Chetwell paid no attention to his wife's grief. His gaze landed on Billie like an arctic blast.

'What could have possessed you to appear in our home with a female constable in tow, especially during this time of grief? You know how strongly I opposed adding women to the force,' the councilor said.

'WPC Harkness is the constable who helped to make the connection between the fact that Audrey was missing and that a young woman meeting her description was injured during the air raid. I thought it might be less of an intrusion on your wife to be accompanied by a constable with whom she had already made an acquaintance,' the chief said.

'WPC Harkness? Are you related to Lydia Harkness?' He swept his gaze from her uniform cap to her sensible black shoes as if looking for a family resemblance.

Billie nodded. 'Lydia is my cousin.'

The councilor's brow creased into a scowl. 'That explains your position with the constabulary,' he said. 'Your cousin was an early champion of the notion that women should be recruited for the police force.'

From the tone of the councilor's voice, Billie felt certain that he had not shared her cousin's enthusiasm for permitting women to serve as constables.

Mrs Chetwell peered past the chief constable and addressed her attention to Billie.

'You are the helpful young woman I met at the information bureau,' Mrs Chetwell said, staring at Billie. 'I should have seen the resemblance to Lydia straightaway.'

Billie took a step towards Mrs Chetwell who extended a small, icy hand. It trembled like a stunned bird Billie had once found outside a window at the rectory and had scooped up to keep it safe from the neighborhood cats until it could regain its senses.

'Yes, I am,' Billie said. 'I am so very sorry things turned out the way that they did with your daughter.'

Councilor Chetwell jabbed a thick finger in the air in the chief constable's direction. 'The only constable you should have brought with you is the one who is dragging our Audrey's reputation through the mud.'

'I am certain that no one in the constabulary would do any such thing, Councilor,' Chief Constable Willis said.

'Then let me disabuse you of that notion. I have it on good authority that one of your constables implied in police court that Audrey was responsible for her own death by being care-less with blackout ordinances,' Councilor Chetwell said.

'No offense was intended,' the chief constable said. 'Although Audrey was cited for a lighting violation at the location where she died, no one truly believes that anyone but the Germans is responsible for what happened to her.'

The councilor took a step towards Chief Constable Willis and jabbed his finger against the senior policeman's chest.

'Say what you will, court testimony is a matter of public record, and my daughter's name has been besmirched. If a lighting violation occurred while she was on the premises, I assure you she could not have known about it. Our Audrey was far too responsible for any such nonsense,' he said.

'Councilor, I am sure the constable in question only meant his comments to help serve as a reminder to others of the need for the blackout to be enforced. He meant no disrespect,' the chief constable said.

'His intentions are irrelevant, but his competence is not. I have distinct doubts that the person your constable claims to have seen at that café even was Audrey,' he said.

'I understand that you wish to keep blame from attaching to your daughter's name, but the fact that she was later found in the same building does lend weight to Constable Upton's report,' Chief Constable Willis said.

'Nonsense. Audrey must have run into the café seeking shelter when the air-raid sirens sounded,' the councilor said. 'The suggestion that she was lurking about the place late at night is frankly preposterous.'

'What I don't understand is what she was doing in that part of the city in the first place. She had said she was planning to meet up with her friend Muriel to attend a dance near the art college,' Mrs Chetwell said. She turned her bewildered gaze from Billie to the chief constable.

'Perhaps she was there as one of those larks the young people get up to nowadays. The war has brought out a spontaneity in much of the city's youth,' he said.

'Audrey was not the sort to run about carousing in the seedier sections of the city. I doubt very much she had ever been there in the daylight, let alone after dark. I'm sure that your constable was simply mistaken and that the young woman he saw was another. In fact, I want his comment stricken from the record.'

'Begging your pardon, sir, but I saw your daughter at the café on the day she died. I can't speak for why she might have been at the premises after hours, but I do know she was there as a customer earlier in the day,' Billie said.

'Were you a friend of Audrey's?' Mrs Chetwell asked.

'I'm sorry to say we were not acquainted. I happened to be in the café on the square when she came in and sat at a nearby table,' Billie said.

'Then how did you know that she was named Audrey?' Mrs Chetwell asked.

'She had a companion who called her by her name,' Billie said.

'And you remembered her name from overhearing someone say it in a café?' Councilor Chetwell asked.

'Your daughter made an impression, Councilor. She was so vivacious that it would have been impossible not to notice her. I was truly saddened to find her there in the café again after the air raid,' Billie said.

'You are the one who found her?' Mrs Chetwell asked, leaning forward and squeezing Billie's hand.

Billie looked over at the chief constable, wondering if she had revealed more than she ought. He gave her the briefest of nods.

'I am. I was out in the street looking for ways to help with any who had been injured when I spotted someone through the window. So I went inside the café and found her. I was so sorry that there was nothing to be done for her,' Billie said, once again glancing at the chief constable. He bobbed his head reassuringly.

'WPC Harkness placed herself in considerable danger trying to assist your daughter.'

'Audrey should be remembered as the patriot and hero she was rather than someone who foolishly caused her own death,' the councilor said. 'How much more does this family have to endure?'

Mrs Chetwell let out a stifled sob and staggered to her feet. Without a word, she rushed from the room. Billie raised an eyebrow at the chief constable to silently ask if she should follow her, but he gave a tiny shake of his head.

'I was afraid this would happen. My wife has been through more than any mother should have to bear. I trust I may count on you to refrain from troubling her further,' the councilor said.

'I am sorry if the constabulary has in any way added to your grief,' the chief constable said. 'Rest assured I will look into the matter of removing Audrey's name from the court records and will leave you both in peace.'

The Chetwell house was out of sight before the chief constable spoke.

'Not all interactions with the public are quite so combative. I hope you will not be dissuaded by this experience from remaining with the constabulary,' he said, keeping his eyes fixed on the road in front of him.

'I am not easily discouraged, sir,' she said.

'You do seem like your cousin,' he said, this time glancing over at her for a split second. 'Did you really see Audrey in the café the day she died or were you just trying to assist me?'

'I wouldn't lie about a thing like that,' Billie said. 'The fact that I saw her at the café and heard her companion call her Audrey was the reason I knew that the body in the café might be the Chetwells' missing daughter.'

'Very clever. Constable Crane said you show real promise,' he said.

Billie didn't know what to say. She was delighted to hear that Avis thought her capable but was not sure she ought to respond with pleasure. After all, should one feel good about a talent for unearthing information that brought such sorrow to others? She thought of poor Mrs Chetwell rushing from the room and wondered what had prompted her outburst.

'May I ask what the councilor meant when he said his family had already endured enough?' she asked.

'He was speaking of their son, James. He was one of the men lost at Dunkirk. They barely had time to grieve his death when the air raid took their only surviving child,' he said.

Billie held her breath. Should she tell the chief constable about her suspicions that Audrey had not been killed by enemy fire? Constable Upton had warned her not to do so. And she had already shared her concerns with Avis. Not only that but the chief constable had promised to do what he could to remove mention of Audrey's name from the police records citing her in the lighting violation. As much as it felt like lying, she bit her tongue all the rest of the way back to the station.

TWENTY

Hull
Special Constable Upton's PNB

Peter stood on the pavement outside the butcher's shop and gave it a once-over. It was a modest, brick-front establishment, but the glass in the windows was sparklingly clean and the meat that hung on the hooks in the display windows was appealing, at least as far as wartime rationing went. A short queue stretched from the front counter halfway across the tiled shop floor as he pushed open the door and set the bell above it jangling.

The butcher looked up and held up a hand as though to ask him to wait for the customers to be served before he could turn his attention to him. Peter poked around the shop, looking over the hams and sausages and a carefully displayed array of chops as he waited for the butcher to take orders, wrap up packets of meat in brown paper and twine, and carefully mark ration cards before sending his customers on their way. He was efficient at his job, however, and Peter did not have to wait long for the butcher to come out from behind the counter and flip the sign hanging upon the door from *Open* to *Closed*.

'I heard you'd be coming by about the bicycle theft. That is why you're here, isn't it?' he asked.

Peter nodded. 'Father O'Connell said that you and your delivery boy might be willing to speak with me about it this morning,' he said.

'Mickey's in the back. He can tell you more than I can, but I'll come along and put in my twopence worth,' the butcher said, wiping his well-muscled hands on his white apron.

Peter followed him into a room located behind the counter.

There, sitting at a high-topped table covered in slabs of beef and a variety of poultry awaiting packaging, was a boy of about fourteen. He was checking over a list, and from the scowl stamped upon his face, it did not appear that the information there contained pleased him in the least. He looked up from his task, and his expression took on a guarded cast as he noticed Peter's uniform.

'Mickey, the constable's here to ask you about Father O'Connell's bicycle. I told him you'd be eager to help him get to the bottom of it,' he said.

Peter wondered if the boy's wariness had been attributed to some other sort of mischief, because as soon as the bicycle was mentioned, his face relaxed and he leaned forward eagerly. Packs of boys had been roaming the city ever since the schools had stopped operating, and Peter had seen the sorts of things they had got up to, none of them terribly criminal, but not the best example of young British manhood he had ever seen, either.

He could hardly blame the kids, though. It wasn't as if children were spoiled for choice of wholesome activities when the Germans were dropping bombs on schools and hospitals, and every kid he ran across seemed to be teetering on the edge of malnourishment. Rationing was hard on everyone, but he could well remember being a young boy growing faster than his mother could let down his hemlines. If he had had to go through that stage while food was being rationed, he was sure he would've been looking for whatever sort of thing could've distracted him, too.

'I'll do whatever I can to help. I was just looking over the list of deliveries and I don't know how I'll be able to manage them all on foot,' he said.

'If you're not able to take care of it, I'll have to get in another delivery boy. Either one to split the jobs with you or to take over entirely if he has his own bicycle,' the butcher said.

Peter felt electricity in the air between the two. He wondered if the butcher had been chomping at the bit for an opportunity to let the boy go.

'Let's see if we can get to the bottom of it before it comes to that, shall we?' Peter said.

The boy's face once again flooded with relief.

'What is it that you want to know?' Mickey asked.

'Why don't you start with where you were when the bike was stolen?' Peter said. 'Was it while you were out making deliveries?'

'It was about three-quarters of the way through my route. I had just stopped at Mrs Mullens's house with a pound of sausages and a stewing hen. I'd only been there for a few minutes when I discovered it had been stolen,' Mickey said.

Peter eyed Mickey's posture and determined the boy was not telling the entire truth. But what reason would he have for making up stories about what had happened at the Mullens's house? Could he have been up to something he ought not to have been while he was there?

'That's a laugh,' the butcher said loudly. 'He's never been in and out of there in under a quarter of an hour; of that I am certain,' he said.

'What makes you think that he was there longer than he claims?' Peter asked, turning towards the butcher.

'It's a constant struggle, isn't it?' The butcher threw up his hands in exasperation. 'All of these women who ask for their orders to be delivered take one look at this kid with his big blue eyes, freckles and the dimples in his cheeks and they decide he looks like he's wasting away. Invariably, they offer him cups of tea and food to go with it. He spends most of his shift bellied up to the table of half the housewives in the city.'

Peter turned back to Mickey and raised an eyebrow questioningly. The boy held up his hands as if to defend himself, but his face had turned a deep red.

'Had you been inside the house for quite some time enjoying Mrs Mullens's home cooking?' Peter asked. 'There's nothing criminal in that. I am just wondering for the sake of the timeline.'

'It never seems polite to refuse. Her son's serving overseas and she's ever so lonely. Besides, if I don't accept something, they take offense. Cycling is hard work. I feel half-starved by the time my deliveries are done, even if I do stop and get something to eat at every house that offers it to me,' Mickey said.

'See, what did I tell you? All the old biddies invite him in one day and then they ring up the next complaining that their deliveries are late. What do they think will happen if all of them distract the delivery boy from going about his business?' The butcher's voice had raised a couple of octaves, and he waved his arms wildly about in front of him.

Peter could only guess that this was a constant and chronic complaint from his customers. He could see that the butcher would be frustrated at the lack of foresight the customers seemed to display. Surely, they should have had better sense about the whole matter if they had really thought it through.

'I'm sure that's correct, sir, but it doesn't help us to get to the bottom of the missing bicycle unless one of these women was in on helping to steal it.' He turned back to Mickey once more. 'How long do you think you were actually in there?' he asked.

Mickey shot a furtive glance at his employer before answering. 'Probably fifteen minutes. I try to hurry as fast as I can, but most of them are very chatty women and they keep foisting slices of cake and biscuits on me. That Mrs Mullens is a very fine baker, and I couldn't help but make a bit of a pig of myself,' Mickey said.

'So the bicycle was simply gone when you came back outside? Someone stole it in broad daylight?' Peter asked.

'That's right. I had parked it at the side of the building in a little alleyway so it wouldn't be blocking the pavement. I didn't think it was particularly in danger as it was the middle of the day and the alleyway isn't a popular route for anyone. It seemed as safe a place as any to leave it,' Mickey said.

'Did you see anyone lurking around the building before you went in to make your delivery?' he asked.

Mickey shook his head. 'I don't think so. There were people walking past, of course. It would've been strange if there hadn't been. The Mullens's neighborhood is not one that I would call bustling, but there are always people going about their business. That said, nobody seemed to be paying any particular attention to me or the bicycle when I left it.'

'Did you see anything on the ground that the thief might've left behind?' Peter asked.

'No, nothing at all. Not if you mean cigarette butts or

footprints or anything like you read in detective novels,' Mickey said.

The butcher snorted. 'Just like a foolish boy to be thinking about detective novels. Mickey, this is a real constable you're dealing with. Don't be so daft,' the butcher said.

Peter didn't like the way the man treated his delivery boy. It was time to put him in his place.

'Actually, that's exactly the sort of thing I had in mind. Tire marks, footprints and sweet wrappers can go a long way to pointing you in the right direction to get an investigation going. Was there anything at all unusual?'

Mickey shrugged. 'I wish there was something I could tell you that would be helpful, but it was as though the bicycle had never been there. The pavement was dry, and it all happened before the air raid so there wasn't the amount of dust and rubble on the ground that could've allowed a trail to be seen. It would've been no great trick for someone to simply wander up and help themselves to it. They could've just pedaled off as if the bicycle was their own.'

Peter had to agree that it would be a simple thing to pinch a bicycle. After all, so many of them had very few distinguishing characteristics, at least from a distance and to casual observation. If someone knew how to ride a bike and act as though they were doing nothing untoward, who would pay attention to a cyclist passing along the city streets? He had passed any number of them on his way to the butcher's shop that very morning. Who was to say that Father O'Connell's bicycle was not one of those he had passed by without realizing it? Which brought another question to mind.

'That doesn't give me very much to go on, but I'll do my best to track it down. Before I go, were there any distinguishing features to the bicycle that might help me to identify it?' Peter asked.

'The bicycle looks pretty much like any other black two-wheeled contraption, but I did add a wooden crate to the front and another to the back in order to hold the deliveries. The crates were from Blackworth Supply Company. Their name was stamped on the outside of the crates, if that helps,' Mickey said.

Peter wrote down the name of the company and tucked his

notebook back into his pocket. 'It's not a lot to go on, but it's better than nothing. I'll let you know if I make any progress.'

With that, he let himself out of the back room and out into the street once more. Before leaving, he flipped the sign back to *Open* and heard the bell jangling over his head. Mrs Mullens's address was not more than a half-mile from the shop. If he hurried, he could take a look at where the bicycle had gone missing and the nearby alley before he started his shift at the docks.

As he walked along, he thought about Sergeant Skelton's admonishment that bicycle thefts were commonplace and not of the highest priority. But Peter knew from experience how important the income a child brought into a household could be. The look on Mickey's face when the butcher threatened to cut in half his potential earnings or to eliminate him altogether had been one that Peter had easily understood.

He wished that Mickey had been able to provide him with more information, but he supposed that would have been an unreasonable expectation. After all, bicycle thefts would not be so common if they were not so easy to pull off. Peter quickened his pace and before long found himself standing in front of Mrs Mullens's property.

It was a part of the city that had been among the earliest to be turned to residential housing when the town fathers had undertaken the massive and occasionally unpopular task of clearing the unsanitary and overcrowded terraced houses of the previous century. Sure enough, there on the side of the building ran a shadowy alleyway. He stepped into it from the pavement side of the Mullens's residence and allowed his eyes to adjust to the gloom.

He looked around and noticed that there was barely enough room for two people to walk abreast down the alleyway. Rubbish barrels and piles of debris dotted its length, and as Peter picked his way from the front towards the back, he glanced up and noticed no windows overlooked it on either side. Not only that but the alley ran between two parallel streets, and after only a short distance, the depth of two buildings built back to back, he popped out on the other side into the sunlight once more.

He felt that he hadn't learned much about what had happened

to the bicycle. It was all the clearer that it would be easy for the thief to get away without being noticed by Mrs Mullens or Mickey. In fact, the only thing of real note was that he found himself standing in front of the heap of rubble that had been the café where Audrey Chetwell died.

TWENTY-ONE

Kingston upon Hull
Dear Father,

How are you? Are you eating? Is it naïve to imagine a care package might reach you? I am sure you would find the time would pass more quickly, or at least more pleasantly, if you were to have a few of your favorite books to read. I am not at the rectory myself at present but am certain Ronald would be happy to send a carton of them to you.

And why am I not at the rectory, I can hear you asking yourself. It just so happens that your cousin Lydia invited me to pay a visit to her in Kingston upon Hull. She has the most breathtaking home right in the city, and she has asked me to stay for just as long as I would like. I know you have lost touch with that branch of the family, but I am delighted to report that Lydia is a font of knowledge about them all. She has been very generous with her memories and stories of them, especially Grandmother Phyllida. Did you know I am the spitting image of her when she was my age?

In other news, there is a matter I wished for you to hear about from me before word reached you from elsewhere. I know Mother was adamant that I not join the services and I believe I have honored that wish, although you may feel I am splitting hairs when I tell you what I have done. The Hull Constabulary has made the decision to add women to their force in order to free up more men to serve overseas. I am one of only two so far. Perhaps

you might disapprove, but I must admit I feel quite thrilled
to answer to the title WPC Harkness.

I shouldn't like you to think it is all pridefulness, though.
There is real work to be done in a place like Hull, and I
am so grateful for a chance to help in whatever way I can.
I went out on a call to a family who had lost their daughter
in tragic circumstances and I thought of you and Mother
and how you provided comfort to the grieving in the parish.
I hope I can do something similar in my role as a WPC.

Should the Germans permit you to send a letter, I would
be very grateful for word back from you. I miss you each
and every day. You are in my heart and my prayers.

Love,
Wilhelmina

She was still agonizing over her decision to keep her questions to herself when they arrived back at the police station. Her reappearance in the company of the chief constable had drawn stares from the other constables. She wasn't sure if it was a commentary on her gender or a reminder not to get above herself on account of being singled out to help the chief constable, but she spent the rest of the shift making tea for a steady stream of male constables and typing up their reports.

With each report she typed up, she found her thoughts wandering to the conversation she had had with Constable Upton at the police court. Had he noted a lack of debris surrounding Audrey's body as he claimed? Had his report mentioned carting her own body out of the building like a sack of flour? Curiosity burned in her like an incendiary bomb on a thatched roof. Hoping that no one would sense anything amiss, she asked where she ought to file the reports. Sergeant Skelton directed her to a bank of metal filing cabinets in a far corner of the room.

She nodded her thanks and made her way calmly to the cabinets. It took her a few minutes to comprehend the system used, but before long she had figured out where to place each of the sheets of paper she held in her hands. She glanced over at the constables scattered around the room. For the most part, they were too busy with their work to pay her any attention.

The only man who looked in her direction had fixed his gaze on her legs rather than on her hands.

She shifted her position to be even more certain her actions would be shielded from view and pulled out the drawer she believed would contain the report Constable Upton filed involving the discovery of Audrey's body. She ran her fingers along the top of the folders until she found what she sought. The sounds of footsteps approached from behind and she slipped the report from the folder, folded it in half and tucked it as quickly as she could between her uniform jacket and her blouse.

The footsteps halted abruptly, and she forced herself to smile as she turned around. Chief Constable Willis stood close enough to peer over her shoulder. The room had grown remarkably quiet, and although the other constables avoided staring at her overtly, she was certain they were attending closely to the conversation.

'Sergeant Skelton tells me you are just about ready to finish up for the day. I am heading out myself. Why don't I drive you home?' he said.

'I shouldn't wish to put you to any trouble,' she said, hoping he would let the matter drop. Not only did she wish to retire to the WPC's cloakroom to sneak a peek at the file in order to return it to the cabinet as quickly as possible, but she didn't want anyone, least of all herself, to consider reasons she was being singled out by the chief constable.

'It's no bother at all. I am happy to do it. Are you ready to head out?' he asked.

She nodded, hoping her discomfort did not show on her face as she made her way past desks filled with constables studiously avoiding eye contact with her. Sergeant Skelton was the only one to indicate that he had noticed the chief constable's offer. He raised an eyebrow at her, then shook his head slowly.

As they made their way along the street from the station, Billie couldn't help but notice that he had not needed to ask for directions to Linden Crescent, or even Lydia's address. Between that and the chief constable's appraisal of her cousin's character, she had to wonder how well he knew Lydia. He barely said a word as they drove along and refused her offer to come inside to greet her cousin. Billie noticed that he waited for her to enter the house before he pulled away.

As she pushed the front door shut, she felt the purloined report rustling beneath her uniform jacket. She slipped it out from under the blue serge and unfolded it carefully. As she skimmed the contents of the report, a knot gathered in her chest. At the police court that morning, Constable Upton had lied to her face. No mention whatsoever was made of the lack of debris surrounding Audrey's body. Billie's name was listed as the person who reported the body to Constable Upton, but her observations were unquestionably omitted.

Audrey's death was attributed to a wound to the head. The report stated that before her body could be retrieved, the entire building had collapsed. Nothing that was written was an outright falsehood, but the picture the report painted left the reader to easily conclude that Audrey had died as a result of an incendiary bomb. What Billie didn't know was whether the omissions from the report were a deliberate attempt to mislead or a simple act of incompetence.

As she read through it quickly once more, she was relieved to note that whatever else he might have lied about, Constable Upton had not mentioned the high-handed way he carted her from the building. She tucked the report back under her jacket as she heard the sound of Lydia's voice call out for Billie to join her. She hurried to the drawing room and paused in the doorway. Mrs Chetwell sat on the sofa next to Lydia, a hand-kerchief clutched in her hand. Even from a distance, it was impossible not to notice her eyes were rimmed with red.

'Hello, my dear. Mrs Chetwell has come by specially to speak with you. I assured her that you would be more than happy to give her a few minutes of your time when you arrived home from your shift this evening,' Lydia said in a voice that encour-aged assent.

'Of course, I'm happy to help however I can, Mrs Chetwell,' Billie said, crossing the room and taking a seat opposite the two older women.

The fading light of the evening passed through the still uncovered windows and the shadows falling on Mrs Chetwell's face made her look all the more wretched. Billie's heart squeezed in her chest. With the loss of her mother, she understood how raw grief could feel, especially in the early days. Mrs Chetwell's face held the same look as those of so many of the people Billie had seen over the years being counseled by her parents when similar tragedies had befallen their own families. Lydia reached out and took Mrs Chetwell's hand and squeezed it encouragingly.

'Go on and tell her what's on your mind,' Lydia said. 'I am quite certain Billie will manage to be discreet.'

Mrs Chetwell gave an almost imperceptible bob of her head and dabbed her eyes with her handkerchief before speaking.

'Ever since you left my home earlier today, I have wanted to ask you a question,' Mrs Chetwell said.

'Anything,' Billie said.

'My husband told me not to keep dwelling on it, but since you were actually there, I thought you could help me to know what happened.'

'What is it you think I can tell you?' Billie asked.

'Since you were the one who found her, the one who saw her before the building collapsed, I want to know if my daughter looked as though she suffered,' Mrs Chetwell said. 'I cannot stop picturing Audrey terrified and trapped in a burning building as the ceiling and the walls crashed in on top of her.'

Billie felt her heart squeeze as she imagined the torrent of emotions that surely plagued Mrs Chetwell. Hadn't she tortured herself for hours on end imagining her mother's last moments? How much worse would such a thing be for a mother? Billie looked at Lydia for guidance, but her cousin's attention was entirely focused on their visitor. She drew in a deep breath and hoped she could find words that would be both truthful and comforting.

'I can promise you I saw nothing that indicated she had suffered in the least. When I first noticed her, I thought she was simply unconscious,' Billie said, hoping that would be of comfort.

'But the café had completely collapsed around her. I went and saw it for myself. Her body had to be retrieved from beneath tons of rubble,' Mrs Chetwell said. A sob wracked her slight frame and Lydia wrapped an arm about her shoulders.

Billie once again felt the wave of helplessness that imagining a loved one's last moments could provoke. She wished desperately to lessen Mrs Chetwell's grief.

'When I found Audrey, the building was entirely intact. It wasn't until a constable entered the café that I knew of any danger from an incendiary bomb. I am certain your daughter had no notion that the building would come down.'

'You said she didn't appear to be hurt?' Mrs Chetwell asked, leaning forward slightly.

'No, she wasn't. I was unable to tell until I felt for her pulse that she had been injured at all. I thought she had perhaps fainted,' Billie said. It would not do Mrs Chetwell any good to hear the gory details of the wound on the back of her daughter's head.

'If she wasn't killed by a bomb blast or the building caving in, then what killed my daughter?' Mrs Chetwell's eyes widened.

Billie looked at Lydia once again for a sign of what she ought to do. Her cousin raised both eyebrows and shrugged helplessly. As Billie looked at Mrs Chetwell's face, she thought of her own grief at not knowing exactly who or what had caused her mother's death. She wouldn't wish that on anyone else. It didn't matter that the police report failed to support her version of the events. Still, she didn't want to falsely raise Mrs Chetwell's hopes that there would be an investigation into Audrey's death.

'I think I should mention that what I saw was seen through the eyes of a private citizen. I would not want you to put more stock in what I have to say because I am now a member of the constabulary. I am still very new to my duties,' Billie said.

'That may well be, but it doesn't necessarily mean your memory is faulty,' Mrs Chetwell said. 'Do you think my daughter might not have died because of the air raid?'

'I cannot say exactly what caused her death, but I can tell you that she had a wound on the back of her head and that there was no debris surrounding her body,' Billie said.

'So there was nothing to be seen that might have knocked her down and dealt a fatal blow?' Mrs Chetwell said, dabbing her eyes once more.

Billie nodded. 'Not unless someone removed it before I arrived.'

'Are you suggesting that someone murdered my daughter?'

Mrs Chetwell sagged back against the sofa as a choking sob rose from her throat.

'I didn't mean to upset you even more by suggesting anything. I just wanted to assure you that Audrey did not look at all as if she suffered,' Billie said.

'But to think she may have been murdered is too, too horrid. Who would ever want to do something so unspeakable to my daughter?' Mrs Chetwell asked, turning her tearful gaze from Billie to Lydia, then back again.

'I wish I could tell you I knew the answer, but there was nothing in the café to suggest who might have been at fault,' Billie said.

A knot tugged itself firmly in her stomach and she wondered if she had done the right thing in mentioning the scene at the café. Mrs Chetwell drew in a shuddering breath, then rose and extended her small hand to Billie.

Billie watched with a lump in her throat and a heaviness in her chest as Lydia stepped out of the room to show Mrs Chetwell to the door. There was only one thing left that she could do for Audrey, or her family for that matter. She took out the police report once more and read through the contents a third time.

Maybe she should have held her tongue, but she couldn't live with herself if she left Mrs Chetwell with as many fears as to what happened to Audrey as she had about her mother. If Constable Upton thought he could simply hide the suspicious nature of Audrey's death in the ruin of a bomb site, he could think again.

TWENTY-TWO

Hull
Special Constable Upton's PNB

Peter brushed off his hands and leaned back in his chair. Even though he was well aware that the criminal element had flourished ever since war had been declared, he had not expected to discover that 250 bicycles had been stolen in the city of Hull between January and May of 1940. It was a simply astonishing number.

Father O'Connell's bicycle was one of so many, the vast majority of which had never been recovered. Peter allowed his mind to drift briefly to the other sorts of crimes that had likely risen as a result of the blackout. He had been worried by the thought of his mother being out after dark, and this made him all the more eager to remind her to be careful when she left the house.

If it was that easy to make off with something as large as a bicycle, how much easier would it be to simply grab the handbag of a woman of his mother's age as she wandered alone by herself in the dark? He didn't like to think of the consequences if she were to be knocked to the ground. An involuntary shudder ran through him as he imagined her sprawled on the pavement, suffering a wrenched ankle or worse, as criminals fled down the street carrying off her hard-won valuables.

He refocused his attention upon the matter at hand. As he flipped through the reports once more, looking for some sort of pattern, none seemed to emerge. The locations of the thefts were spread throughout the city, and the ages and conditions of the bicycles had little in common either. The one thing that was similar about the victims was their approximate age or station in life. Prosperous men over forty weren't inclined to spend much time astride a bicycle instead of piloting their own automobiles about town. The victims tended to be either quite young or of lower social standing. Peter's jaw tensed as he considered how such a loss would impact those citizens.

Having possession of an automobile was one of the ways to remark upon one's wealth without saying a word. Such divisions in class even penetrated the police force. The city had put out a special call to recruit residents who owned automobiles for the constabulary, with a plea that they use their vehicles to help in the performance of their duties. Those men who had responded to that request had even set themselves apart from the rest of the constabulary by forming their own social club.

But not everyone could afford such a luxury. Peter understood just how valuable a bicycle could be to a person who did not have access to a motorcar, and right there in black and white in front of him was the evidence that 250 individuals had suffered such a loss in the space of less than six months. His chest burned when he thought of it. He clearly remembered the relief that came of the opportunity to borrow Father O'Connell's bicycle when he was the same age as the butcher's delivery boy.

As he eyed the stack of reports outlining the details of the thefts, a new thought occurred to him. Were the thefts in some way connected, not to the victims or their locations, but to a wish to acquire them for a reason that was more organized than it first appeared? Could there be some kind of black market in bicycles occurring in their city? Since none of the bikes had been recovered, Peter had to wonder if it was a lack of effort on the part of the police department or if it had more to do with the organized and businesslike behavior of the thieves. Was there some sort of criminal organization network in the city that stole bikes, repainted them or disguised their appearance in some way and sold them on, making a large profit from each sale?

Or could it be something even more nefarious than that? The vast majority of the victims of bicycle theft had been those who had volunteered for some sort of war effort. Many of the adults who had lost their bicycles were firemen or local wardens. The children whose bicycles were stolen often served as fire spotters and messengers for the police department or other auxiliary forces. Was it possible that the bicycles were being stolen as a way to thwart these people in the commission of their duties? Could the theft of the bicycles be some sort of enemy activity that had gone unnoticed?

His mind began to race as he considered that he might have unearthed something far larger than the simple theft of the local parish priest's bicycle. Were there Germans and other enemy aliens sneaking about Hull, filching bicycles in an effort to erode the carefully constructed infrastructure of the defense of the home front? As much as he hated to think such a thing might be possible, he felt a stir of excitement that he might have uncovered something of importance.

As he leaned back further in his chair and tented his hands in front of his eyes, a vision of WPC Harkness filled his mind. He could see her face as she had appeared at the police court, waggling her finger under his nose and suggesting that something criminal had occurred in the café. He was getting as bad as she was, allowing his imagination to run wild. Surely a bicycle theft was just a bicycle theft, wasn't it?

Still, it couldn't do any harm to look into the thefts with a more open mind. He couldn't dismiss the memory of Audrey Chetwell's lifeless body and the total lack of debris nearby. WPC Harkness was right. The death couldn't be convincingly attributed to the air raid. He bent back over the stack of reports once more with an eye towards making connections between them somehow. He might be jumping to conclusions just as readily as WPC Harkness, but that didn't mean he was wrong.

TWENTY-THREE

Kingston upon Hull
Dear Candace,
    It seems so long since I've heard from you. When you have time, please write with any news, both your own and any from home . . .

Billie tugged at the collar of her uniform, hoping her face did not look as guilty as she felt. She had spent the night dreaming fitfully of Audrey's body and her mother's being buried under a towering mountain of crumpled police reports. She had awoken before dawn from a nightmare in which Constable Upton confronted her as she tried to secretly return his falsified statement to the filing cabinet. She chided herself for her fears and pushed open the door to the station. With every step she took, the irrational fear that the police report, hidden in her handbag, was somehow obvious to everyone in the room grew stronger.

She plastered her most stoic look upon her face and squared her shoulders as she approached the counter behind which stood the formidable Sergeant Skelton. The sergeant held a telephone receiver to his ear and made conciliatory noises now and again. Billie's heart stuttered as his gaze landed on her. He held up a large square palm like a traffic warden for her to stop and wait.

As the sound of the voice on the other end of the telephone grew louder, she felt the sergeant's stare grow more and more piercing. Her stomach lurched as she realized she recognized the caller's voice. By the time Sergeant Skelton returned the receiver to its cradle, his face was red and small beads of sweat clung to his receding hairline.

'WPC Harkness, can you imagine who was on the telephone?' he asked, leaning over the counter and jabbing a blunt finger at her.

'Was it Councilor Chetwell?' Billie asked.

'Got it in one. If you were a man, I'd suggest that you ought to consider joining the detective force. Since you're only a chit of a girl, I'm not sure I even want to suggest that you keep your uniform on long enough to make me a cup of tea before I toss you out of here on your scrawny backside. Any idea why the councilor called?' he asked.

'I'm sure I couldn't say, Sergeant,' Billie said.

'Since you were able to guess that it was him, you must have some inkling why he would have taken time out of his busy schedule, not to mention his stupor of grief, to call to complain, can you?' he said.

Billie felt all eyes focusing on her as she stood there in the center of the room. None of them felt friendly or supportive. Out of the corner of her eye, she spotted Constable Upton standing near the bank of filing cabinets, holding a thick stack of papers. The look of pity on his face served to put a bit more steel in her backbone. She never wanted to be pitied but certainly not by the likes of Constable Upton.

'Did he say that he objected to my conversation last night with his wife?' Billie asked.

'You're right again. He said you'd taken it upon yourself to convince his poor, grieving wife that their daughter's death was suspicious. Mrs Chetwell was so overwrought that a physician had to be called in to administer a sedative.'

'That is not exactly what happened, sir,' Billie said, forcing herself to look the sergeant in the eye. 'Mrs Chetwell appeared unexpectedly at my cousin's home and wanted to ask me about the circumstances in which I found her daughter's body. She was haunted by the notion that Audrey had been crushed to death by a burning building. It seemed a kindness to be able to assure her otherwise.'

'It isn't for you to make unauthorized statements to members of the public, no matter what sort of sob story they tell you,' the sergeant said.

Billie opened her mouth to reply, but the sergeant held up his hand once more.

'The councilor went so far as to mention how much he disapproved of women serving in the constabulary, and, based on your performance, I would have to say that I agree with him. If it were in my power to do so, I would dismiss you on the spot,' Sergeant Skelton said.

Billie could not bring herself to look in Constable Upton's direction once more. She kept her eyes firmly fixed on the sergeant's face, feeling her own flaming with both shame and indignation.

'But it's not within your power to do so, now is it?' Billie heard a voice say.

She turned and saw with relief Avis Crane barreling down the corridor, waggling a finger in front of her. 'I have sole discretion over the women in the department and how they are to be reprimanded, not you. Constable Harkness, follow me.'

TWENTY-FOUR

Kingston upon Hull
Dear Mrs Palmer,
    Thank you so very much for your generous parcel of fig bars and other treats! It was most kind of you to think

of me and I must confess it was just the thing to take
some of the sting out of a difficult day!
   Love,
   Wilhelmina

'Would you please explain what I just witnessed?' Avis asked. She gestured towards the seat opposite her own at the desk and settled into her chair. 'Close the door behind you. It won't do for us to be overheard.'

With a sinking feeling, Billie shut the door behind her and sank into the wooden chair opposite Avis's desk. She felt a trickle of sweat run from the bottom of her hairline down her neck and under her collar. Despite the relative coolness of the temperatures in the north, she seemed to continually find herself in situations that caused her to break out into a full sweat. For just a moment she longed for the relative predictability of her life in Barton St Giles. Then she thought of the last confrontation she'd had with her mother and decided that it was unlikely that this would be worse than that. She took a deep breath and launched into her story.

'I'm afraid I got off on the wrong foot with Councilor Chetwell. I made the mistake of expressing doubt to his wife as to the cause of his daughter Audrey's death,' Billie said.

Avis arched an eyebrow at her and leaned slightly forward. 'You did what?' she asked.

'When Mrs Chetwell told me that she was haunted by the idea of her daughter dying in a fiery building collapse, I told her that she was not harmed in that way. The idea that her daughter was killed under other circumstances occurred to her on her own, but it seems her husband didn't see it that way,' Billie said.

'Are you sure she could not have died as a result of the air raid?' Avis said.

Billie nodded vigorously. 'Absolutely. In the statement I made to Constable Upton the night of the air raid, I said that there was no debris found around Audrey's body that could account for her being struck on the back of the head and killed in that manner. But the report doesn't include that statement. Here, take a look for yourself.' Billie removed the report from her handbag and passed it across the desk.

Avis arched an eyebrow again. She read over the report quickly and then looked back at Billie. 'Why did you have the report in your handbag?'

Another trickle of perspiration trickled down Billie's back. From the look on her superior's face, it appeared her career as a constable might be over almost before it had begun.

'After I visited the Chetwells with the chief constable, I wanted to be sure that the report accurately included my statement, but I didn't want to appear to be checking up on a fellow officer. I took it home with me to read without being overseen,' Billie said.

'Do you suspect Constable Upton of deliberately falsifying the report?' Avis asked.

'I don't know what else to think. When I saw him at the police court after I was sworn in, he claimed to have faithfully recorded my statement. But, as you can see, there is no mention of it in the report.'

'Have you asked Constable Upton why the report does not include your statement about the lack of debris?' Avis asked.

'Not yet. I had only stepped into the station when the sergeant confronted me,' Billie said.

'You violated regulations and jeopardized your position when you removed the report from the station. What would have made you take such a risk?' Avis asked.

'I thought that if it had been me lying on the floor of the café, my parents would've wanted whoever had done that to me to be brought to justice rather than simply chalking it up to another loss at the hands of the enemy,' Billie said.

Avis looked her up and down thoughtfully before leaning back in her chair and drumming her fingers on the top of the desk.

'You must understand that being the victim of a deliberate homicide casts a particular shadow over the dead young woman. Nothing else about her will be more remarkable than the fact that she was the victim of such a heinous crime. Surely, you can understand how her family would find such a notion distressing,' Avis said.

Billie had not considered it that way before. She could well imagine her mother would have shuddered at the thought of being associated with something as unseemly as murder and surely would not have wanted it attached to Billie's name. Still, it offended Billie's sense of justice that it was more important to observe those finer feelings than it was to hold someone accountable for a crime.

Besides, who could guarantee that Audrey would be the only victim of such a person? Wouldn't closing one's eyes to the possibility endanger the public? Wasn't the entire kingdom concerned with the greater good at present? Everyone was asked to make sacrifices in wartime. Allowing a murder to be swept under the carpet so that no one felt additional pain ran at cross purposes with everything else going on.

'It was not my intent to make a terrible ordeal any more difficult for the Chetwells. If you think I should resign, I will,' Billie said. She felt a wave of sadness pass over her as she smoothed her uniform skirt nervously with her hand.

'I have no interest in dismissing you from the constabulary. In fact, I believe that you are exactly the sort of young woman we should encourage in our ranks. That said, you must keep in mind that you are shouldering an enormous responsibility, not only to the population but to all of the other women who would one day serve as WPCs. People like Sergeant Skelton and Councilor Chetwell are looking for any excuse they can possibly find to support their prejudice against women becoming officers. Any misstep you make will add fuel to their arguments, and that is not something I wish to allow them the pleasure of doing,' Avis said.

'Should I simply forget my concerns about what happened to Audrey in order to make room for other women to serve on the force?' Billie asked.

'Certainly not. But you will have to become more adept at doing the very thing women have always done. You will have to find some wiggle room in the existing situation, to take your chances where you can and hold your tongue more often than your peers. You will have to allow the fact that you are a highly visible constable, and one who is carrying the future on her shoulders, to shape your actions.'

'Is that the end of it, then?' Billie asked.

'Unless Constable Upton is willing to go on record supporting your claim that there was no debris surrounding that poor girl's body, officially the matter will be declared an unfortunate result of enemy action, nothing more,' Avis said.

'So are you saying there won't be an investigation into what happened to Audrey Chetwell?' Billie asked.

'I didn't say that. I said there will be no official police stance on the case. That does not mean that someone with a keen gift for observation should not keep asking discreet questions.'

Billie sat back in her chair, stunned. Not only was she not going to lose her job, but she was being trusted to work on a real investigation and a secretive one at that.

'You want me to start asking questions myself? Won't that make things even worse with Sergeant Skelton and the councilor?'

'I think the best thing we can do at present is to get you out from under the watchful eye of Sergeant Skelton. I'm going to send you on patrol. I'll arrange for Constable Upton to take you along with him,' Avis said.

'I doubt the sergeant will want me to tag along with any of the male constables, regardless of his feelings towards them. He seemed to think I wasn't even qualified to make the tea,' Billie said.

'What the sergeant wants is not my concern – nor yours either. I want you out of the police station and I also want you to have the opportunity to speak with Constable Upton about the inaccuracies in the report. Just do your best not to let him form the impression you are investigating anything. Do you think you can do that?' Avis asked as she slid the report back across the desk.

Billie didn't know whether she could pull off something like that. She did know she was willing to give it her very best try. She stood and tucked the report back into her handbag.

'Absolutely.'

TWENTY-FIVE

Hull
Special Constable Upton's PNB

S ergeant Skelton had made it sound like a compliment when he had insisted that he allow WPC Harkness to shadow him for the rest of the shift. As soon as Avis Crane had shepherded the new policewoman to the safety of her office, the sergeant had pulled him aside and explained that if they were going to have to put up with women on the force, the least they could do was to make sure they were taught how to perform their duties by someone who knew how it should be done. He had shot a disparaging glance at a pair of war reserve constables loafing by the tea cart, idly dunking biscuits into steaming mugs as if to emphasize the point. No sooner had he been given that dubious compliment than Avis Crane appeared in front of the sergeant's desk once more, declaring the new recruit was to be sent out on patrol. Which was how he found himself striding along the streets of Hull, garnering curious stares from the citizenry.

Of all the women to join the force, he found himself mightily annoyed that the one to have actually done so was WPC Harkness. He had realized she was trouble from the very first moment he spotted her standing over a dead body in a building about to go up in smoke. What sort of a woman would put herself into such a position?

Not that he didn't admire her bravery. It was just that she was utterly outside of his experience of women, a fact for which he was profoundly grateful. He wasn't sure he wanted to become accustomed to the sight of women driving lorries, launching barrage balloons or wearing military uniforms. He was quite sure he didn't want to get used to patrolling the beat with one.

She didn't gripe, though; he had to give her that. Despite the fact that his stride was twice the length of hers and she was slightly out of breath simply trying to keep up, she never voiced a complaint all the way from the police station to the neighborhood they were assigned to patrol. She simply kept trotting along beside him, peppering him with questions about the sorts of incidents they might encounter and protocols for going about their jobs. He tried his best to fulfill his obligation to her as a fellow officer and a trainee without making her feel as though he was encouraging her interest. Perhaps she would grow weary of playing policeman and would decide to turn in her uniform by the end of the day. It wasn't until they stopped under the shade of a towering brick building that she asked a question that surprised him.

'When I saw you at the police court giving evidence about the lighting violation involving Audrey Chetwell, I was surprised to hear the owner of the café say that she was just a customer like any other. Did that surprise you, too?' she asked.

He turned and looked at her with new interest. At the time he had thought it strange that the café owner would be surprised by someone occupying her establishment after hours. He had assumed that she was lying about her connection with Audrey Chetwell in an effort to wriggle out of the fine. With discouraging frequency, he found that people were willing to lie in order to save relatively small sums of money. He suspected their efforts had more to do with a sense of accomplishment at putting one over on the authorities than with a desire for thrift.

'I don't know how things are where you're from, but around here there are plenty of people willing to give false evidence in court,' he said. 'What are you getting at?'

He watched her face as a slight crinkle appeared between her eyebrows. She tipped her head slightly and stared up as if the answer were written in the sky above the city. When she turned back to meet his gaze, she seemed quite certain.

'I'm just saying I think that it makes no sense. I'm wondering if she had a reason for lying. Since we both know Audrey wasn't killed in the bombing raid, and the owner of the café said she did not give her permission to be in the building after hours, I have to ask if those two things are connected, don't you?' she asked.

Peter wondered how WPC Harkness had come to have such

a suspicious bent of mind. He should have thought of it himself. Still, it seemed unlikely that something untoward had happened, didn't it? Why would anyone, least of all a middle-aged café owner, want to harm as lovely a girl as Audrey Chetwell?

'Are you suggesting that the café owner killed her?' he asked.

'I'm suggesting there might be more to the story than she admitted at the police court. When I was at the café the afternoon of the air raid, I seem to remember Audrey greeting the waitress as if she knew her,' she said.

'Just because this is a larger city than the place you're from, it doesn't mean that people are unfriendly or anonymous. People everywhere tend to stick to areas near to their homes or offices for the majority of their daily needs. Audrey may have been a frequent customer at the café, and the waitress had a passing acquaintance with her because of it. What sort of waitress would she be if she was unfriendly to the customers?' Peter said.

That got her. He watched as she crossed her uniformed arms over her chest and gazed up at the sky once more.

'Tell me the truth. Did you see any evidence in that building before the roof came down that Audrey Chetwell had been struck on the head by falling debris?' she asked, turning to face him once more.

In his mind's eye, he could still see her standing over Audrey's body, pointing to the floor surrounding it and asking him what might have struck her down.

'I admit I saw nothing that explained how she came to meet her death in the café, but I said as much in my report,' he said.

'Curiously, your report on file does not mention the lack of debris surrounding her body.'

'You're certain about that?'

'Yes. I saw it with my own two eyes.' She batted her eyelashes at him in a way that he found most disconcerting, and for a second all other thought vanished from his mind. 'Take a look for yourself.' She reached into the pocket of her uniform jacket and retrieved a folded piece of paper which she held out to him.

He gave himself a bit of a shake and reached for the paper. He unfolded it and felt his blood begin to clamor in his ears as he read over the contents.

'Where did you get this?' he asked.

'I found it in a filing cabinet at the station. There seems to be no mention in it of the lack of debris surrounding Audrey's body.'

'Someone has altered my original report,' he said.

She cocked a dark eyebrow at him. 'Now, why would anyone want to do a thing like that?' Before he could respond, she bolted away from him in the direction of the shouts of an elderly woman and a much younger man racing off, an oversized handbag in his hand.

TWENTY-SIX

Kingston upon Hull
Dear Candace,
    Your letter describing your training was so heartening.
I had a rather disastrous day of things myself and it was
so cheering to hear I am not the only one still learning
the ropes of a new position . . .

I f she was completely honest, she would have to say things had not got off to a particularly good start. It seemed that there had been something lurking beneath Sergeant Skelton's decision to send her out on patrol. She had been foolish not to consider that she might have proved a thorn in Constable Upton's side.

But from Constable Upton's reaction when she had stuck out her hand, that's exactly what he felt she was. The sergeant had sent them to a street where a gang of small boys had reportedly been throwing rocks at store windows as well as dashing back and forth across the street, impeding traffic. Sergeant Skelton ordered them to go and make their presence known to dissuade such unruly behavior. Her new partner wheeled on his heel and strode out of the building without a word to her. She hurried after him, almost breaking into a run to keep up.

She fell into step beside him on the pavement, not wanting to admit she had no idea where to find the street to which they had been assigned. The city was still so new to her and, to be honest, a bit frightening and overwhelming. She had known every street and lane and even cart track in her village, but the only streets she had become familiar with to any degree in Hull were the ones that took her from the train station to her cousin's house, and many of those appeared altered by the bombing.

She had heard that things moved faster in cities than they did out in the country, but she hadn't properly understood what that meant until she had arrived in Kingston upon Hull. Everyone seemed to be whizzing about. Cars moved faster; people bustled past with a determination she rarely had seen. She found it both invigorating and unnerving at the same time.

She covered her nerves by asking a steady stream of questions about the constabulary and what might be expected of her. With what she hoped was subtlety, she worked the conversation around to the café owner and the omissions from the report.

She had to admit that he seemed genuinely surprised when she told him his report didn't mention the lack of debris or any question of how Audrey came to die in the café. She found herself wondering if someone else had altered it behind his back. If she had found it a simple thing to remove the report from the files, surely someone else could have done so as well. But before she could consider it further, she heard someone cry out. Up ahead, an elderly woman stood pointing at an adolescent boy who was streaking away from her down the street. Billie pelted towards the woman as fast as her legs would carry her.

'He snatched my handbag,' the woman said, waving her arm in the direction of the retreating boy.

Billie turned and raced after him. She thought she would lose him at the corner, but the fear of being run down by an approaching lorry filled her with a sudden surge of adrenaline. Fueled by the knowledge of how dangerous it could be to be struck by a vehicle, she lunged forward with more speed than she would have thought possible. A man pushing a cart filled with produce slowed the youth's progress, and with an extra push, Billie caught up to him. She launched herself in the air and knocked him to the ground. When Peter arrived a few seconds later, she had the young man pinned on the ground beneath her, a knee firmly in the small of his back.

'I don't believe this bag matches your outfit,' Billie said.

Peter pressed his boot down on the thief's arm firmly enough for the boy to release the bag. Up close, it seemed he was likely no more than fourteen years old. Peter bent down and helped lift him to his feet. She tapped the handcuffs clipped to her belt and gave Peter a significant look as if to ask if she should do the honors. He nodded. She unfastened them and attached them to the boy's wrists behind his back. Peter took hold of the chain between them and led the boy off in the direction of the handbag's owner.

She hurried along beside him, not quite sure how to interpret the look she had seen on his face when she had glanced up and spotted him at her side. Her mother had always accused her of being too much of a tomboy, and she had gained few points with the other ladies in the village for her unorthodox behavior. She wondered if what she had seen on his face was the same sort of silent rebuke she'd seen so many times before. She told herself it hardly mattered. She was here to do a job and she was going to do it. As they approached the elderly woman, she recognized the same sort of astonished look.

'Here's your bag, ma'am,' Billie said, handing it back to her.

'In my day, a young lady did not throw herself through the air and tackle boys to the ground,' the woman said.

'Then I suppose, back in your day, a woman such as yourself would prefer to have her valuables disappear with a fleeing youth,' Peter said.

Billie felt a lump rise in her throat as he gave her a curt nod, then turned his attention back to the thief.

TWENTY-SEVEN

Hull
Special Constable Upton's PNB

He didn't know what to make of it. One minute WPC Harkness had been standing at his side, pestering him with questions, and the next she had streaked off down

the street in pursuit of a local hooligan in an even more unlady-
like display than the one she had put on at the café. He had
been sure she was a goner when a passing lorry had come
within a hair of crushing her beneath its wheels. When he caught
up to her and discovered her knee planted in the thief's back,
he didn't know whether to congratulate her for her quick reflexes
or report her to their superiors for sheer lunacy.

But what had really astonished him was the reaction from
the victim. The W in WPC wasn't something he was eager to
get used to, but in his book an insult to any member of the
constabulary was an insult to them all. Besides, the look on
WPC Harkness's face when he had told the older woman off
was one he wouldn't soon forget. She was quite attractive when
she wasn't accusing him of lying. Or putting her life in danger.

She was uncharacteristically silent as they made their way
back to the station with the handbag thief. She had even excused
herself as he led the boy to the lockup. When he returned, she
was sitting at a desk opposite his, typing.

'I hope you don't mind but I went ahead and started typing
up the report of the incident while you were getting the suspect
booked,' she said.

He noticed that she had typed more than halfway down the
sheet of paper when he returned, and another sheet was lying
face down on the desk beside the typewriter as if it had already
been completed. He heard the bell on the return bar of the
typewriter clang and then the sound of the roller bar spinning
as she yanked the page from its grasp. She stacked the pages
together and handed them to him.

'I'd appreciate it if you would look these over before I turn
them in to the sergeant. I want to be certain I filled everything
out correctly. Sergeant Skelton doesn't seem like someone you'd
want to give any excuse to criticize you,' she said, thrusting the
two sheets of paper at him.

'In my experience, he's not,' Peter said.

He reached out and took the papers she offered him. As he
read through the report once and then a second time even more
slowly, he could not quite believe what he saw. Somehow,
without phrasing the report in such a way that constituted lying,
WPC Harkness had managed to leave out any mention of the

fact that she apprehended the suspect without any assistance on his part.

The contents of the report made it sound as though the two of them had taken care of the incident together, and in any way that was possible, she had made sure to highlight the part he had played. If no one had seen what had happened, they would never know she was the one who knocked the boy to the ground and made the actual arrest. A hot spurt of anger filled his chest.

He thrust the papers back at her. 'What do you mean by this?' he asked, drawing curious glances from nearby officers as well as members of the public.

'Wasn't everything present and correct?' she asked him, a worried look crossing her small face.

'You know it isn't.' He leaned in close to her and lowered his voice. 'I told you before that I don't falsify reports, not even those that shade the truth to make me look good.'

She leaned back slightly and looked him square in the face. He had the impression she was testing him. She really did seem convinced that he was not above bending the truth, and for the life of him he couldn't understand why.

'I see. Would you prefer to write it up yourself?' she asked.

'No. You need to learn to do it correctly for yourself. If you are going to be a help rather than a hindrance, it is important that you do things by the book.' Peter realized too late that he had raised his voice again and that everyone in the station was staring.

'It wasn't my intention to cause difficulties. I only want to be helpful,' she said, dropping her gaze to the papers in front of her.

Something in her posture made him regret how harshly he had spoken.

'I'm sure that the woman whose handbag was recovered was grateful for your service,' he said.

'I wouldn't be so certain of that. But perhaps she was more inclined to feel that way after you reminded her that things could have turned out differently,' she said.

Peter didn't know what to think of any of it. He had thought she would turn out to be absolutely infuriating, and indeed she could be. But he couldn't believe she hadn't taken the opportunity to gloat over her success on her first day on patrol. If he had been in her place, he was not at all certain he would have been so gracious. In fact, as he thought back to the pride he had taken in his first arrest as a constable, he felt even more astonished at her generosity.

She might be a woman, but she truly had behaved like a gentleman, even if her behavior out on the street had been anything but ladylike. And all for the retrieval of a stranger's bag, especially when that stranger had not appreciated the efforts made but had pointedly derided her.

Suddenly, the sergeant appeared at their side with a cup of tea in his hand. He snatched up the report and skimmed it quickly. Sergeant Skelton grunted and then put his cup down on top of the report, leaving a damp, brown ring on the neatly typed surface.

'It seems I was wise to put the two of you together. It looks like you make an effective team. I have half a mind to make it a permanent situation,' he said. 'What do you think about that?'

The room had grown quiet, and Peter could feel the other officers listening without appearing to do so. Peter glanced down at WPC Harkness's earnest face. He wasn't going to embarrass her in front of the whole station. She deserved better.

'I'm sure you know best,' he said.

As the sergeant strode back to his desk, he leaned towards Billie. Under his breath, he said, 'Do you really think things don't add up about Audrey Chetwell's death?'

She looked at him, her eyes widening just slightly. She darted a glance over at the sergeant's desk and gave the barest of nods.

'Then I guess we had best investigate,' he said.

'Right now?' she asked, making to rise from her chair.

He shook his head. 'You've had enough excitement for one day. I'll think it over tonight and I'll let you know what I come up with.'

'You aren't just fobbing me off, are you?' she asked, the crinkle of skepticism appearing between her brows once more.

'If I had wanted to get rid of you, I wouldn't have brought it up in the first place,' he said. 'Besides, after the way you tackled that boy today, I suspect you wouldn't be that easy to shake off, even if I wanted to.'

With that, he stuck his cap back on his head and strode towards the exit before he thought better of his offer and changed his mind.

> *Kingston upon Hull*
> *Dear Frederick,*
> *How I wish I knew where to send this letter, for there is so much I wish I could tell you. How you would tease me for my behavior today . . .*

Billie left the police station with a lightness of heart and an eagerness to stop at the library to see if Lydia was still at work. Luck was with her, and when she entered the lobby of the large building, her cousin looked up from behind the desk where she was adjusting her fashionable hat with her gloved hands.

'You're just the person I've been longing to see,' Lydia said. 'I have a favor to ask of you, but first I want to hear all about your first day.' She came out from behind the desk with a wide smile across her face and took Billie by the arm, guiding her towards the exit.

Billie couldn't help but imagine how her mother would have reacted to any newsy tidbits about her job as a WPC. She could just imagine the scowl upon her face even if Billie had omitted to share the incident involving the bag snatcher. She wondered if Lydia would approve if she knew all the details of her exploits. Would she respond more like the old woman who accepted assistance in retrieving her handbag and then criticized Billie for having succeeded?

She was tempted to keep the details to herself but decided that to have a life she truly wanted to live would require being honest about who she was and what she did. It was vastly preferable to prioritizing outmoded rules of society over pitching in with what had to be done as the need arose.

She drew in a deep breath and commenced her story. She told Lydia about the dressing-down she had received from the sergeant on account of Councilor Chetwell's telephone call. She went on to describe the conversation she had had with Avis, even remarking on the omissions from the police report. Her cousin said nothing as they wound through the busy streets of

Hull. But when she described launching into the air in order to bring down the thief right there on the pavement for all to see, Lydia stopped dead in her tracks and turned to face her.

'If I didn't know any better, I would be absolutely certain I was listening to Grandmother Phyllida describing how she dealt with a burglar,' Lydia said. 'But tell me, how did Constable Upton seem to take to your company on patrol?'

'I don't think he was best pleased, and frankly I wasn't all that happy to be sent out on patrol with him, either. After all, he was the one who followed me into the café the night of the air raid,' Billie said.

The corner of Lydia's scarlet-tinted mouth twitched upward. 'After finding you in a burning building, I expect he wasn't all that surprised when you flung yourself down the street in pursuit of a thief,' she said.

'I didn't ask him. All in all, I think things went better than they might have done. I made sure to write up the report in such a way that shared the credit for the arrest,' Billie said.

Lydia gave her another smile. 'Very clever of you, my dear. If you are going to have any access to power in an organization, it's best not to alienate others who were there before you. Most men would not take too kindly to appearing bested by a female colleague.'

'That was my thinking exactly,' Billie said.

They reached the corner where the bank had once stood. Still, no one had removed the two enormous safes from the center of the square, but an attempt had been made to clear the rubble surrounding them. They stood as a ghostly reminder of what had happened such a short time before.

'I'm sure you've heard enough about my day. What was the favor you wanted to ask?' Billie said.

'I shouldn't like to trouble you, but I would feel better talking it over with someone. It's my habit to read the *Hull Daily Mail* every morning, and a couple of days ago a letter to the editor caught my eye. With all of the disruption from the air raids, it simply slipped my mind until today.'

'What did the letter say?' Billie asked.

'It was an admonishment to librarians, booksellers and univer-sities to take more care with any maps of their cities and the surrounding countryside in their possession. The writer claimed there had been reports of incidents involving foreigners requesting such maps in London and that it would be no more than our duty to keep an eye on such things throughout the country,' Lydia said.

'So you thought it best to take a look at the map collection at the library?' Billie said.

Lydia nodded. 'In a quiet moment this afternoon, I did just that. I checked the collection of maps we have listed in the card catalogue against the actual contents held in the library.'

'Did you find any discrepancies?' Billie asked.

'I'm sorry to say that I did. A very detailed map of Princes Dock and the surrounding area is missing. I'm really quite worried about what that might mean,' Lydia said.

'Have you ever had something like this happen before? Don't libraries often have items that go astray?' Billie asked.

'We most certainly do. There are any number of reasons that people might filch a book rather than check it out, and they aren't always nefarious reasons. Children sometimes help themselves to reading material they think the librarians might not allow them to access or books they would rather their parents not know interested them. And there are adults who would rather that no record was kept of their reading interests. I cannot tell you how often copies of *Lady Chatterley's Lover* go missing.'

'Couldn't that just be the case here with the map?' Billie asked.

'It could be, but that letter created doubts in my mind.'

'Is it possible that the map has intrinsic value? Could someone have wanted to sell it? I know that antique maps are often quite valuable,' Billie said.

'That is true, but the map in question was the most recent map of the dock area. Before maps were being regulated in the bookshops, it was the sort of thing one could find in a tourist guide. What worries me is that I can't think of any wholesome reason why it should have gone missing,' she said.

'Are you sure it wasn't simply misfiled somewhere or that it didn't slip underneath or behind a cabinet or shelf?' Billie said.

'I thought of that, too. After all, it does no good to borrow trouble before all possibilities are examined,' Lydia said. She exhaled deeply. 'Which is why I pulled out and double-checked every map in the collection, scoured every drawer and shelf in the map room, and even pulled furniture away from the wall to verify nothing had slid in behind. I can absolutely assure you that the map is not in the room. I can't say that it categorically is nowhere to be found in the library, but it would be unlikely for it to go unnoticed for long.'

Billie didn't like the sound of that. She liked the expression on Lydia's face even less.

'What are you going to do now?' Billie asked. 'Is there someone you should inform?'

'That's just what I'm doing. The letter to the editor mentioned that should librarians become aware of any such discrepancy, they ought to inform the local constabulary at once. That's you, is it not?' Lydia said. She placed her hand on Billie's sleeve and leaned forward expectantly. 'I thought if you were to take this information to Avis, it would be by far the best route to take.'

'But I'm brand-new on the job. Don't you think there's somebody far more qualified whom you ought to tell about such an important discovery?' she asked.

'Why ever would I do a thing like that when I have the perfect opportunity to give my beloved cousin the chance to be a part of something more important than making tea for the male constables and typing up reports? Besides, Avis is exactly the sort of person to take this information to. She is both level-headed and disinclined to be dismissive of reports simply because they are made by women.'

'If it is as serious as you suspect, maybe you should take your concerns to the chief constable,' Billie said. 'He had some very favorable things to say about you today.'

Lydia smiled and shrugged.

'Arthur is a lovely man, but I have more confidence that Avis would find a way for the information not to be used by the city council as grounds to dismiss me.'

'But surely the loss of the map cannot be considered your fault, can it?' Billie said.

'Councilor Chetwell is well known for his opposition to

women serving in any roles of responsibility, even as librarians. How his wife has put up with him all these years I simply cannot fathom. He was one of the loudest voices decrying the addition of women to the constabulary here in Hull. If the royal police inspector had not made a surprise inspection of the city a few weeks ago, I doubt you would have been admitted to the force.'

'Councilor Chetwell said something about disapproving of WPCs when I was at his home yesterday. How did the council come to vote to allow women to serve?'

'When the inspector visited, he attended a council meeting and went on record to say he was aghast that a city the size of Hull had not actively recruited women to the constabulary. He admitted he could not force the city councilors to hire women but said he would be sure to mention it to the king in his report if they refused to do so.'

'Councilor Chetwell can't have been any too pleased to be put under that sort of pressure,' Billie said.

'He was livid. The National Council of Women had been after the council for months to include women as WPCs in order to free up more men for the services. Even when we pointed out that women had been of enormous assistance as constables in the Great War, the council refused to vote to include them.'

'It was a lucky thing that the police inspector just happened to pay a surprise visit to Hull, wasn't it?' Billie said. She looked carefully at Lydia, a suspicion forming in her mind.

'Luck plays very little part in most successes, my dear. The police inspector and I have known each other even longer than I have known Councilor Chetwell. He was simply delighted to accept my invitation to visit for the weekend with his wife. She and I were at school together,' she said with a wink.

'Does Councilor Chetwell know you were the reason the inspector came to visit?' Billie asked.

'He undoubtedly suspects it. I have never made any secret of my opposition to most of his positions. He and I have butted heads for years. It has made my position at the library tenuous at times, but I have weathered the storms – so far, at least.'

Billie flinched at the thought that her own actions might have made Lydia's position more precarious. Was the councilor the sort of man who would take his anger out on her cousin?

'Do you think my conversation with Mrs Chetwell has made matters even worse?'

'I wouldn't think him so small as that. However, I would not be surprised if a man so understandably consumed with grief would be glad of the distraction a crisis like enemy activity at the library would provide. It would be in my best interest for this to be handled discreetly and without prejudice,' Lydia said. 'Avis is the one to be told.'

'Are you sure that it wouldn't be best coming from you?' Billie said.

'I think it would be best coming from a fellow officer. Please promise me that you will tell her about it first thing in the morning,' Lydia said, leaning forward eagerly.

Billie thought back to the last time a woman asked her to keep a promise. She thought about her mother's pleading look, much like the one on Lydia's face, when she had tried to extract a promise that Billie would not join the forces. Her stomach turned as she remembered her refusal to give her mother that satisfaction and how those had been the last words she had ever heard her mother utter. How could she possibly repeat that mistake?

TWENTY-EIGHT

Hull
Special Constable Upton's PNB

By dawn, Peter was itching to follow up with the café owner before his shift at the docks. He dressed quickly and headed out of the door. If he had really thought about it, he would have realized where his thoughts were leading even before he had spent such a restless night. After WPC Harkness showed him the discrepancy in the report he filed, he had made a note of the café owner's home address. He unfolded the slip of paper he had left in his pocket and consulted his mental map as to where he might find her residence. It was not too far out of his way, and he determined to take his chances and see if she might be both at home and awake when he stopped by.

The woman who opened the door to his sharp rap looked decidedly less pugnacious than the one who had stood in the dock at the police court only days before. A kerchief covered her head, and she wore a faded housecoat that had seen better days. But rather than slippers, she wore a pair of sturdy shoes upon her feet and held a duster clutched in her gnarled hand. She reminded him of his mother when she had things on her mind that she did not wish to discuss. His mother always said there was nothing like a good turnout of the house to fix whatever ailed her. She scowled at him as if she did not recognize him out of his police uniform.

'May I help you?' she asked.

'I'm here to ask you a few more questions about the woman found dead in your café,' he said.

She squinted at him, and then her eyes widened with recognition. 'You're that constable, aren't you?' she asked.

'Guilty as charged. I know it's a bit early to call on you,' he said.

'I've been awake for two hours at least. I can't seem to get off the schedule the café demanded, even though there is no place to go to anymore. If you want to sell freshly baked goods in your restaurant, you have to get up mighty early in the morning to prepare them,' she said.

'I thought that might be the case, which is why I risked stopping by on my way to my job at the docks,' he said.

'At the docks? I thought you were a constable?' she asked.

'I'm a special constable. I volunteer on the force after my job as a dock inspector is over for the day or on my days off. We all have to do our bit for the war effort, don't we?' he asked with a shrug.

She looked him up and down, and made a harrumphing noise. She inclined her head down the hallway.

'You'd best follow me, then, young man.'

He wiped his feet carefully on the doormat placed on her front step and then followed her down the hallway. It reminded him strikingly of his mother's own with its narrowness and family photos clinging to either side. No windows allowed light to penetrate the narrow space, but a glow from the far end made him suspect they were headed for the kitchen.

Sure enough, she led him into a bustling center of domesticity filled with warm, yeasty smells. She wrapped her gnarled hand around the handle of a Brown Betty teapot and pointed it at the table as an offer to take a seat. She poured out two cups of tea and carried them to the table. She lifted a cloth tea towel off a mound in the center of the table to reveal a pile of scones and assorted small buns.

'Help yourself. You look like you could use a good meal. You must be run off your feet if you're working so many hours. Tell me, why is it that a young man like you isn't serving overseas?' she asked.

It was a question he bristled at every time it came up, but as he looked at her face, he could see that she asked out of curiosity rather than judgment. He lifted a fruit-studded scone from the plate and took a bite before answering.

'I'm in one of the reserved occupations so I'm forbidden to enlist no matter how much I might want to. Serving in the constabulary is my way of doing what I can do under the circumstances,' he said. 'I don't particularly like handing out fines for lighting violations.'

'I'm sure you had no malicious intent. We all have to do our bit to help out, and I'm sorry for the way I behaved at the police court. I think the whole situation just brought out the worst in me. It was a terrible thing to lose the café, and then to discover that poor girl had been in my building left me feeling responsible somehow.'

'But it's not as if you're the one who chose to drop bombs on your neighborhood, is it?' Peter said, keeping his eyes trained on her face as he took another bite of the scone.

She seemed to be such an average sort of woman, a salt-of-the-earth type, and he hated to imagine that someone like her might be involved in the types of aid to the enemy they were constantly warned not to provide either through thoughtless slips of the tongue or deliberate activity.

'That may well be, but if I had known she was in there and

not properly blacking out the windows, I would have done something about it. Then maybe she wouldn't have ended up dead,' she said.

'You're absolutely sure you did not give her permission to use your building after hours?' Peter asked.

'I most certainly did not. You could have knocked me over with a feather when I was told that a body was removed from the café. I have no idea how she got in there or what she might have been up to,' the woman said, pushing the plate closer to Peter, having noticed he had finished his scone.

He helped himself to one of the buns and sat thinking for a moment. As he bit into it, he thought the Germans had a lot to answer for when they destroyed her eatery. She was a remarkably good baker, and he could see how her business would help to raise the morale of anyone who entered her establishment and had a chance to sample her wares.

'Are you the only owner?' he asked.

'I am since my husband died three years ago,' she said.

'It seems like a lot to keep up on your own. Do you have any staff?' he asked, recalling that WPC Harkness had mentioned a waitress, but he wanted to see how she would respond.

'My daughter, Sally, has been helping out ever since I lost my husband. She decided to stay close to home instead of joining up in the services or heading off to work in one of the armaments factories, unlike so many others I could mention.' The woman sniffed as if to wordlessly complain about such behavior. 'Although I don't know how much longer she's going to be able to avoid serving in some capacity. With the registration of unmarried women, I worry that she's going to be conscripted into the war effort anyway.'

It had been a matter of some controversy that women were to be conscripted along with the men, but Peter thought it was a wise move on the part of the government. During the last war, there weren't enough citizens involved in the effort to truly support the forces. With that in mind, a campaign to recruit women had been in effect for months.

'Did you have any sense that your daughter was friendly with the victim?' he asked.

'Sally is friendly with just about everyone. You can't very

well be a waitress and do otherwise, can you? Besides, it's not in her nature to be standoffish. Why do you ask?'

'I just wondered if the woman found was in some way more connected to your establishment than perhaps you had realized,' he said.

The woman looked up and squinted at him sharply. 'What are you suggesting?'

'I'm trying to make sense of how she happened to be in your café after hours. I thought maybe Audrey Chetwell and your daughter were friends and had arranged to meet there to go to the cinema together. There are many of them nearby.'

The woman's face relaxed and she settled back in her chair and lifted her teacup to her lips. 'All I can tell you is that Sally never mentioned any such thing to me. She's a grown woman and can keep company with whomever she pleases, but I would expect that if she knew that young woman, she would have mentioned it. It's not the sort of thing that happens every day, now is it?' she said.

'Thankfully, it isn't. Does Sally live here with you?'

'She does, but that doesn't mean I am privy to all her business.'

'Is she home now?' he asked.

'She stayed overnight with a friend last night, but she said she would be back home to spend this evening with me. Did you need to speak with her, too?'

'Yes. May I call around again this evening?'

'Two visits in one day from a handsome man in uniform? Why not? I'd love to give the neighbors something to gossip about.'

Peter pushed back his chair and picked up his hat.

'I appreciate your time. And thank you for the scones. I shouldn't like my mother to hear it, but they were at least as good as hers.'

Before he could leave, she pressed a paper sack with more scones into his hand and patted him on the shoulder as he headed back out of the door. As he left, he had the strong sense that she truly had no idea what Audrey Chetwell could have been doing in her café and had nothing to do with her death. Which begged the question, what in the world was Audrey doing there?

TWENTY-NINE

Kingston upon Hull
Dear Candace,
   How are you getting on with your male colleagues? I
had thought it might be easy enough for me to navigate
the complexities of it all considering I had so much practice
getting along with my brother and his friends, but it really
isn't the same in the least . . .

T he station pulsed with activity when Billie arrived, and
most of the other constables barely glanced at her as she
entered the building and made a beeline for Avis's office.
She rapped upon the door and entered when bid to do so. Avis
sat in her usual spot behind the desk, looking as unflappable
as ever.

'You look as though you're bubbling over with something to
tell me. How did you get on yesterday with Constable Upton?'
Avis asked.

'It was a bit rocky at first, but I think things went better
than they might have done,' Billie said.

'Any news regarding the report on Audrey Chetwell?'

'I asked him about it, and he seemed genuinely surprised that
the report on file didn't include the absence of debris,' Billie said.

Avis leaned back in her chair and tented her hands in front
of her face. 'Did he now? Do you believe him?' she said.

'I do. I think someone else changed it after he filed it.'

'What changed your mind?'

'At the end of the shift, he asked if I truly thought Audrey
had been the victim of foul play. When I said I did, he suggested
that we investigate,' Billie said.

'In that case, I suggest that anything you and Constable Upton
undertake you keep as quiet as possible. Sergeant Skelton will
surely object to anything either of you wishes to pursue. Was
there anything else?'

'I also have a message from my cousin Lydia that she
insisted I deliver in person rather than relying on a note or the
telephone.'

'I assume it's a matter of discretion, then?' Avis leaned
forward in her seat once more.

Billie nodded. 'Yes.' She lowered her voice. 'Lydia noticed
a map of the Hull docks is missing from the library. She
wanted someone in authority to know but felt concerned that
she would be blamed for the theft or dismissed as hysterical. She suggested you were the perfect person to take the
matter seriously without assuming she was at fault for what
had happened. Apparently, there's been a bit of interest in
replacing her with a political appointee,' Billie said.

'There are members of the city council who would be eager
to reward a supporter with a position in city government. One
doesn't think of the library as a branch of the government, but
the librarian is a position that is appointed by the councilors
and a job many would enjoy having,' Avis said. 'Does she have
any sense of how long ago the map was taken? It's a potentially
serious matter.'

'I'm afraid not. She was only moved to check the maps at
all because of a letter she read in the newspaper. Someone had
written in to say that maps had gone missing from London
libraries; the writer wanted to encourage other librarians to be
more vigilant, especially with maps featuring sensitive or
important areas,' Billie said.

'Thank you for bringing this to my attention. I'll look into
that while you do your best to make some inquiries behind the
scenes about Audrey. Any idea where you'll start?'

'I have no idea whatsoever,' Billie said.

Avis scraped back her chair and stood. 'I'm sure you'll think
of something. After all, that's why I hired you.'

As Billie walked back down the corridor, a boy of about fourteen called out to her from the switchboard room. He waved a
piece of paper over his head and gave her a wide grin as she
slipped into the small room to take it from his outstretched
hand. Her cousin had called and left a message to say that their
visitor from earlier in the week would be waiting to meet with

her in a conference room at the library at noon. Billie apprised Avis of her intention to meet with Mrs Chetwell and received her blessing to take as long as she needed away from the police station.

After spending the rest of the morning typing reports and enduring curious stares from visitors to the station, Billie was grateful to leave the clamor for the hush of the library with its soaring ceilings and beckoning rows of books. For just a moment, she wondered if she had made the right decision in joining the police force; there were far fewer pitfalls to tumble into within the walls of the library. But then she thought of her mother and the danger that had overcome her on a quiet country lane. There was no path in life untouched by risk. Surely it was best to immerse oneself in pursuits where the value outweighed the cost.

As she approached the glass door of the conference room, she decided she had indeed made the right decision. The older woman sat facing the door, her gaze lowered to her lap. Although her hair was pinned carefully in place and her clothing looked as though she had dressed with care, she still appeared desperately wan. As she heard Billie approach, she glanced up at the door and her face brightened ever so slightly.

'Thank you so much for seeing me. I wasn't sure you would after the call my husband made to your sergeant.'

Billie took a seat in the chair next to her and pulled her police notebook out of her pocket. She searched her handbag for a pencil; finding a stub of one at the bottom, she turned towards Mrs Chetwell.

'I am at your service. What is it that you wished to speak to me about?'

'I only have a few minutes before I have a Women's Voluntary Service meeting, but I cannot stop thinking about our last conversation.'

'I never meant to upset you so,' Billie said. 'I am truly sorry.'

'It isn't your fault. My son was shot down and presumed dead, so we don't have any sense of what exactly happened to him. I cannot bear for the same to be true of my daughter. My husband would not understand going behind his back to come

and speak with you, but I must know what happened to her,'
Mrs Chetwell said, leaning slightly forward.

'What is it that you would have me do?' Billie asked.

'I want whoever is responsible for her death to be held to
account. I am asking if you will do your best to discover who
that person might be,' Mrs Chetwell said.

'My superior suggested that this sort of inquiry can be painful
for the family. Are you sure you are willing to expose yourself
to more grief?'

'My husband is absolutely appalled at the notion that Audrey
might have been a deliberate target. Audrey was his little prin-
cess, and he would rather not risk knowing the truth. Unlike
him, I am under no illusion that my daughter was perfect; I
would find it a comfort to know the truth, whatever it might be.'

'I can't promise that I'll be able to figure out what happened
to your daughter, but I can assure you that I'll do my best.'
Billie said. 'But I will need your help to get started.'

Mrs Chetwell nodded. 'I am happy to assist in any way I
can, but you must promise to be discreet. My husband cannot
know I spoke with you again, for both our sakes.'

'Agreed. Let's start with an obvious question. What could
Audrey possibly have been doing at that café after hours?' Billie
asked.

'I've asked myself that again and again, and I truly have no
idea. Audrey had grown rather distant lately. In fact, she had
expressed an interest in finding a place of her own,' she said.

'That seems surprising considering you have such a spacious
home and there is a housing shortage with so many people
pouring into the city for work. Did she tell you her reasons for
wanting to find a place of her own?' Billie asked.

Mrs Chetwell shook her head. A crinkle appeared between
her blue eyes. 'When I asked, she just said something about
how much more convenient it would be to have rooms near the
art college.'

Something about the tone of her voice made Billie believe
that Mrs Chetwell had not given a lot of credence to her daughter's explanation. She knew very well that there were lots of
reasons why a woman of Audrey's age might not want to discuss
all the details of her personal life with her mother. Hadn't she

kept secrets from her own mother? However, it could also be that whatever was causing Audrey to seek the privacy of her own place could have led to her death. While Billie hated to pry, it was part and parcel of the job. She had often seen her parents ease bits of information from parishioners who could not bring themselves to open up without prompting, even though they had come to the rectory seeking counsel and assistance. It seemed Mrs Chetwell needed similar coaxing.

Billie softened her voice. 'It sounds as though perhaps you did not believe that was the entire reason for her interest in finding a place of her own.'

'I feel rather guilty about it, but no, you're right. I suspected there was far more to it than that. Not to put too fine a point on it, I was worried that she was conducting a relationship with someone of whom we would not approve. Audrey was a very headstrong girl and would not have appreciated any interference from either her father or me, especially concerning the people with whom she chose to associate,' Mrs Chetwell said.

Billie watched as Mrs Chetwell tugged at her gloves, adjusting the fingers and the cuffs this way and that. If she had to guess, she would say that there was more Mrs Chetwell could tell Billie about her daughter, given the right encouragement.

'Was there someone in particular that you thought might have been the source of her interest? Did she say anything that made you doubt her reasons for seeking a place of her own?' Billie asked.

'It was just more of a feeling. She had changed since she had taken up with the students at the art college. I didn't mind her learning to sketch or to dabble in paints. I liked those sorts of things myself when I was about her age and thought it seemly for a young woman to be in possession of artistic ability,' Mrs Chetwell said.

'Had she made any particular friends at the art college of whom you did not approve?' Billie asked.

'There was no one I could mention for certain. It's more that an artistic crowd is not really our sort, if you see what I mean. Mr Chetwell and I are sensible people. We value practical matters and don't really understand the appeal of the sort of lifestyle so many of those students partake in. And, frankly, the staff as well,' she said, pressing her lips together in a firm line.

'Do you think that her association with people at the art college led to some sort of undesirable behavior on her part?' Billie asked.

She knew that artists had a reputation for living lives that were considered a bit fast and loose compared to the average citizen. But was it really such a concern at an art college in a city like Kingston upon Hull? It wasn't as though Audrey had run off with a group of impressionistic painters to the Caribbean. Still, her family was a prominent one in the city, and Mrs Chetwell seemed obsessed with appearances. Perhaps there was nothing more to it than that. Still, if there wasn't, she had very little more to go on than when she had entered the room.

'I shouldn't like to say undesirable, exactly. It was more that they were a distraction from the sorts of relationships we would have preferred that she foster. For example, there was a nice young man from the engineering school that was interested in Audrey. He would have been most suitable, but when I suggested she encourage him, she simply laughed and said she had her mind on rather a more interesting catch. I hate to think what she meant by that.'

Now they were getting somewhere. 'Do you know the name of the engineering student?' Billie asked.

'Orson Hewitt. Quite a suitable young man, as I said. He's in the last few months of his course and then intends to apply to the Territorials as an engineer, although he may be required to remain on the home front as there is such a high demand for men in his field,' Mrs Chetwell said.

'If he is an engineering student, did she know him from somewhere other than the college?' Billie asked.

Mrs Chetwell shook her head. 'No, he was a new acquaintance; the engineering school and the art college have close ties. The engineers need to be involved in learning to draft their designs, and so there is an overlap between the disciplines. Some of the engineering classes are held on the art school campus.'

'So, you met this Orson Hewitt, then?' Billie asked.

'I met him on two or three occasions. He seemed to simply appear at functions where I happened to be with Audrey. I thought it was rather sweet that he was following her about like a lovesick puppy.'

Could Orson have been the young man Audrey had been with at the café the day Billie arrived in Hull?

'Did Audrey have any other friends who might have valuable information?' Billie asked.

'I would contact Muriel Matthews. Her parents have been friends of ours for years, and the girls have known each other all their lives. I'll give you her address.' Mrs Chetwell reached out for Billie's notebook and neatly printed the information on the bottom of the page before handing it back to her.

'Do you happen to have an address for Orson as well?' Billie asked.

'I seem to remember that he lives in the dormitories at the college. I'm sure if you were to check with the staff at the engineering school, they would be able to point you out to him with ease. You don't think he had something to do with Audrey's death, do you?' Mrs Chetwell asked.

'I have no idea. But I think it's safe to assume that people closer to your daughter's age might know things about her life that she was disinclined to share with her parents. You must remember what it was like to be her age and have secrets of your own,' Billie said as kindly as she could.

'It seems so long ago I barely remember it, but I suppose you're right. I had best be getting to the WVS meeting.' With that, Mrs Chetwell stood, then paused and patted Billie on the shoulder. 'Thank you for all you are doing. Please keep me informed should anything come up that you think I should know about.'

THIRTY

Kingston upon Hull
Dear Constable Bridges,
  I am writing to thank you for how kind you were when you arrived at the rectory to deliver the news of my

mother's accident. Since last we met, I have joined the
ranks of the Hull Constabulary and I have found myself
in a similar position. I am now aware of how difficult it
is to be on the delivery side of such a message as well as
the receiving end. It is a dreadful job and one I had not
fully appreciated until now . . .

She used the telephone at the library's front desk to telephone Avis with an update on her progress and to ask
permission to track down Audrey's friends before returning
to the station. She placed a telephone call to the Matthews
family home and was assured that Muriel would be happy to
meet with her. Lydia provided directions to both the art college
and Muriel's address, and in no time Billie found herself
standing before a house built on the same scale as the Chetwell
residence.

Once again, an old-fashioned sort of servant led her through
a grand hallway to the interior of the house. As they went along,
Billie could not help but make comparisons between the understated hall of the Matthews home and the ostentatiousness of
the Chetwells' entryway. The maid rapped discreetly upon a
paneled door at the end of the hall and opened it on to a small,
bright room where the daughter of the house awaited her. A
rather plain-looking young woman of about Billie's age rose
and dismissed the servant before turning her appraising gaze to
her guest.

'You know, I wondered if your telephone call was some sort
of prank. I wasn't aware there were any WPCs in Hull. How
absolutely thrilling,' Muriel said, lowering herself on to a sofa
and gesturing for Billie to be seated beside her.

'So far there are only two of us. There is room for more if
you are of a mind to join the constabulary yourself,' Billie said.

'How amusing, but I am sure your visit here is not one bent
on recruitment. How may I help you?'

'I am following up a few things involving the death of Audrey
Chetwell, and her mother suggested you would be one to ask
as the two of you were friends,' Billie said.

She kept her attention fixed on Muriel's face. Muriel's mousy
brown hair was twisted and pinned into an approximation of

the latest style, and her lips were painted in the same bright scarlet she had seen on Audrey that day at the café. But any resemblance to the dead woman ended there. Her eyes were set slightly too close together to be appealing, and her chin receded enough to be called weak. If her hostess had not been so well bred, Billie felt certain she would have rolled her eyes.

'Our parents were the ones who were friends. Audrey and I were constantly thrown together over the years because of that fact. I rather think my parents hoped that Audrey would rub off on me. I think if they knew her as well as I did, they'd be rather more relieved that she hadn't,' Muriel said.

Billie looked at Muriel with interest. After what she had seen in the café, Billie could understand how Audrey might rub some other young women the wrong way. To Billie, Audrey had seemed sophisticated and confident. But she supposed it was possible that if she had been constantly compared with her, she might have grown to resent it. For a young woman so lacking in personal charm as Muriel seemed to be, Audrey's presence could have been exceedingly grating.

'It sounds as though Audrey had another side to her that her parents and yours did not see,' Billie said.

'She certainly did. It makes me sick the way her father and everyone else seem to have nothing but the highest regard for her. It isn't as though she was a particularly useful person,' Muriel said. 'But now that she is dead, her father is making her out to be the poster girl for patriotic duty.'

'You don't think she merited that sort of praise?' Billie said. 'I had assumed that she was involved in all sorts of volunteer efforts in Hull from what her father had to say.'

Muriel snorted. 'Audrey was far too busy with her own affairs to have much time left over for something as mind-numbingly thankless as serving at one of the women's auxiliary canteens, or, God forbid, something as tiresome as fire watching,' Muriel said. 'To hear her parents boast about her, you'd think she was spending every spare minute pitching in at every available opportunity, but the truth is her efforts were far more personal.'

'How did she really spend her time?' Billie asked.

'Like me, she was a student at the art college, which I'm

sure explains how she came to be so very busy,' Muriel said with a tinge of scorn in her voice.

Her face shone with malicious triumph, which Billie found entirely off-putting. What could be so worthy of criticism about attending an art college? While Billie understood that not everyone thought the arts were a practical career pursuit, Billie had the impression that the Chetwell family was not one that was concerned with their daughter pursuing an occupation that provided a comfortable living. Billie suspected that the primary role of a daughter in that family would be to make a good match and that such a thing would not be hard to do. Especially for a girl as attractive and charming as Audrey had been.

'Was she devoted to her studies, then?' Billie asked.

'She fancied herself to be a talented painter, but I understood that she was perfectly willing to spend more of her time as a model if asked by the right person,' Muriel said.

Billie wondered if what Muriel had to say was completely born out of spite and jealousy or if Audrey had been involved in something at the art college that would have called her character into question. She knew that artists often had a reputation for making choices in their personal lives that were contrary to those that were respected by general society. Was that enough to inspire Muriel's comments or was there more to her insinuations?

'And who would the right person be?' Billie asked.

'One mustn't speak ill of the dead,' Muriel said.

'Would you be speaking ill if you offered an explanation for how Audrey came to be found in the café where she died?' Billie asked.

Muriel looked up at the high ceiling with its intricate plaster molding before answering.

'I'm sure I couldn't say. People of our set don't spend time on that side of the city as a rule. But, come to think of it, perhaps that was what she was after.' A vaguely repellent smile stretched across her face.

'Are you suggesting that Audrey was trying to avoid being seen by those who knew her?' Billie asked.

'The only thing I will suggest is that you should ask your questions at the art college. I am sure someone there will be of more help than I will ever prove to be.'

With that, Muriel stood and gestured towards the door. Billie thanked her for her time and asked for the shortest route to the art college before taking her leave. After reaching the drive, she looked back at the house. She could have sworn Muriel stood barely concealed behind a net curtain, watching her go.

Just as Mrs Chetwell had suggested, it was a simple enough thing to make inquiries and to locate Orson Hewitt. A cheerful young woman in a paint-stained smock directed her to a mostly empty classroom. As she peered through the open doorway, she realized with a start that the young man bent over a thick book spread open on the table in front of him was the same person who had met Audrey in the café. Her heart thumped raucously in her chest as she recalled the way Audrey had winced when he had grasped her wrist. The image of the sticky wound to the back of Audrey's head flashed into her mind as she stood there. She dismissed from her mind a sudden urge to have the sturdy presence of Constable Upton beside her.

Orson Hewitt must have felt her eyes upon him because he lifted his head and looked up at her. He started as though she had come across him doing something he ought not. Did he have a guilty conscience? Despite her misgivings about being alone with him, she was determined to find out.

'Good afternoon. I am looking for Orson Hewitt and I was told I would likely find him here,' she said, stepping into the room and hoping her voice rang with a sort of easy-going authority.

'Well, you found me,' he said, eyeing her uniform guardedly. 'Although I cannot imagine what business a member of the constabulary might have with me.'

'I hoped that you might be able to give me some information about Audrey Chetwell.' Billie kept her gaze fixed on his face, searching for signs of discomfort at the mention of Audrey's name. Once again, Orson flinched.

'Why would you ask me about Audrey? She was killed in the air raid,' he said.

'There are a few things that need to be cleared up before the case can be officially closed. My questions should only take a few minutes of your time.'

Billie didn't wait for his agreement but pulled up a chair from an adjoining worktable and sat down. She took her notebook and pencil from her uniform jacket pocket and turned to a fresh page. She noticed a line of almost imperceptible sweat had formed just above Orson's top lip. She wasn't sure if it was a result of concentration on his work or a moment of panic at being questioned by the police that had caused it. For all she knew, it could be attributed to discomfort he felt with women in general or WPCs in particular. No matter the cause, he was clearly reluctant to speak to her. Perhaps he would loosen up if she presented him with some encouragement.

'I was given your name by Audrey's mother who said that you were just the sort of young man she was pleased to see her daughter spending time with,' Billie said.

From the way one of his eyebrows lifted, she could see that Mrs Chetwell had not communicated that information to him herself. Nor, apparently, had Audrey. A flush of color crept up his pale neck, and his posture relaxed ever so slightly at the compliment.

'I am happy to hear it. I thought very highly of Audrey,' he said.

'Mrs Chetwell said that she encouraged Audrey to socialize with you since she thought you to be a sensible man with good prospects ahead of him. Would you say that you spent a lot of time together?' she asked.

His back straightened once again, and the muscles of his jaw tightened.

'We were together off and on, but not as much as I would have liked,' he said.

'I thought the two of you were quite close from what her mother had to say. She mentioned that she had the impression Audrey had formed a strong attachment to a man she knew from the college, and she was hopeful that it was you,' Billie said.

It wasn't exactly a lie. While Mrs Chetwell hadn't thought Audrey was attracted to Orson, she had definitely held out hope that she was wrong about her suspicions.

'I wouldn't say that we were more than good friends. I would have liked to have been the one she cared for in that way, but she seemed far more interested in someone else, no matter how I tried to warn her off him,' Orson said.

The blush crept rapidly up his neck and moved to his cheeks. Billie wasn't sure if it was embarrassment or anger that caused it, but whatever it was, he was experiencing a strong emotion.

'It can be very difficult not to have one's feelings reciprocated. Even more so if one's rival is someone unsuitable.' Billie paused to give Orson a chance to respond. When he held his tongue, she continued. 'Mrs Chetwell did say she was concerned about some of the sorts with whom her daughter was keeping company. She said she worried about the artistic crowd and the influence it was having on Audrey.'

'She should have been worried. Audrey could have done better than Byron Trent,' he said.

He looked almost startled, as though he had revealed a secret he had held in for a long time.

'Is Byron Trent an art student?'

'He might have been at one time. Now he is one of the most popular professors here. Audrey took classes with him.'

'Do you think she was involved with him in a way that went beyond the relationship between a student and a professor?'

'I am certain of it. She walked around all goo-goo-eyed whenever she spotted him. She was always fawning over him, and I often saw them walking together or skulking about the campus, whispering when they thought no one was watching. But I knew it wouldn't last and I was right,' he said.

Billie stopped her scribbling and looked at him conspiratorially. 'Did something happen to come between them?'

'I wasn't following them, mind you; I have too much pride to lower myself that way.'

'Of course,' she said encouragingly.

'But I happened to find myself in the same corridor where her class meets the day that she died. Neither of them saw me, but I spotted them. They were having the most terrific row.'

'Are you sure it was an argument? Were you able to hear what was said?'

'Audrey said she had had enough and wanted to call it quits. She turned to walk away, but he grabbed her by the arm and pulled her back. He said she couldn't up and leave him, that

he didn't know how he could go on without her and that he
desperately needed her.'

'Did you hear her response?'

'There wasn't one. I was just about to intervene when she
yanked her arm away and hurried off without another word. I
watched him staring after her. From the look on his face, I would
say he was absolutely furious.'

'Did he call after her or anything?'

'No. He just stood there, watching her retreating back,
clenching and unclenching his fists. If Audrey hadn't been killed
in the air raid, he would be the one I would blame for her
death.'

THIRTY-ONE

Hull
Special Constable Upton's PNB

He arrived back at the house on North George Street
with a growling stomach and a hope that Mrs Nichols
might be on hand to offer another round of her baked
goods. Honestly, he was getting to be as bad as the butcher's
delivery boy, looking for handouts from the housewives in the
community.

He mounted the front step once more, and after a brief wait,
a young woman answered the door wearing a smock covered
in soot. One dark curl slipped out from underneath the kerchief
wound around her hair and lay against a vivid birthmark. Her
face was flushed, and she wiped her brow with the back of her
hand, smearing it with a sooty smudge.

'You're the constable that visited Mother this morning, aren't
you?' the young woman asked, holding the door open wide and
waving him inside. She told me you would likely be by this
evening,' she said.

'I have a couple of questions to ask you,' he said, suddenly
remembering the woman's name was Sally.

'I'd be happy to have a break. Ever since the bombing raid, my mother's been in a tizzy about keeping busy. I don't mind if she wants to work herself to the bone to keep her mind off what happened, but I wish she'd leave me out of it. I think I have more than earned a few minutes away from blacking the stove and riddling the coals,' Sally said. 'Mother's out speaking with a builder about what it will take to get the café up and running again, so I have time for a chat.'

He followed Sally back to the kitchen where her mother had entertained him not long before. He took the same chair he had sat in on that visit and forced himself not to look longingly at the teakettle sitting on the hob. If Sally didn't offer him a cup, he certainly wasn't going to ask. Besides, everyone was doing their part to conserve fuel to the best of their ability, and reducing the use of cooking fuel was one of the ways to make the biggest impact. That and minimizing heating water for bathing.

'I wanted to ask you if you knew how Audrey Chetwell came to be in the café after hours,' Peter said. 'From what we know about her, it doesn't make sense that she would be there. She wasn't an employee, even if it was off the books, was she?' Peter asked, hoping that his voice invited confidences.

'I wondered if anyone would ask about that. I've been expecting Mother to do so. It's a measure of how upset she must've been over the bombing that she hasn't thought to question it herself,' Sally said.

'Are you the one who made arrangements for her to be there without your mother's knowledge?' Peter asked.

Sally nodded. 'I didn't see what harm it could do. I certainly didn't think Audrey would end up in the wrong place at the wrong time because of it. It just seemed harmless,' Sally said.

'What exactly did you let her do?' Peter asked.

'Audrey had this way of sort of charming you into offering things. I found myself not charging her for a second sandwich or offering to bring her extra milk for her tea. There was just something about her that made you want to do her favors and gain her goodwill. When she mentioned how she was looking for a place to meet someone without the prying eyes of her parents, I asked her if she wanted to use the café after hours,' Sally said.

'That's quite a generous offer for you to have made,' Peter said. 'She must have been quite a charmer.' He thought back to the lovely girl he had handed the citation to and could understand how someone might make such a proposal.

Sally shrugged. 'It was nothing really. Besides, I live with my mother, so I know how much a girl wants a bit of privacy now and again.'

Peter thought he detected a note of bitterness in Sally's voice. Had she resented her own mother's attention to her personal life? Jean Nichols had sounded as though she was happy to allow her daughter to make a life of her own when she spoke of her that morning, but perhaps there was a vast difference in their interpretations of what a lack of meddling might look like.

'Did she accept your offer?' Peter asked.

'She jumped at it. Somehow, I found myself offering to have a key cut for her to use, as long as she promised that she would leave everything just as she found it when she arrived. I knew my mother wouldn't be particularly happy for her to be in the building unsupervised at night. Mother's quite a cautious woman; there are no other employees besides me in the café because she doesn't trust anyone but family with her business,' Sally said.

'Your mother never suspected a thing?' Peter asked.

Sally shook her head. 'Once there was a near miss. About a week or so ago, I needed to go to the café earlier than my mother in order to meet a delivery. When I arrived and went into the storeroom, I found Audrey fast asleep on top of a coat spread out on the floor. She had her head propped up on a bag of flour as though it were a pillow. If my mother had been the one to arrive first, she would've found her and then the game would've been up,' she said.

'Did Audrey say why she was sleeping in the storeroom?' Peter asked. 'It couldn't have been very comfortable, and from what I understand, she's not the sort of person who would enjoy roughing it.'

'That's just what I asked her. She said that she had been there until late and didn't want to go back to her parents' house in the middle of the night in case she woke them. She said she had tried to stay awake, but she just couldn't keep her eyes open. But the thing is, I didn't believe her,' Sally said.

'You didn't believe her reason for being there?' Peter asked.

'I didn't believe that she suddenly decided to stay because it was late. It was the height of summer after all, and she would've had no need for a coat. She must have brought it with her, and that suggests to me that she had planned to stay there overnight all along.'

'Did you say that to her?' Billie said.

'I didn't want to cause an argument, and since I arrived before my mother, there was no harm done. I did tell her she needed to make sure to leave before she fell asleep again. I reminded her that my mother would not be happy if she found her there after hours and that I would also be catching an earful. I told her that if she wanted to be able to continue to use the place, she must promise never to bed down in the café again because I couldn't answer for the consequences,' Sally said.

'So she had never stayed overnight at the café before that?'

'Not that I was aware of. From the fact that she was meeting someone in such an unorthodox way, I was pretty certain that it was not someone her parents would approve of.'

'What do you think was wrong with him?' Peter asked. He could think of many reasons why his mother would not approve of a woman he might choose to take an interest in. She would have a lot to say about girls outside their station and even more about those who were not Catholic.

'If I had to guess, I would say that he was married. Otherwise, they could likely spend time together at his place, now couldn't they?'

Sally looked at him as if his brain was made of mashed potato. Although he had not led a particularly sheltered life, his thoughts didn't run quickly to that kind of behavior. He was as red-blooded as the next man, but he believed if you married someone, you kept your vows.

'Did she happen to mention the man's name or any other details about him?' Peter asked.

'No, she didn't have anything to say except what I just told you. In fact, after I scolded her, she gathered up her things and cleared out abruptly,' Sally said.

'You've been very helpful,' Peter said. 'I'll let you get back to your work. I wouldn't want you to have any trouble with your mother for not getting more done on her list.'

'You're not going to tell my mother about what I did, are you?' Sally asked as she got to her feet. 'I don't think she would be very understanding, and I can't see how it makes any difference now.'

'If it doesn't need to come up, I won't mention it. But it may come out anyway. Perhaps you should tell her yourself before-hand. She might be more understanding than you think she will be,' Peter said.

'I very much doubt that. I love my mother, but we don't always get along, and I am never inclined to give her any more reasons to quarrel with me,' Sally said, leading him back down the hallway to the front door. She pulled it open and gave Peter a tired smile before shutting it behind her.

As he made his way down the immaculate steps from the house to the pavement, he wondered who the man Audrey met at the café might be. Was he involved in her death? He was suddenly struck by the urge to talk over the possibilities with someone. He wondered how long it would be before he saw WPC Harkness again.

THIRTY-TWO

Kingston upon Hull
Dear Mildred,

How like you to take the time to send along a note asking after my health and inquiring about my activities here in the north. I am happy to allay your fears as to the people and life in a city. The people are very welcoming and friendly, and although there is a great deal more traffic and noise than in Wiltshire, I have found it all invigorating and enjoyable. And while I will confess that I find it does require a diligent ear to become accustomed to the accent of some of the locals, I have enjoyed making rather a

game of it and thus have not found the adjustment particu-
larly difficult . . .

B illie came upon Professor Byron Trent exactly where
Orson suggested she might find him. The smell of oil
paints and solvents filled her nose before she even reached
the doorway to a large, airy studio. She threaded her way
between wooden easels and rolling carts whose surfaces were
covered with coffee cans filled with brushes and mounds of
paint-stained rags. The professor's back was to the door as Billie
entered the room, but he turned as soon as her footfalls echoed
along the wooden floor.

Although the professor was at least a decade older than the
students attending the college, Billie could easily see how
Audrey Chetwell might have found him far more attractive than
her contemporaries. With his dark, wavy hair and broad shoulders, he gave the appearance of someone in robust good health.
The way he glanced up at Billie, as though he felt equal to
managing whatever life might send his way, made him seem
all the more attractive. He was certainly a more likely specimen
for Audrey's affections than the weedy and unsure Orson Hewitt.
Billie felt quite sorry for the lovelorn engineering student. There
was no way Audrey would have been interested in him if the
man standing before her was on offer.

But that raised the question, didn't it? Had the professor been
on offer? Orson certainly seemed to think so. He had bristled
with resentment when speaking Byron Trent's name. Billie
wondered if it was a question of him trying to cast blame on
another for something he had done. Orson wouldn't be the first
man to turn violent when thwarted in the pursuit of romantic
interest.

'May I help you?' the professor said, closing the gap between
them with a few long strides.

'I certainly hope so. Are you Professor Byron Trent?' Billie
asked.

The man nodded slowly, keeping his eyes fixed on her face. 'I
am. And you appear to be a police constable. You're not here to
arrest me, are you?'

There was a flirtatious quality to his voice that Billie found disconcerting. She wasn't used to being teased in quite that way. After all, a rector's daughter in a tiny village was unlikely to be the sort of girl all the local lads pursued. Perhaps if she had been a more rebellious sort, the conquest of her would have been a feather in someone's cap worth having. But as she had not been inclined to go out of her way to encourage the interest of young men in Barton St Giles, they had left her mostly to herself.

She wondered if his tone was calculated to fluster her and she felt her spine stiffen in response. His attitude might have charmed the students in his classes, but it was not something that predisposed her to warm to him. She found herself suddenly reevaluating how attractive she found him to be.

'I have no such intention at present but perhaps by the end of our interview I will have changed my mind,' Billie said.

'Then I'd best mind my manners,' he said. 'I can see that you are here in an official capacity, so I will treat this as a professional encounter. What can I do for you?'

He gestured towards a desk tucked into the corner of the room and the chairs flanking it. Billie followed him and took a seat, pulling out her notebook once more.

'I'm making inquiries into the death of Audrey Chetwell, and your name has come up in the course of the investigation.' She looked at his face and tried to discern whether or not Audrey's name evoked any sort of guilty reaction.

'Such a tragic loss Audrey's death was,' he said. 'Of course, I am happy to help you in any way that I possibly can, but I don't understand why the police would be looking into a death caused by an air raid.'

'There are just a few things that we need to clear up for our reports before we can consider the case entirely closed. I'm sure you understand there are protocols that must be followed in any unexpected death,' Billie said.

She hoped she sounded as though she knew the ins and outs of police procedure sufficiently to dissuade him from digging any further into her authority to be asking him questions. He seemed to take her excuse in his stride because he leaned forward over the desk and held his hands apart as if to indicate he was open to questions.

'Of course, you must. What is it that you want to know?' he said.

'I understood that you were someone who knew Audrey quite well. Would you say that she was a student with whom you had a close relationship?' Billie asked.

'I have a close relationship with most of my students. That tends to happen in art classes,' he said.

'Would you say that you had particularly singled Audrey out for extra attention?' Billie asked.

'I suppose that someone with a jealous or suspicious mind might have seen my interactions with Audrey as beyond the typical. But I assure you, Audrey was above and beyond the typical both as an artist and as a human being. It was a pleasure to spend time with her and to encourage her in her studies.'

'You say that it was a pleasure to spend time with her, but I have a witness who is willing to report that on the day that Audrey died, you were seen arguing with her here in the college. Can you confirm that's true?' Billie asked.

Professor Trent leaned back in his chair and gazed at her silently for a moment as if determining how much to reveal. Billie stared right back, even though it made her stomach squirm to discuss such things with someone who was both her elder and a man. It was as though her mother was keeping up a running chatter in her head, admonishing her for her rudeness.

'I did have an argument with Audrey and, considering what happened only hours later, I can only say how much I regret it. I wish we had parted company on better terms than we did since we were never able to speak again,' he said.

Billie had the sense that he was speaking sincerely but she didn't necessarily think that let him off the hook as to whether or not he might have been involved in her death. It was certainly possible to both have made a mistake and live to regret it.

'What was the source of this argument?' Billie asked.

'I can't see how that matters now that she's dead, especially considering the manner in which she died.'

'The witness implied that perhaps your relationship was a

romantic one and that Audrey wished to break things off with you,' Billie said.

'I expect you've been speaking with that engineering student who was more often than not trailing along in Audrey's wake,' Professor Trent said. He waited for Billie to confirm his assertion. When she didn't, he continued. 'No, of course, you can't tell me who said such a thing. That would be unprofessional, wouldn't it? Audrey and I were not lovers, nor were we entertaining the notion. I'm a happily married man.'

'The witness mentioned overhearing Audrey say something about quitting and that you insisted she could not. You were seen grabbing her by the arm in a manner described as violent. You deny this conversation took place?' Billie asked.

'I don't deny that the conversation took place at all. I told you that I argued with Audrey. I simply say that it was not about what your witness claims it to have been.'

'Would you mind telling me what it was about, then? I'd like to hear your side of the story,' Billie said.

'Audrey told me that she wanted to leave the art college. She said that the war effort was more important than any self-indulgent educational pursuits could possibly be. I told her there was more than enough time both to volunteer for the war effort and to attend classes.'

'And you thought resorting to violence would convince her to change her mind?' Billie said.

'I'm sorry to say that I lost my temper. You have to understand that Audrey had real talent. It's not every day that I encounter a student with so much potential. We have many young people enter the college simply as a way to thumb their noses at their families. Others just want to dabble in sketching or watercolors. Can you imagine how refreshing it is to have a student with the type of true artistic inclination that Audrey had?' Professor Trent asked.

His voice had raised by a few notches, and there was a gleam in his eye that had not been there before. Billie noticed a furrow that had developed between his eyebrows as if he had found the notion of Audrey abandoning her art painful.

'It sounds as though you were invested in her success,' Billie said.

'Undoubtedly. I even offered to try to secure a commission with the War Artists Advisory Committee for her if she really was determined to increase her involvement with the war effort. After all, what greater good could an artist do than to be involved with a program like that?' he said.

Billie eyed Professor Trent with new interest. She was familiar with the WAAC and had even flirted with the idea of sending in a proposal of her own not long after war had been declared. The committee had been created to help document wartime life for posterity. An artist was granted sketching permits by the committee if he or she had sufficient clearance with the local authorities, along with sufficient skill as an artist, to merit one.

Throughout the countryside, and in cities as well, artists were busy at work recording the way life had been in England before the bombs began to fall. Artists worked feverishly to capture bucolic scenes of rolling hillsides and peaceful fields or architectural gems such as cathedrals and other public buildings. No one knew for sure how much might be changed by the course of events to come, but everyone was certain that nothing would ever be quite the same after it was all over. By sketching and painting and gathering together such images as they produced, at least a little part of England as it had been could be preserved.

There were also artists who were hired for salaried positions as well as those who were given commissions to carry out certain sorts of work on a piece-by-piece basis. Some artists were embedded with troops and spent their time recording the way life transpired for those in the services. Others served on the battlefront, sketching from the front lines almost as though they were wartime photographers, wielding a pencil or a paint-brush rather than a camera.

Commission work was highly competitive, and if Professor Trent had offered to help Audrey to procure one, it spoke volumes. Both about his faith in her abilities and his own clout in both the artistic and governmental fields. Perhaps Professor Trent was more connected than one might first assume of a man tucked away in a small city art college.

'You must have believed in her a great deal, then,' Billie said.

'She was the most promising student I ever had. I certainly wouldn't have done anything to dissuade her from continuing her education or to harm her in any way. And as to the other implication, I have absolutely no interest in romantic entanglements with artists. As a group, we are far too much trouble to be worth it. I am much more likely to show interest in sensible women with a practical turn of mind,' he said.

Billie couldn't be sure, but she felt as though he was leering at her once more. There was something quite wolfish about him, and she felt the hairs on the back of her neck begin to rise. She thought fleetingly of Constable Upton once more.

'I only have one more question for you. Where were you at the time the air raid was going on?'

'I was where any sane person would be, in an air-raid shelter,' he said, broadening his toothy smile even more.

'And where might that shelter have been located?'

'I'm happy to say I'm fortunate enough to have one in my back garden. I was in there all night with my wife,' he said. 'If there is nothing else, I do need to return to my work.'

'I am sorry to have troubled you at work. I'll just need your home address in case I have any further questions for you,' Billie said. She wouldn't swear to it in court, but she didn't think she imagined the look of concern that passed over the professor's face as he gave it to her.

The Trent house was located in a neighborhood Billie had not yet visited during her time in the city. While the houses were far more modest than those on Linden Crescent, it was still the sort of area that one would describe as respectable. Billie was not at all sure what to expect from Mrs Trent when she stepped up to the front door and rapped upon it with more confidence than she felt. What sort of woman would she imagine paired with the professor? Before she had sufficient time to mull it over, the door opened and a thoroughly ordinary woman in her mid-thirties stood before her. In one swift glance, she seemed to take in Billie's uniform and both calculated and discounted reasons for her arrival.

'How may I help you, Constable?' she said, as though she opened her front door to find a member of the police force standing there as a matter of course. For all Billie knew, perhaps she did.

'I've just been speaking with your husband, and there is a matter I must verify with you,' Billie said.

'Well, then, you must come in,' she said, pulling the door open wide and gesturing for Billie to follow her. 'I hope you don't mind if I continue with my mending while we chat.'

Mrs Trent led her down a short hallway to a cozy sitting room facing the back garden. An overstuffed sofa and a pair of comfortable-looking and well-used leather wingback chairs were positioned near an ornately tiled fireplace. A workbasket holding a heaping quantity of clothing sat on a low table between them.

'I shouldn't wish to disturb your work. I know how those things can pile up,' Billie said, pointing towards the basket. 'I don't expect I shall need much of your time.'

Mrs Trent nodded and gestured towards one of the leather seats. She sat on the sofa and plucked a dark sock from the basket. From a small box to her left she removed a wooden darning egg and slipped it inside the sock. With practiced movements, she threaded the needle and began slipping it in and out of a hole, pulling the gaping threads together neatly, a bit at a time.

Many was the time Billie had seen her mother make exactly the same sort of repair. Her father and brother seemed forever to be wearing holes in the toes and heels of their socks, and as the rectory was not a living that provided endless funds, repairs were an important part of maintaining the family budget. Besides, her mother had equated wastefulness with sinfulness, and as most of the sock was still useful, she could not countenance replacing it if it could possibly be repaired.

Her mother had been ahead of her time in her efforts to make do and mend. The entire country was being admonished to make such efforts, whether they had been in the habit of doing so or not. Women everywhere were learning how to let down hems for children's clothing and to turn facings back to front to make cuffs and collars appear fresh and serviceable long after they might have consigned such garments to the ragbag. Although Billie had not always appreciated what had felt like parsimony, she had been grateful to her mother for teaching her the habit of performing such alterations and repairs long before the government was asking the population to do so. From the way Mrs Trent swiftly and neatly completed the task, Billie had to assume she was not new to such activities herself. She folded the sock neatly and placed it on the sofa beside her before reaching for a shirt and a needle threaded with white.

'So why are you here to speak with me?' she asked as she drew the thread up through the holes in a button and began fastening it firmly to the garment.

'Did your husband happen to tell you anything about the death of one of his students?' Billie asked.

'You're speaking of Audrey Chetwell, of course,' Mrs Trent said, pausing briefly in her work to meet Billie's gaze. Billie nodded. 'Yes, Byron was quite distressed by what happened to Audrey. Of course, it was in the newspaper as well.'

She thrust the needle back down through the button, and Billie wondered if she was applying more vigor to her jabbing than she had done before Audrey's name was mentioned.

'Yes. In order to close the investigation into Audrey's untimely death, there are some questions. I'm just verifying a few things your husband had to say,' Billie said.

'I'm sure my husband had a great deal to say about someone as lovely and talented as Audrey. I've never known him at a loss for young women to praise, and Audrey was simply the latest in a long string. That is what you're getting at, isn't it?' Mrs Trent asked, giving the thread a yank.

'When I spoke with your husband, he made it very clear that there was nothing about his interactions with Audrey beyond those appropriate between a devoted professor and a talented student,' Billie said.

'I'm sure that is exactly what Byron would say. He's very fond of the role of doting professor. If only he were as fond of that of the devoted husband,' Mrs Trent said as she reached for a pair of tiny, black-handled scissors from her workbasket and snipped off the excess thread. 'I suppose he tried to convince you that he was not romantically involved with her or any other student, didn't he?'

'He did deny that anything about his involvement with Audrey extended beyond that of a teacher and a student. You don't sound convinced?'

'You're an attractive young woman. You say you spoke with my husband yourself?' she asked.

'Yes. I just came from the art college,' Billie said.

'You tell me, then. Did my husband seem to be flirting with you when you first arrived? Was there anything about him that implied that he was evaluating whether or not you might be an easy conquest?'

Heat rushed to Billie's cheeks. Her face grew hotter still as Mrs Trent sighed and shook her head.

'I'm very sorry, my dear. It's almost like a sneeze or one's knee jerking when rapped upon during a physical examination at the doctor's surgery. Byron cannot seem to keep himself from trying it on with any young woman who comes across his path. You'd think that your uniform might have proved daunting, but I expect, knowing my husband as well as I do, that it only intrigued him all the more. As happy as I am that women are being admitted to the constabulary, there may be some uncomfortable times ahead of you.'

'So you don't believe his claim that he was not involved romantically with Audrey?' Billie said, trying to keep her voice even.

She had no idea how to navigate a conversation that involved admitting to a woman that her husband had tried to flirt with her.

'People say it is a tragedy that we are involved in war once again. You know, I don't see it that way. There's something about one's life being in jeopardy that clarifies situations and makes it possible to speak about things you found unmentionable before. A year ago, I would not have considered airing my private business concerning my marriage. With the world in such chaos, it seems quite a small matter indeed to tell you that my husband has been terminally unfaithful throughout our marriage.'

'So Audrey's not the first woman he has become involved with?' Billie asked.

'Of course not. Artists are a different sort of creature entirely. When we married, I thought perhaps ours would be an exceptional relationship. But over time I became accustomed to his exploits and found ways to ignore them. I knew that Byron was seeing other women, but I also knew that he always returned to me. But now, as so many people are behaving recklessly, I do wonder if he might just leave,' Mrs Trent said.

A flicker of pain flashed across the older woman's face, and Billie looked down to see a drop of blood fall on the white shirt just below the newly attached button. Mrs Trent did not notice the spreading stain but simply left her hand bleeding against the snowy fabric.

Could Professor Trent's argument with Audrey have involved him suggesting a permanent arrangement in their relationship? Had he offered to leave his wife? Had it spooked her and caused her to try to break it off? Had she demanded that he do so, and he refused? That would explain her insistence that she would quit whatever had been happening. It would also explain the violent display when he grabbed her by the arm.

Of course, she only had Orson's word that the confrontation had been a physical one. From a distance, even without an agenda to serve, it could be difficult to tell how forceful one held another; in fact, the only person who could have accurately assessed that was Audrey. That said, Mrs Trent had as much reason for wanting Audrey out of the way as Orson Hewitt did – perhaps more. It was one thing to be distressed by something one could never have. But was it quite another to be concerned about what one stood to lose?

'Your husband claims to have been in your garden shelter during the air raid that took place this week. Can you confirm that?' Billie asked.

Mrs Trent met Billie's gaze. 'I'm afraid that I can't.'

'Are you saying that your husband was not with you during the air raid?' Billie asked.

Mrs Trent looked down at the blood on the shirt and let out a sigh.

'I don't know where my husband was, but I can assure you he wasn't with me. I was on my own with the dog, just as I am most evenings. If the circumstances were different, I would have suggested you ask Audrey about my husband's where-abouts that evening, but, sadly, that is no longer possible.'

THIRTY-THREE

Hull
Special Constable Upton's PNB

When Peter reported for his shift that evening, one of the boys who served as switchboard operator rushed up to him, waving a piece of paper. He shoved it into Peter's hand before racing back to the room crammed with switchboards, wires and stools, upon which perched a half-dozen boys. Peter unfolded the note and swiftly read the contents. A bicycle matching the description of the one he sought had been turned in at an auxiliary station on the other side of the city.

He checked with the sergeant on duty, thankfully a man providing coverage during Sergeant Skelton's day off, and apprised him of his plan to view the bicycle. As he was making his way back towards the door, he spotted WPC Harkness slowly moving towards him along the corridor that led from the women's cloakroom. The look on her face suggested she had a great deal on her mind. He lifted a hand in greeting as she approached.

'Are you on duty this evening?' he asked.

'Actually, I'm just finishing up my shift. It looks as though you're about to start one,' she said.

'That's right; I just got in. I'm on my way to the Queen's Gardens station,' he said.

'You aren't transferring to another station, are you?' she asked.

Peter felt his heart lift as he noticed she sounded disappointed at the thought of him leaving.

'No, I'm going over there to follow up on the investigation into the parish priest's missing bicycle. It was stolen while a butcher's delivery boy was borrowing it, and I've been trying to locate it for them. The station called and left a message for me saying that a bicycle matching the description I sent out has been turned in at the station.'

Constable Harkness gave him a beaming smile. 'Well, that's good news,' she said.

'It is. He'll be very glad to get it back,' he said.

'I'm sure he will, but I meant it was good news that being saddled with me on patrol the other day hadn't made you decide to transfer to another station where you wouldn't be plagued by my presence any longer,' she said.

Peter had thought that he had done a good job of hiding his irritation at being forced to allow her to tag along with him. Maybe he had not been as subtle as he had thought.

'I wouldn't have considered your presence to be a plague. All new officers get ribbed about their value to the force when they first join up. You don't expect to be treated any differently just because you're a woman, do you?' he asked.

He was gratified to see she stood up a bit straighter and a defiant look flickered across her face, chasing away the defeated one.

'Of course not. I hope the bicycle turns out to be the one you are looking for,' she said.

'Do you have any big plans for this evening?' he asked.

'Nothing that can't wait. I have a book that I've been enjoying reading, but it will still be there later. Why do you ask?'

She tipped her head to the side like a small bird, and her cap shifted slightly on her head. He wondered if there had been no uniform headgear small enough to fit her properly. It had been a struggle to advocate for uniforms for the special constables and even those involved with the war reserve. It must have been an even greater scramble to find something suitable for the WPCs to wear. With only two of them serving so far, the kinks were still being worked out.

'If you don't have anything better to do, you could come with me to the Queen's Gardens station, and I could introduce you to some of the chaps over there. We don't overlap with them very often, but it's always good to see a familiar face if you show up at the same accident scene or air raid,' he said.

He lowered his voice a bit. 'Besides, I have some things to tell you about that matter we discussed yesterday.'

A wide smile spread across her face, and he felt a little guilty at how grateful she seemed to be offered a friendly overture.

'I'd like that. I have a few things to tell you, too,' she said.

He held the door for her as they passed out of the station, and she smiled once more. As they walked along, the pavement still radiated some of the day's warmth, even though the air around them had grown cooler. The sun had not yet set but it had sunk below the height of the tallest buildings with only a glow peeking out between buildings from time to time. He had the sense that she was not yet entirely comfortable with the city from the way she kept close to his side as the night grew darker and shadows gathered in.

She had seemed such a formidable force when he had seen her in the café bent over Audrey's body that he had not considered how much courage it might have taken her to do so. After all, wasn't she a country mouse who had found herself in a big city as some remarkable chaos was unfolding? It certainly hadn't been a very warm welcome for her on any front.

He launched into a summary of his visits to Mrs Nichol's house and the discovery that Audrey's presence at the café after hours was a mystery to the owner but not to her daughter. He left out mention of any eating he might have done while he was there.

'I thought Audrey seemed particularly friendly with the waitress,' she said. 'Sally offered a different take on Audrey from her parents, didn't she?'

'She wasn't critical of her, but she did make her sound as though she could be someone it was hard to refuse, whatever the request. It seems she was a popular girl,' he said.

'Not with everyone,' she said.

Peter's eyes widened as WPC Harkness told him about her surprise meeting with Mrs Chetwell, as well as her interviews with a student named Orson and a professor named Trent. He listened with surprise as she relayed her conversations with Muriel Matthews and Mrs Trent. She looked up at him expectantly as she told him that Mrs Trent had cast the professor's alibi into doubt.

'It was a remarkably informative day, and yet I still don't feel as though I've got very far,' she said.

'You may not be getting as far along as you'd like but you're certainly making headway. After all, you've managed to come up with several suspects and even a few motives. It's more important than my bicycle investigation.'

Peter felt just the slightest bit envious of her success. As useful as he felt the retrieval of Father O'Connell's bicycle might be, he couldn't truly say that he would not have rather spent his time in pursuit of a murderer. There was something far more laudable about bringing that sort of criminal to justice than those who would likely turn out to be a ragtag group of miscreant children.

'You mustn't say that. Your priest's bicycle is changing the lives of people who are still living them. What is the butcher's boy supposed to do if he can't make deliveries? I don't expect he does the job purely for the fun of it, even if all the house-wives in Hull are feeding him. Surely his family relies upon his income. No matter what happened to Audrey Chetwell, it's safe to say she's beyond such worries.'

Peter looked at her with fresh eyes. Billie's voice was the cultured southern sort that never dropped aitches or contracted words by eliminating vowels, unlike his own. She had an air of gentility about her that suggested she came from money. He found it difficult to imagine that she truly had any notion of what it was like to wonder if her purse would stretch to cover the bills.

Although the reputation of the Church was not one of lavish living, the basic needs were guaranteed to be met. Besides, he had understood that many of those who entered the clergy were men of means who took up the cloth as a sort of charitable act rather than a vocation chosen to support them financially. He had simply assumed that she and her family were typical do-gooders. Her empathy towards those who did not come from such a background surprised him.

She spoke as though she knew exactly of what she spoke. Perhaps, he told himself, she was as good an observer of the people in her father's parish as she was of those they questioned while on an investigation. He could not imagine her wondering if the gas would be turned off or her mother would go without dinner so that she might have a full belly that night.

Before he could think of a suitable response, the Queen's Gardens police station appeared in front of them, and she took a few eager steps ahead of him as though she was even more excited by the possibility of this case being solved than he was himself. They pushed open the plate-glass doors and entered the lobby. In no time they were led to a back room where surrendered property was stored.

Sure enough, it was Father O'Connell's trusty machine. He immediately recognized the way the bicycle seat tipped slightly to the left as well as the rust spots freckling the wide chrome handlebars. The fruit crates lashed to it were just as the butcher's boy had described. Peter inspected the bike for signs of damage and was relieved to find there were none. WPC Harkness seemed equally interested in poring over it as though there might be some sort of clue to where it had been. As he bent over to squeeze the rear tire to check for leaks, she let out an excited squeak.

'What's this?' she asked, reaching her hand into the depths of the fruit crate. She held up a scrap of paper and stepped towards the bulb hanging from the ceiling in order to inspect it more closely. Peter came up alongside her and looked at it as she tipped it this way and that. It was a pale-blue bit of paper with black letters printed upon it. Hardly larger than a postage stamp, it was impossible to read any words other than *at* and *for*. More letters were missing than were present. Still, it was the only bit of evidence as to the bicycle's whereabouts.

'It's impossible to say for sure considering how small that is, but I suppose I could ask the butcher's boy if it's part of the wrapping from one of his deliveries. Probably, it will turn out to be nothing, but you never know,' Peter said. 'Well spotted, WPC Harkness.'

Even in the dim lighting of the storage room, he thought he noticed a faint flush rising to her cheeks. Perhaps it would not be such a bad thing to have her on the force. She was extremely detail-oriented if her discovery of the scrap of paper was anything to go on.

'Whatever it is, I would hang on to it if it were my case.

Someone ought to be held to account for the theft, and that
might be the only thing that ties the culprit to the crime,' she
said as she handed him the scrap of paper. He nodded and
slipped it into his wallet for safekeeping.

'The first order of business is to take the bicycle back to
Father O'Connell. Do you want to help me take it to him?' he
asked. Once again, her face lit up at the chance to be included,
and once more he felt ashamed of the way he had felt about
her accompanying him on his rounds.

'Is it on the way towards Linden Crescent?' she asked. 'I am
still not quite sure of my way around the city, especially after
dark.'

A flicker of worry flitted across her face, and he wondered
again if she was uncomfortable walking about in a city. Or
perhaps it was the darkness that bothered her most. Either way,
it made no difference. Something crouched uncomfortably at
the back of her mind.

'No, it isn't. But Linden Crescent is right on the way to my
boarding house,' he lied.

THIRTY-FOUR

Kingston upon Hull
Dear Frederick,
*   This evening I made the acquaintance of a Catholic
priest and I must confess he was not at all as I had imagined one to be . . .*

Peter wheeled the bicycle all the way to St Brigid's, slowing
his steps far more than he had on their first shift together.
Billie wondered if her nervousness at being out in the
darkness showed. Every time the sound of a motorcar or trolley
reached her ears, she tried to hide her rising panic, but from
the way he leaned in close until the vehicles passed, she was
not sure she had kept her fear hidden. Thankfully, he made no
mention of it and they soon reached their destination.

Father O'Connell was not as she had imagined he would be. For one thing, he had a strong Irish accent rather than that of the locals as she had expected. Truth be told, he was at least as easy to understand as Peter. For another, he was warm and welcoming and not at all standoffish. Her parents had always made Catholics out to be rigid, formal sorts of people with rules that were strict and very different from their own. As there were none of them to be found in Barton St Giles, she had no evidence that their beliefs might be faulty.

In fact, the father was so delighted at the return of his property he tried to convince them to join him for a cup of tea or even a tot of whisky. Peter had raised a questioning eyebrow at her as if to leave the decision to her, but before she could make an excuse not to delay her return to the safety of Lydia's house, the sound of an air-raid siren rang across the city. Peter sprinted to the doors of the church and stepped out on to the pavement.

'Perhaps you should take cover, lass,' the priest said, gesturing towards a row of pews. Billie had read the pamphlets that recommended sheltering beneath a table or under a staircase if it was not possible to access another form of protection. Remembering the damage to the city from the previous raid, she thought the pews looked entirely unequal to the task.

'Isn't there a public air-raid shelter nearby?' she asked, shouting to make herself heard over the clamor of the relentless sirens.

Father O'Connell shook his head. 'They are setting them up just as fast as they can, but for now the church serves as the shelter for this neighborhood.'

As if to emphasize his words, a throng of people streamed in through the church's open doors. Billie's heart fell as she realized that Peter was not one of them.

'He'll be out in the street if I know our Peter,' the priest said. 'He was never one to be early to church.' He turned from her and began comforting the huddle of people who stood looking dazed.

Billie imagined the dark and her mother and the traffic streaming by. None of that seemed to matter as she heard the sirens and thought of Peter standing in the street behaving as a member of the constabulary should in a crisis. She had told her mother she wanted to be of real use. Well, now was her chance. She took a steadying breath and raced out into the dark to look for Peter and to see how she could help.

She found him in the center of the street, shouting and pointing towards the church. Planes roared overhead, and Billie watched in horror as an incendiary landed only a few yards from where he stood. She raced towards him and asked what she should do.

'Go back into the church,' he shouted. 'Father O'Connell could use your help.' From the look on his face, Billie could see he was not speaking to her as a fellow officer but as a woman.

'You aren't leaving until everyone else is inside, are you?' she shouted up at him.

'No,' he said.

'Then you'll get to safety in half the time if I help.' Before he could protest, she raced off down the block to a cluster of people attempting to force the door of a corner shop.

It seemed as if time stretched interminably before the street was emptied of people, but finally Peter waved at her to follow him. They raced up the steps and shoved the church doors firmly shut behind them. Soot covered his face and her hat had gone missing in the fray. As they each crawled under neighboring pews, he shook his head at her.

'You did well out there, partner.'

A lump rose in her throat at the word 'partner'. 'For a woman?' she asked.

'For anyone. You can be sure the sergeant will hear about how well you represented the constabulary.'

She could not think of a gracious way to accept such an unexpected bit of praise, so she changed the subject.

'Providing we manage to make it out of here,' she said.

'I have a feeling you might be the sort to manage just about anything life throws at you.'

THIRTY-FIVE

Kingston upon Hull
Dear Canon Reeves,
   Thank you for your concern for my well-being and your
offer to provide me with letters of introduction to members
of the clergy here in Hull. Despite any rumors it appears
you have heard to the contrary, I am very well situated in
the home of my father's thoroughly respectable cousin.
Please do not feel troubled in the least on my account . . .

B illie looked through the wavy glass of the sidelights and recognized Muriel Matthews standing on the front step. Muriel shifted restlessly from one foot to the other and continually checked her outfit, flicking at imaginary lint on her sleeves and adjusting her hat. Wishing she had bothered to get dressed before descending the stairs, Billie turned the knob and forced herself to offer a welcoming smile.

'Good morning, Miss Matthews. What brings you here?' Billie asked.

'May I come in? I'd rather speak to you without everyone on the street wondering about my business,' Muriel said, looking over her shoulder.

Billie stepped back and allowed her to enter. Muriel looked all around appraisingly. She had the look on her face that Billie expected had been on her own when she had first seen Lydia's home. If Muriel had been a less well-bred young woman, she likely would have passed comment about modern vulgarity. As it was, she simply permitted her eyes to widen slightly before returning her attention to fidgeting with her clothing.

'I don't suppose you'd like to join me in a cup of coffee?' Billie asked.

'I don't mind if I do. I left the house this morning before having any breakfast,' Muriel said, following her towards the kitchen.

Whatever brought Muriel to see her must be a matter of some importance, Billie thought. She added some coffee grounds to the percolator and set it on the hob before turning her attention to the table where her guest had taken a seat with her back to the rear of the house. The blackout curtains had been drawn back and the windows were flung open. The sound of the city filtered in through the screens, along with a warm breeze and the sound of bird call.

For just a moment Billie felt a slight pang of homesickness for the grounds of the rectory. On a summer day such as this, she would have delighted in sneaking off to the garden with a book, a flask of tea and an apple in search of a quiet nook in which to immerse herself in some grand adventure penned by an author she would never meet. Dappled sunlight would filter through the canopy of the rectory's grove of peach trees, and flocks of tiny sparrows and finches would twitter in the leafy canopy above her.

She could almost hear her mother calling her name, entreating her to participate in some good work or other intended to support the village. Muriel cleared her throat, and Billie blinked at finding herself standing in Lydia's kitchen. She sat at the table opposite Muriel and attempted to behave as a hostess ought.

'If you stopped by to see my cousin, I am afraid she's already gone off to the library for the day,' Billie said.

'Actually, I'm here to see you. I had an unsettling telephone call from a friend of mine late last evening and thought I'd best come by and set the record straight. I stopped in at the police station, but they said you were on a later shift. I made the sergeant at the desk give me your address,' Muriel said.

Billie could easily imagine Sergeant Skelton enjoying the notion of allowing a member of the public to track her to her private residence. She wouldn't be a bit surprised to hear that rather than having the information dragged from him, he had simply offered it up to both rid himself of Muriel and to bother Billie in one fell swoop.

'What is it that you think I can do for you?' Billie said. She wondered exactly who Muriel's friend was. Was it possible that Professor Trent had been turning his attention towards

Muriel as well as Audrey? While the two young women had little in common as far as appearances went, they were both art college students, and if Mrs Trent was to be believed, her husband was not likely to turn down the opportunity to avail himself of whatever female companionship might be in his orbit.

Muriel had made it sound as though she resented Audrey and her connection to the professor. Had she been jealous of the attention and preference he showed to the dead girl? She supposed it was possible that Muriel had a connection with Mrs Trent. That would be another good reason why she would have been so harsh in her assessment of Audrey's behavior with the professor. Muriel had indicated that she spent much of her time involved in volunteer efforts in the city. Perhaps she knew Mrs Trent from one of the volunteer organizations and felt some form of loyalty towards the older woman.

'Orson said you seem to think that he might have had something to do with what happened to Audrey. Not that that makes the least bit of sense considering the Germans were the ones who killed her. That said, I can't see you have any reason to go about upsetting him. His exams are coming up very shortly, and he doesn't need anything to distract him from his studies,' Muriel said.

Billie was surprised at the vehemence with which Muriel stated her case. Orson Hewitt had not been as upset by her questions as Muriel herself seemed to be. Was it possible that she was interested in Orson for some reason herself? Perhaps that was the nature of her dislike of Audrey. Maybe Muriel had set her cap at him, and when he had turned his attention to Audrey, she had been overcome with jealousy.

'I only had a few questions for him about Audrey and can't imagine why he would have taken any of them so much to heart that it would impede his studies. Did he tell you that was the case?' Billie asked.

Muriel shook her head. 'No, he didn't. But I could tell that he was very upset by the whole situation. I told him that he shouldn't give it another thought as I would set you straight immediately,' Muriel said.

'Set me straight about what exactly?' Billie asked.

'About his lack of involvement in whatever it is that you seem to think happened to Audrey. He simply could have had no part in any of it, whatever you might imagine it would be,' Muriel said.

Billie wondered why Muriel was quite so worked up about her questioning Orson. Although she was new to interviewing suspects and following leads, she didn't think she had implied Audrey might have been the victim of foul play. Did Muriel herself suspect that something had happened to Audrey that could not be explained by the air raid? Was she in some way complicit in what had happened?

She certainly seemed to dislike Audrey enough to make her a viable suspect. But was she cool-headed enough to cosh another person over the head and leave her for dead on the floor of the café? Could she have helped Orson to do so?

'What makes you so sure that he had nothing to do with anything untoward?' Billie asked. The sound of the percolator bubbling behind her filled her ears as she kept her eyes trained on Muriel's face.

'Because he was with me. We had gone out to a show together and were trapped in the cinema for hours during the air raid, that's why,' Muriel said, crossing her arms over her chest. She lifted her chin defiantly as if to prompt Billie to question her story.

'Were you often in the habit of going to the pictures with Orson Hewitt?' Billie asked. While it really would make no difference to an alibi at the time, she did wonder what reaction Muriel would have to the question.

'Actually, it was our very first date, if you must know,' Muriel said.

'And what a memorable one it must've been,' Billie said.

'What do you mean?' Muriel said, squeezing her upper arms with her hands.

'I don't think I would be likely to forget being trapped in a cinema with a bunch of strangers during an air raid. As a matter of fact, the exact same thing happened to me and I can't get it out of my mind.'

'No, of course, you're right about that. I'm sure that is something we will be able to tell our grandchildren about one day,'

Muriel said, pushing back her chair and standing. 'I just thought you should know he couldn't possibly have had anything to do with Audrey's death. I hope you put that in your report before you file it. I can see myself out.'

The percolator stopped thunking, and Billie rose to lift it from the hob. As she poured herself a steaming cup of coffee, she wondered what the real reason for Muriel's visit had been. Had it been to provide Orson with an alibi or to give herself one?

As she stepped out on to the street, she was sorry to note the city looked no better in the morning than it had the night before when the sirens had stopped and she had emerged from the church along with Peter and dozens of shocked residents. He had walked her all the way to Linden Crescent, even though she insisted she could find her way on her own. Everywhere along the route to the police station was strewn with evidence of the air raid. At the end of one terrace of houses, a lump rose in Billie's throat when she spotted a single stalk of snap-dragons thrusting defiant yellow blooms skyward despite the mound of debris surrounding it.

For a moment she felt despair and wondered if there was simply no point in trying to do some good amid such chaos. But then she caught sight of a man hoisting a sheet of plywood into place across a window whose glass had been blown out. He was whistling a light-hearted tune, and between the blows of his hammer, she recognized the tune as one her mother had often sung. As long as there was someone willing to face the difficulties with a cheerful song on their lips, the least she could do was to give her best efforts to the job of constable. She glanced at the large clock in the square up ahead, pleased to see she had made good time even at a leisurely pace.

Despite the delay caused by Muriel's visit, she still found she had enough time to check the women's cloakroom for a uniform cap to replace the one she had lost the night before. After locating one on a high shelf, she opened the cloakroom door and heard Avis's voice floating down the hallway towards her. Something in her tone made Billie pause. She waited in the cloakroom's shadowy depths, the door barely cracked open, for her superior to pass by. At first, she could not quite identify the voice of the man speaking with Avis, and then it clicked into place like a final puzzle piece. Her boss was speaking with Professor Trent.

She held her breath as they passed the cloakroom, hoping Avis would not notice her there. Before they reached the end of the corridor and the sight of those assembled in the open lobby, they paused and faced each other. Avis lifted her gaze up towards the professor, an urgent look on her face. He reached out a hand and patted her arm reassuringly before turning and striding away.

Billie was not sure she could identify the emotion flitting across Avis's face as she watched his retreating back, but she was quite certain that it was not something she had ever experienced herself. Whatever was passing between Avis Crane and Professor Trent was clearly important to her supervisor. The question was, what could it be? Billie thought of Mrs Trent's suspicions that her husband was unfaithful and the professor's own assertion that he preferred women of a practical bent. Avis certainly fitted that description. Could it be that the two of them were romantically entangled? If he was a suspect in Audrey's death, would that affect the way Avis pursued the case? Although it gave her no pleasure to do so, she determined she would have to ask Avis about it.

She tucked her pocketbook under her arm and stepped out of the cloakroom and into the hallway. Avis wheeled around with a startled look upon her face.

'Billie, I didn't know you had reported for your shift already,' Avis said.

'I've only just arrived. Was that Professor Trent I saw you talking with?' Billie asked.

'I don't believe he said his name was Trent. He was simply a member of the public who wanted to make inquiries about the information bureau. He was trying to trace a family member who he believed had left the city after the air raid,' Avis said. 'Let's get you settled with your assignments for the day. I think I'm going to have you take care of some typing and filing that have been piling up.'

With that, Avis strode off towards her office without another word. As Billie watched her walk away, she could think of no good reason for her boss to have lied to her.

THIRTY-SIX

Hull
Special Constable Upton's PNB

Peter felt as though his chest was about to burst into flames. Everywhere his eye landed, there was another one of the damned things. The wind off the water caused them to flutter and swirl and lift and spin. All about him, people were making a grab for them, and Peter felt wave upon wave of fury.

He ran after the blowing papers as quickly as he could, snatching them and stuffing them into a stack clamped beneath his arm. Two or three members of the public joined his pursuit, and between them they did their best to round up the leaflets. He wasn't sure he could ever remember being quite so angry in all his life.

Day after day, men and women and boys barely out of short pants were giving it their all to keep the Germans from rolling over England the way they had mowed down their neighbors on the continent. It was hard to credit that someone had the audacity to spread such filth right there at his dock. While he wished he could say that there was no one who grumbled about the sacrifices being required or who supported fascism, it sickened him to think someone would be so brazen as to carpet the docks with fascist leaflets. As soon as he had rounded up what he could, he retreated to the relative privacy offered by a stack of crates and took a closer look at one of them.

There, printed in bold black ink, was an invitation to the reader to tune in to the new British Broadcast Channel for the truth about the war and the Axis Powers' agenda. He had heard all about this supposedly new radio station and the type of propaganda it spewed from the other side. He had to give them credit for naming it something that could be abbreviated to BBC in order to sow confusion. Unfortunately, more subjects of the Crown tuned in than was good for morale. Leaflets like this didn't help.

It wasn't just the content printed upon them; it was also the audacity with which they had been distributed. If they couldn't control the type of message that was spreading within the borders, how could they have any hope of fighting back the Germans on foreign soil? It was exactly the sort of thing calculated to undermine, and sadly it often worked.

His hand trembled with rage as he looked down once more at the page in front of him. Then, with a start, he took a closer look at the paper. It was pale blue and the border around the text looked familiar. Clutching the papers tightly to his chest, he fished into his back pocket and retrieved his wallet. Carefully, he pulled the scrap of paper WPC Harkness had discovered in the fruit crate attached to the priest's bicycle. He held the scrap against the top leaflet in the stack and felt his breath catch in his chest.

The color of the paper was a perfect match and the border around the text was, too. He placed the scrap of paper over a spot he felt it matched up with and noted how the pieces of the missing letters lined up to complete the words. He looked up and down the dock for the place from which the papers could have been distributed. Given the scope of their spread, he guessed that it was likely someone had tipped them down on to the dock from a point somewhere above his head. He glanced up and saw one of the gangway bridges that spanned from one walkway to another to help workers easily navigate the crowded port area.

The leaflets had been on the dock for some time, given the fact that they were blown about for a great distance and were soaked with the overnight dew. He returned the scrap of paper to his wallet and then made his way towards the bridge where he stood in the center and looked down. If someone had the intention of distributing a great quantity of printed material to a prime demographic of discontented workers, this would be the perfect spot to release it. He wouldn't allow such a thing to happen again, not on his watch. He'd work his shift at the dock and then he would ask about subversive behavior in the area. Not everyone will be willing to print such rubbish, but he was sure that he knew someone who knew someone who would.

Another even more disturbing thought occurred to him. Could the bicycle have not really been stolen at all? At least not by a stranger. Could Father O'Connell have taken his own bicycle back and used the excuse of a theft to cover for his activities or those of some of his associates? Like it or not, he was going to have to tax the priest with his suspicions, or at least ask some questions that would not credit either of them.

Kingston upon Hull
Dear Candace,

I had to write to tell you of a letter I received from the Canon. It seems that someone alerted him to my hasty departure from the village. It seems the poor man was laboring under the impression that I was likely in need of a home for wayward girls. I shall leave it to you to imagine who might have put such a notion in his head. After I recovered from the shock, I was rather touched that he would put pen to paper to mention such a difficult subject and that he would offer to be of assistance in such a practical and caring way.

I hope all is as well as can be with you. Do write when you can! I love hearing your stories of night watches and manning – or should I say womanning – the barrage balloons!

Love,
Billie

After double-checking the details of the last report, she stacked the papers neatly together, then discovered her own desk contained no stapler or paperclips of any kind. She carried the reports down the hall to Avis's office and knocked upon the door. When she received no response, she tried the handle. It turned smoothly under her grasp and she stepped in.

A stapler sat upon Avis's desk and she reached for it and pressed down on it before discovering it to be empty. With a strong feeling of unease at violating her superior's privacy, she told herself it couldn't be helped and began opening the drawers of Avis's desk in search of staples. Drawer after drawer revealed no results, just stacks of paper and previously gathered reports, pens, pencils and packets of sweets. Billie was not sure where else to look until her gaze landed upon another door in the small office.

She crossed the room and opened it, discovering it held a coat hook and shelving for supplies. A whole department's worth of carbon paper, typewriter ribbons and citation pads were tucked away in the corner of Avis's tiny space. Billie wondered if it was some sort of a commentary on the value the department placed on Avis that her office would be the one required to give over extra storage space for the good of the whole station. She couldn't imagine Sergeant Skelton making room for such things in his domain.

As she lifted a box of staples down from an upper shelf, her glance landed on a folder tucked into the back of a lower shelf. She wondered if it had simply been forgotten and would be best filed away among the other manila folders tucked into the various cabinets in the main area of the station. She opened it to determine where it ought to be returned to, and her breath caught in her throat.

Her heart pounded in her chest and the feeling of unease she had had when she caught Avis in a lie about Professor Trent came flooding back. Although she could not be certain that what she was looking at was the same missing map Lydia had reported to her earlier, she could think of no good reason why Avis would have a map of the docks hidden away in the back of her supply closet. How would she have come to have it in her possession? And why would she have not mentioned it to Billie when she listened to Lydia's concerns?

Who exactly was Avis Crane and what was she doing at the police department? She could think of absolutely no loyal patriotic reason why Avis would have such a document in her office. She had no idea what she should do. Should she replace the folder in the closet and pretend she hadn't seen it? Should she report the fact that she found it to Lydia? To Sergeant Skelton? Should she tell Peter?

She couldn't see how it would be the right thing to remove it. After all, if she took it out of Avis's closet, she couldn't prove that that was where she had found it. And who would believe her anyway? She was new to the job, new to the city and quite possibly in over her head. She was trying to decide what to do when she heard footsteps coming along the corridor. She quickly shoved the folder back into the closet and quietly shut the door. She leaped to the visitor side of Avis's desk and reached for the stapler poised to pretend she was attempting to use it.

The door opened behind her, and Sergeant Skelton stood there, an urgent look upon his face. 'Have you seen WPC Crane recently?' he asked.

Billie shook her head, her throat dry with anxiety. 'No, not recently.'

'Damn that woman. She's always underfoot when she isn't needed and she's not here when she is. I suppose you'll have to do,' he said. 'I'm going to need you to come with me for an interview.'

'Has something happened?' Billie asked.

'I'll say something's happened. A professor from the art college has gone and got himself murdered. We've got to deliver the bad news to his widow, and I thought it best to have a WPC at the scene in case she goes into hysterics,' he said.

'And you want me to be the one to do it?' Billie said.

He threw up his arms in the air as if completely exasperated. 'I don't see any other women hanging about the station that could do it, do you? Grab your uniform cap. We've got to head over to the Trent residence straightaway,' he said, striding out of the door without a backward glance.

She took one last look at the supply closet and then rushed after him.

Billie wasn't sure how a widow was supposed to act when receiving the news that her husband had been suddenly and tragically killed, but she was uneasy about the way Mrs Trent took the news of her husband's murder. Everyone behaved differently in trying circumstances; she knew this from the many occasions when those in need of consoling had appeared at the door of the rectory, their lives shattered beyond all recognition.

Still, Billie couldn't help but feel as though Mrs Trent took the news with far more aplomb than she had when the village

constable had brought her the news of her own mother's death.
Sergeant Skelton had broken the news with a gentleness Billie
would not have expected him to possess. Rather than the blus-
tering and cross man who glowered at female officers, he played
the role of a kindly uncle or even father confessor. It was a
side of him that Billie had not expected existed, and despite
herself she found that she admired the way he managed to
deliver terrible news and yet still seem to be on the alert for
whether or not Mrs Trent might have been involved.

'Can you think of any reason why someone would wish to
do your husband harm?' Sergeant Skelton asked gently.

Mrs Trent managed a raised eyebrow and a weary smile at the
question. 'There were a great many people who had reason to
wish my husband ill. Your constable must have told you that my
husband had a reputation for being unfaithful.' Mrs Trent looked
at Billie over her steaming cup of tea and took a slow sip.

Billie felt Sergeant Skelton stiffen ever so slightly as he shot
her a sideways glance. She had managed to keep it from him
that she had spoken with Mrs Trent previously concerning her
husband's alibi for the time of Audrey's death. Now it seemed
she would have some explaining to do once they were on their
own.

Still, he seemed to be more interested in discovering what
else Mrs Trent knew and preserving a unified front for the police
department than in scolding her then and there. Billie let out a
silent sigh of relief as he kept his attention focused on Mrs Trent.

'I'm sure that WPC Harkness was quite thorough in your
previous conversation, but I'd like to hear it from you myself.
There were other women that caught his eye?' he asked gently.

'There were indeed. In fact, almost all other women seemed
to catch my husband's eye and likely the rest of him as well.
Audrey Chetwell was merely the most recent,' she said, carefully placing her teacup on the table beside her and leaning
back gracefully against the sofa.

'Since your husband was found at the college, I don't suppose
you would be able to provide an alibi for where you were last
night?' he asked.

'I was where I so often find myself, Sergeant. I was at home,
alone,' she said. She gestured towards a wicker basket near her

feet where a wire-haired terrier lay guarding his mistress's feet. 'Well, except for Toby, that is. He's a far more faithful companion than my husband ever was.' She reached forward and stroked the dog's rough fur.

'I don't suppose the dog would be able to vouch for you in a formal statement,' the sergeant said.

'I'm afraid you're just going to have to take me at my word. I'm not in the habit of lying, and certainly not to members of the constabulary,' she said.

The sergeant had not asked Billie to take an active part in the questioning, but she could no longer hold her tongue. It was likely the sergeant was going to have her head for interviewing Mrs Trent earlier. She might as well hang for a sheep as a lamb. She drew her notebook from her pocket and flipped it open, making a show of looking at her notes.

'It's interesting that you should mention that, Mrs Trent. According to my notes, I asked about your husband's whereabouts at the time of the air raid,' she said. 'Do you remember making that statement?'

Billie couldn't be entirely certain, but she felt a look of wariness had crept into Mrs Trent's face.

'I seem to recall you asking me something about that. Why should it matter now?'

Billie couldn't bring herself to look at the sergeant but rather plowed on ahead as if he wasn't sitting next to her, his blood coming to a boil.

'It goes to your general truthfulness. Based on your previous statement, either you were not telling the truth or your husband wasn't. He claimed to have been in the shelter in the garden. You stated that you knew nothing about him being there.'

'I don't see how that means for sure that I was lying or that he was. I didn't know anything about him being there, but I did not say that he wasn't. Byron and I had a tremendous row before he left for the college that morning. He hadn't come into the house when the air raid began, but that does not mean that he hadn't returned home,' she said.

'And why is that?' the sergeant asked.

'Not only do we have an air-raid shelter in the back garden, but we also have a shed where he often would spend evenings painting and drinking and undoubtedly thinking about other women. He actually entertained models there from time to time. There is every possibility that he returned home and went straight out to his studio and, when the air-raid sirens went off, simply hurried into the shelter.'

'But you didn't join him there?' Sergeant Skelton asked.

'No, I didn't,' she said.

'Why not?' Sergeant Skelton asked. 'I would've thought that if you had a shelter in the back garden, that would be the first thing you would do. Weren't you on the premises at the time?'

'I was here all right. The fact of the matter is I never trusted that the shelter was as safe as staying in the house. Byron and I had argued about it many times. He made me agree to use it, but I found that when the air-raid siren went off, I simply couldn't force myself outside into the dark. I grabbed Toby and headed for the closet under the stairs. They say you are as safe there as in a shelter. For all I know, Byron was in the shelter at the time. What I don't understand is why he would have claimed I was there with him,' she said.

'Is it possible that your husband suspected you of needing an alibi for the time Audrey Chetwell was killed?' Billie said.

Sergeant Skelton and Mrs Trent both looked at her sharply.

'I should have thought it very surprising for him to do such a chivalrous thing. Besides, we all know that Audrey died in the air raid. So I suppose that disputes the notion that you are safe inside a building,' she said.

'Do you have any idea who would have had a reason to harm him?' Sergeant Skelton asked.

'I suppose Audrey's father could have done it. He was none too pleased when I told him about the way his daughter was carrying on with my husband. Of course, I expect he wasn't the only one who was angered by my husband's exploits. When it comes to suspects, I am sure you will be spoiled for choice,' she said.

Before Billie could ask a follow-up question about Mrs Trent's conversation with the councilor, the sergeant shot her a warning look. He thanked the widow for her time and left his card in case she needed to get hold of someone in the constabulary. He advised her that she should not leave Hull and that someone would contact her with the details of when she could collect her husband's body from the morgue.

Billie braced herself for an outburst from the sergeant for interrupting during the interview, but none was forthcoming. As they climbed into the police car and headed back towards the station, he seemed lost in thought. Perhaps Peter had put in a good word for her, as he said he would when they were in the church. She turned her thoughts to the other women Mrs Trent mentioned and whether one of them could have been Avis. She was still trying to decide whether or not to mention what she had seen pass between them the day before when Sergeant Skelton broke the silence.

'The chief constable's not going to like this, but we're going to have to interview Councilor Chetwell. I can't believe I'm saying this, but I am going to suggest that you sit in on the interview,' he said. 'I'll have one of the uniformed officers pick him up and bring him to the station. You be ready and waiting when I call you.'

'Why would you want me to be part of the interview? After all, you know that he has nothing but complaints about women constables in general and me in particular,' Billie said.

'Exactly. I want to put him on the back foot by having you in the room. Besides, if it goes down as badly as I expect it will, you will make a perfect scapegoat with the chief constable,' he said, giving her a truly unpleasant smile. 'It will serve you right for interviewing suspects behind my back.'

THIRTY-SEVEN

Hull
Special Constable Upton's PNB

Peter stepped from the bright, warm sunshine of the rubble-strewn street into the shadowy gloom of the church's interior. As his eyes adjusted to the cool darkness, he moved his gaze about and caught sight of a flicker of movement near the altar. The white-haired priest in his black robes faded into the background of the nave. Peter's boots made a sharp sound as they tapped along the stone floor, and Father O'Connell turned to him and raised a hand in greeting.

'Back again so soon, Peter? I suppose there's no chance you're here for confession, now are you?' he said with a smile.

Ironic, Peter thought, considering his line of work. 'Perhaps, but only if you are the one doing the confessing.'

The priest stepped closer and pointed towards the pew at the front of the church.

'You haven't brought the young lass along with you this time, then?' he asked, looking past Peter's shoulder, a wicked grin on his face. He sat down and crossed his legs beneath his long skirts. Peter sank down beside him and pulled his notebook from his pocket.

'I thought it best you and I chat in private,' Peter said.

'This looks to be an official sort of visit, my boy,' Father O'Connell said. 'Should I be concerned?'

'I suppose that depends on what you have to tell me. I found something disturbing during my shift at the dock and I'm hoping you don't know anything about it,' he said.

He held out one of the leaflets he had found blowing about the bank of the river and kept his eyes trained on Father O'Connell's face as he read it over.

'Do you think I had something to do with the making of this?'

'I hate to think you did, but my duty requires me to ask if you had any part in it,' he said.

'What would make you bring this to my doorstep?' Father O'Connell said, neatly sidestepping an answer.

'I found a piece of one of these leaflets torn off and wedged into the fruit crate that was attached to your bicycle. When I discovered it, I didn't know what it was from. It wasn't until I collected well over a hundred of these leaflets blowing about the banks of the Humber that I recognized it.'

'But my bicycle had been stolen. You're the one who returned it to me. Why would you think I had anything to do with these leaflets if it wasn't in my possession?' the priest asked.

'We both know your loyalties have in the past been somewhat conflicted,' Peter said.

'Peter, my loyalties are never conflicted. First and foremost, they are always to God and his Church,' the priest said.

'So you haven't decided to provide aid to some fellow Irishmen in their quest for independence?' Peter searched for signs of guilt on the priest's face as best he could in the low light.

'Are you accusing me of something?'

'I am not accusing, merely asking. You have been known to speak out publicly about your feelings on the subject.'

Although Ireland had declared itself neutral in the conflict, there were persistent rumors that the Irish Republican Army would welcome the opportunity to aid in a German victory. It wasn't necessarily so much that they supported the particular agenda of the Nazi party but rather that they were adhering to the adage that problems in England were opportunity in Ireland. Father O'Connell had never been one to keep his opinions on the conflict between the two countries a secret.

'I consider it my duty to speak the truth. The last war damaged relations between the Irish and the English, and this one is simply dredging up more bad feeling.'

'Any specific bad feelings you might know about?'

The priest waggled a bony finger in Peter's direction. 'Some folks like to think that the problems are behind us and that everyone will pull together to fight a common enemy, but that's just a bunch of foolishness. Emotions are still running high. But it is not the place of the Church to stoke such fires.'

Peter couldn't disagree that many people on both sides of the issue were riled up. In fact, there were men scheduled for trial for attempting to blow up a public building in protest at the English in Northern Ireland. Which made the questions Peter had for Father O'Connell all the more pressing.

'Does the Church have anything to say about fascist literature being scattered along the banks of the Humber right where impressionable dockworkers might find it?'

'The Church has nothing to say about such things. But it does have a great deal to say about the role of a priest keeping quiet about those things that he knows when confided in him during confession. You know as well as I do that not all the information at my disposal is mine to share,' he said.

'Are you saying that you have knowledge of these leaflets because of something revealed in the confessional?' he said.

'I'm saying nothing as direct as that. That said, I assure you that any information I would have about subversive activity would have come to me through the confessional, not through my own actions. I hope you will believe that,' he said, leaning slightly forward.

'I'd like to believe it; you know I would. But this is a very serious matter and cannot be allowed to go unchecked. If you have any information that you could share with me about how such leaflets could even come into existence, I would appreciate it. I'm not saying you are involved with these, but I am saying I am very well aware that you would know how such a thing could be done and I would appreciate it if you would point me in the right direction of how these came to be printed,' Peter said.

Father O'Connell leaned back against the pew once more. Peter heard a creak as the priest's weight pressed against it. The older man closed his eyes for a moment and exhaled deeply. He opened them and once more cleared his throat.

'I don't think I would be in violation of my vows to tell you that such things are often created on the fringes. In this day and age, it is not easy to get a hold of printing machinery, so I would not expect it to necessarily be in the hands of a private party.'

'Are you saying a professional printer would have created these?' Peter asked.

'No. Most professionals wouldn't touch something like this with a barge pole. They'd be facing prison if they did – especially now.'

With the expanded powers of the Defense of the Realm Act, more and more liberties were being shut down. Peter couldn't say he felt that was a bad thing, but it did mean the priest's words made sense. The mere act of printing such material could result in imprisonment and possibly more. With the passage of the Treachery Act in May, the necessary level of proof required for condemning someone to death had lowered shockingly.

'So, if it wasn't something that a typical printer would take on and the equipment would be too difficult for a private citizen to possess, where else might we find those who have the capacity to print them?'

'Some of the wealthier parishes print their own service sheets and other religious materials. But don't get your hopes up, Peter. My poor parish doesn't run to such extravagances.' The priest gave him a sad smile.

'What other sorts of places might have the capability?' Peter asked.

'Some civic organizations, if they had enough backing. Hospitals perhaps if they were large enough. Certainly, you could find such a thing at colleges and universities. In fact, institutions of learning are generally hotbeds of radical activity. If it were me, I would start with one of those,' the priest said.

'Would you say that an art college would be particularly conducive to such lines of thought?'

'I would say it would most certainly be the sort of place one would expect to find students eager to rebel against the establishment and engage enthusiastically in alternative views of the future,' the priest said.

Peter felt a thrill of connection prickle along his spine. He was startled to realize how eager he was to share the information with WPC Harkness. He could just picture her face when he suggested they interview members of the art college newspaper staff. Why was that, he wondered?

Kingston upon Hull
Dear Mrs Hughes,
    I wanted to let you know how sorry I was for the way my mother insisted you release me from my agreement to enlist. I have found another way to serve that I think you will agree is of value to the war effort . . .

Billie assumed that Sergeant Skelton would be the one to conduct the interview with Councilor Chetwell, so she was surprised that the chief constable was the ranking officer in the room when she arrived with her steno pad and pen. Her stomach turned over at the sight of Chief Constable Willis. Her ears rang with the sergeant's suggestion that the situation was tailor-made to produce the kinds of conditions that would lead to her dismissal.

Still, the chief constable betrayed no misgivings at her presence in front of the councilor. She was beginning to develop the notion that, as in families, there could be tension between the members of a group, but dirty laundry was not aired to outsiders. Under the wary gaze of the councilor, she took her seat at the far side of the room and opened the steno pad in her lap. She uncapped her pen and held it just above a fresh sheet of paper, to all appearances the chief's dutiful secretary prepared to do his bidding.

'I appreciate your willingness to give us some of your valuable time, Councilor,' the chief constable said. 'I'm sure you can understand why we would want to get to the bottom of this matter as quickly as possible. It does the city no credit to have a murderer on the loose.'

'I can hardly but agree. But I cannot see how it is that you would need to speak with me about this most unfortunate event,' Councilor Chetwell said.

'I understand that you are well acquainted with both Mrs Trent and her husband,' the chief constable said.

'I wouldn't claim any intimacy with the Trents, but I certainly would not deny having been acquainted with them for some time.'

'According to the society columns of the *Hull Daily Mail*, the Trents were frequent guests at your home as well as at outside social engagements that you also attended,' the chief constable said. 'That sounds to me as if you knew them quite well.'

'The fact that we socialize with them does not mean that we are close. I'm sure you understand the distinction,' Councilor Chetwell said.

The chief constable nodded. 'Of course. Would it be fair to say that both of the Trents were also acquainted with your daughter Audrey?' he asked.

Billie watched out of the corner of her eye as the councilor's posture stiffened. His face suffused with color, and he began to open and close his mouth like a fish stranded on a riverbank.

'What are you implying, exactly?' he asked. He glanced over at Billie and the depth of color filling his face grew even deeper.

'As much as it pains me to bring up any sort of ugliness in

connection with your recently departed daughter, it has been alleged that she was having a romantic entanglement with Professor Trent,' he said.

'That's preposterous. Who would say such a thing about Audrey?' he said.

'His wife, apparently,' the chief constable said.

'Well, this is the first I've heard about it,' Councilor Chetwell said.

'Are you quite sure about that? In an official witness statement, Mrs Trent claimed that she informed you about it at an event where you were the speaker. Isn't that right, WPC Harkness?' the chief constable said, turning his attention to Billie.

She flipped back a page in her notebook and pretended to consult it. In truth, no part of the investigation required notes for her to recall it. Every conversation felt permanently branded on her memory.

'Yes, sir. I took down a statement to that effect earlier today. When asked for possible suspects in the death of her husband, she mentioned the councilor might have been involved,' she said, looking at the chief constable and then at the councilor.

'And did she say why the councilor might have wished her husband harm?' the chief constable asked.

Again, Billie made a pretense of consulting her notes. 'She said she asked the councilor to take his daughter in hand and to see to it that she left Professor Trent alone.'

'This is nothing more than an example of the fevered imagination and tendency towards gossip that women are so inclined to indulge in,' the councilor said.

'Really?' the chief constable said, raising an eyebrow.

'Absolutely. This girl's behavior is exactly what caused me to vote against adding women to the police force in our city despite the heavy-handedness of outside forces,' the councilor said. 'I wish to God I had not been outvoted. My daughter was a person of high moral character and not at all the sort who would put herself in the degrading position this creature suggests. I categorically refuse to listen to this sort of nonsense.'

The chief constable looked over at Billie, and her heart stuttered in her chest.

'I was concerned that you might say something along those

lines, so I telephoned Mrs Trent myself. Do you know what she said?' he asked.

The councilor shifted slightly in his seat. Billie wondered if he was given to heart complaints of his own. His face had turned the same worrying shade of aubergine as that of one of her father's parish deacons just before he fell over dead during a dispute with the choir director over music proposed for the Easter services.

'I would not deign to guess,' he said.

'She claimed she approached you after you gave a rousing speech extolling the morality of women on the home front to the Women's Voluntary Service. She says she told you that you ought to see to the moral fiber of your own home before speaking about it in public. Mrs Trent said she embarrassed herself by flat out accusing your daughter of having an affair with her husband,' he said. 'What do you say to that?'

The councilor sagged forward on his arms and buried his head. For one horrifying second, Billie thought perhaps he was going to burst into tears. When he lifted his head, unshed tears glistened in his eyes as he cleared his throat to respond.

'She did accuse Audrey of having an affair with her husband. It was exactly the sort of thing no father should ever hear. After she died, I wanted to put it straight out of my mind. The only thing I have left of my daughter is memories, and I wanted them all to do her credit. You must understand that.' He looked from the chief constable to Billie and then back again.

'Of course, I can understand how you felt, but you must appreciate my position. I must ask you to account for your whereabouts at the time of Professor Trent's death.'

'I should have thought my position as a city councilor would put me above suspicion, but I can see that you have a nasty turn of mind. Perhaps that's what comes of allowing women into the constabulary. When did you say that he was killed?'

'Sometime in the night. The medical examiner thinks it probably occurred during the air raid.'

'I was attending a function at my social club; the air-raid sirens went off as I was on my way home. I hurried into the shelter in Victoria Square to take cover until the all-clear was sounded.'

'Can anyone vouch for your whereabouts? Did you encounter

anyone in the shelter of your acquaintance who would recognize you?' the chief constable asked.

'Sadly, no. I cannot claim to be such a local celebrity as to attract that sort of notice. I left the club on my own and entered the shelter in anonymity. I assure you that I was nowhere near the art college last night.'

Peter was waiting for her in the corridor when she followed the chief constable out of the interrogation room. He pulled her aside and explained the leafleting at the docks and his hunch that they should check the art college for evidence that the leaflets had been printed there.

They hopped on a tram bound for the college, and she filled him in on the interviews with Mrs Trent and the councilor on the way. They arrived soon after and a quick look at the campus map revealed the location of the newspaper office. Billie wasn't sure that she would have thought to look at the college and admired Peter for putting two and two together.

She caught herself sneaking glances at him out of the corner of her eye as they made their way through the corridors of the building that housed the newspaper office. He really was not as stern as she had first taken him to be. In fact, he had gone out of his way in the last couple of days to make her feel more welcome than anyone besides Avis Crane.

The thought of Avis made her feel a heaviness that she wished she could shake. She had hoped that the councilor would not have been able to provide any sort of an alibi for the time of Professor Trent's death and that she could put her mind at ease about Avis's activities. But his claims to be in the bomb shelter during the air raid seemed entirely reasonable. She pushed such thoughts out of her mind as they reached the room with a plaque attached to the door marking it as the student newspaper office.

Peter turned the knob, pushed the door open, then stood aside and waited for Billie to enter first.

A young man with thick spectacles and a cleanly cropped head of hair stood holding up a newspaper. He looked up as Billie approached, then lowered it to the desk in front of him.

'Please tell me you're here to volunteer to work on the

newspaper,' he said, looking her up and down 'We don't have any women on the staff, and you'd make quite a decorative addition.'

Billie felt her cheeks begin to warm. Then Peter stepped out from behind her and stood at her side.

'I'm sorry to disappoint you, but WPC Harkness and I are here in an official capacity for the constabulary. Who might you be?' he asked.

The young man pushed his glasses back up the bridge of his nose and swallowed. His oversized Adam's apple bobbed up and down over the deep V of his Fair Isle sweater vest. Splotches of ink speckled his pale-blue shirt, and Billie thought she detected spatters of paint dotting his nose. Compared with Peter's tidy police uniform, he appeared disheveled. A surge of gratitude passed through her at the way her fellow officer included her in the professional cloak that was the constabulary.

'I'm Gregory Williams, the editor of the student newspaper. Is there a problem, Officer?' he asked, his gaze darting about the room as if someone had decided to hide in there in an effort to flee from the law.

'We have questions about your printing facility and those who have access to it. Am I to assume that you have a staff that involves more people than just you?' he asked.

'That's right. But it's a small staff. There are only four of us and, frankly, two of them don't put in very much effort. We used to have five members but recently one of them dropped out,' he said. 'That's why I'm here all by myself today working on the paper. The edition is supposed to go out this evening.'

'Who are these other members? Do they attend the college, too?' Billie asked.

Gregory nodded and then paused. 'Well, mostly they are members of the art college. The person who just left the staff actually attended the engineering school,' he said.

Billie and Peter exchanged a glance. 'Was he an engineering student named Orson Hewitt?' Billie asked.

'How did you know that?' he asked.

'It's our job to know things like that,' Peter said. 'Who had access to the printing equipment?'

'All of the members of the newspaper staff had access to it, although I was thinking about being a little more concerned about who was coming and going after the way that supplies have been disappearing from the room,' he said.

'You've been experiencing thefts?' Billie asked.

'We've had a real problem with missing paper. I don't suppose it would've been such a big deal, except now there's such a push to conserve paper that we've cut back on the amount we are allowed to use. About half a ream has gone missing. And there's less ink than there was a few days ago, too.'

'Could any of the staff have used the printing equipment without you knowing about it? Is there any way to tell?' Peter asked.

Gregory shrugged. 'I'm not here around the clock. This isn't a professional newspaper office. Anybody could have come and gone without observation if they timed it right,' he said.

'When was the last time it was used by Orson Hewitt? Has he been around lately?' Billie asked.

'Why are you so interested in Orson?' Gregory asked.

'Just answer the constable's questions, please,' Peter said.

'He was here not long ago as a matter of fact. There was some woman with him I didn't recognize, and he didn't introduce her. When I asked him what he was doing here, he said he just felt a little bit nostalgic about the place and that he wanted to drop by before he got too caught up with studying for his final exams.'

'Did you believe him?' Peter asked.

'I didn't have any reason not to. I thought it was kind of rude the way he didn't introduce the woman, but maybe she was shy or something. She kept trying to hide her face. But then I decided it was perhaps because of the birthmark.'

'What sort of a birthmark?' Billie asked with a mounting feeling of excitement.

'It was a pretty big one. I can understand why things like that would make her feel reserved in front of strangers. She was a pretty girl otherwise; I can say that about her. She was blonde, of about medium height and had quite a rounded figure, if you know what I mean.' Gregory gave Peter a wink, and Billie felt mounting impatience.

'When exactly did you see them here?' Peter asked.

'It was the night of the first air raid this week. I saw him here not long before the sirens went off. I remember thinking that I hoped they had found some place to get under cover since it went off not more than fifteen minutes after they left. After what happened to Audrey, I suppose we were all lucky to make it through as undamaged as we did.'

'Did you know Audrey?' Billie asked.

'Not as well as I would have liked to, but I had a few classes with her. Her death kind of brought the danger into reality more than anything else. It makes you feel sort of reckless – you know what I mean?' he asked, turning his glance from Peter and then to Billie.

'I certainly do,' Billie said. 'Do you remember which side of her face the birthmark was on?' Billie asked. She felt Peter's eyes on her questioningly.

'The left. I'm sure it was the left. I do a lot of portrait painting and she was quite intriguing. As a matter of fact, I made a sketch from memory after she left. I think I left the notebook I doodled it in here in the office, in my desk.'

Gregory headed for a desk at the back of the room and yanked open a drawer. He dipped his hand inside and pulled out a battered composition notebook. He held it aloft and carried it triumphantly to the constables.

'Here it is. This is her.'

He held the notebook open to the page with the sketch and tapped on a small drawing at the bottom of a page. There in front of them was a remarkable likeness of Sally Nichols.

THIRTY-EIGHT

Hull
Special Constable Upton's PNB

If Peter had to guess, he would say that Muriel Matthews was a very angry young woman. Perhaps it had been unfair of him to barge in on her at home and stir up a flap with the servants, but he didn't care. He and Constable Harkness split up upon leaving the art college. They decided that she would head off to find Sally Nichols and demand an explanation as to her involvement with subversive newspaper printings, while he would take on Muriel Matthews and her false alibi. WPC Harkness had told him that Muriel seemed to be one of those young women who felt spiteful and inferior compared with her peers. All Peter could see of the woman who stood before him was a spoiled little rich girl. The surroundings she lived in were opulent by his standards, and the fact that they had a servant open the front door said more about their social standing and wealth than anything else might have done.

Servants had been difficult to acquire since the Great War, and he had never met anyone in possession of one. Truth be told, on occasion his mother 'did' for some of the wealthier women of her acquaintance when they were entertaining and needed an extra set of hands to help prepare the food for parties or to clean up afterwards.

All in all, he couldn't see what in the world she had to be so grumpy about. She was a decent-looking woman – not beautiful by any stretch of the imagination, but pleasant enough and with all the right parts in all the right places. He might not notice her in the crowd, but she certainly wouldn't repel anyone by her appearance. Well, except for the scowl stamped on her face. If she wasn't careful, she'd end up with a permanent set of lines running between her eyebrows before her time.

He did not feel the slightest inclination to treat her with kid gloves. As soon as she appeared in the drawing room where the servant had stashed him while looking for her, he pulled out his notebook and made a point of appearing intimidating and completely official.

'Are you one Muriel Matthews of twenty-three Grosvenor Street?' he asked, remaining standing even though she had indicated he might take a seat opposite her on a delicate-looking settee.

She nodded warily. 'What's all this about, Officer?'

'You made a statement to my colleague, WPC Harkness, regarding an alibi for a man of your acquaintance, Orson Hewitt, on the night of the nineteenth of June. Is that correct?'

'I can't see how it matters to you, but yes, I told WPC Harkness that I had been with Orson on the night of the air raid. So what?' she asked.

Even though she had a defiant tone to her voice, Peter could see her body language tensing and going on the defensive. It was time to go in for the sting.

'Do you intend to stick by that story?'

'Yes.'

'I must caution you that lying to the police in the investigation of an unexplained death is a very serious crime indeed.'

'I don't know what you mean,' she said, her lower lip beginning to tremble.

'I happen to know that you were not with Orson Hewitt that night. I spoke with the editor of the art college student newspaper, and he claims to have been with him at the same time you said you were with Orson at the cinema. I think it would be far better for you if you made a clean breast of it, don't you?' he said.

He had lowered his voice to a gruff tone and made a point of writing down the questions he was asking. Her glance kept flicking between his face and the notebook perched upon his broad hand. She fanned her face with her hand and cleared her throat.

'I suppose there's no point continuing to stick to that story. What is it that you want to know?' she asked.

'Why did you lie about being with Orson the night of the air raid?' he asked.

She let out a deep sigh and shifted in her seat. 'Well, it's really rather embarrassing. I'm afraid that I'm one of those women who has found herself in the uncomfortable position of being far fonder of a man than he is of me. I did have a date to meet Orson at the art college to go to the cinema. But when I arrived, he told me that he was unable to meet me and that something had come up. He shut the door in my face quite rudely but not before I caught a glance of a woman's foot behind him in the room.'

'I should not have thought you would give a false alibi to someone who treated you that way,' Peter said.

'I suppose you've never really been in love, have you?' she asked. She sighed again.

'We're talking about you, miss,' Peter said. 'What did you do next?'

'I'm not proud of it but I lurked around waiting to see if he would come out. I wanted to catch a glimpse of the woman he was with and see what I was up against. Imagine my surprise when not much later he came out of his room with a woman I would have described as plump and even slightly disfigured if you considered her birthmark.'

'That still doesn't explain why you gave him an alibi,' he said.

'I followed them. I followed the pair of them to the newspaper office and then all the way to a café on Victoria Square.' She leaned back wearily against the sofa and crossed one attractive, stocking-clad leg over the other. Peter felt a jolt at the mention of a café. Now they were getting somewhere.

'What happened next?'

'The young woman beckoned for him to follow her into an alley alongside the café. They were down there for just a moment and then she let them into the café with a key. I waited and watched for ten minutes or so before Orson came back out through the door.'

'What would make you think he needed an alibi for simply visiting a café?' he said.

'Because in the light coming through the crack in the door, I saw Audrey. She had walked him to the door and spoke with him before he left. She looked very agitated, and he looked none too happy either. Later, when I read the address of the café, I realized it was the same establishment. I didn't want anyone to think that Orson had anything to do with her death and I didn't want to admit I had followed him. It would make me look pathetic,' she said. A tear rolled down her cheek, and for a moment Peter felt slightly sorry for her.

'Do you know where he went next?' he asked. 'What makes you think he didn't re-enter the café?'

'He ducked back into the alley and came out riding a bicycle. It was hard to see anything in the blackout, but there was just enough light from the moon for me to make out his figure as he rode away. I tried to follow him, but he outpaced me very quickly,' she said.

It all made sense and seemed a likely enough story. Why would she make something like that up if it wasn't true? In fact, she was right to say that it put her in a very bad light. He would not have wanted to admit such a thing if it were him. Then another thought occurred to him.

'What did you do next, when you realized you couldn't follow him?' he asked.

'I boarded the public bus for home,' she said.

'If I asked the servants or your family, could they corroborate your story of coming home?' he asked.

'No, they couldn't. The bus was still on the road when the air-raid siren went off. We were nowhere near a public shelter. The driver pulled over to the side of the road and I sat there with all the other passengers for hours. By the time I got home, my mother was absolutely hysterical. I'm sure she would be happy to tell you that if you feel you need to put her through it,' Muriel said.

Something in the tone of her voice and the look on her face made Peter believe she was telling the absolute truth. It would be good to corroborate her story with her mother, but he was eager to go and confront Orson with what he knew about his involvement with the bicycle theft and the leaflets.

'Is your mother at home right now?' he asked.

'No, she's off doing something useful for the war effort. I'm sure one of the servants would be able to confirm my story since my mother apparently roused the whole house and made quite a scene about it. Shall I call one of them in?' she asked.

After only a few minutes' delay, he had confirmed with three separate servants that Muriel had been away from home that night and had arrived in the early hours with the story that she had been stuck on the bus. Any further confirmation of her whereabouts would have to wait until he could track down the bus driver. He thanked her for her time and hurried out as quickly as he could in the direction of the nearest police call box. He had to get a message to Billie.

THIRTY-NINE

Kingston upon Hull
Dear Father,
You have been on my mind so often as I have been
working on a case involving a father and daughter . . .

B illie was surprised at how much had changed since she had entered the café on the day she arrived in Kingston upon Hull. When she had first met Sally Nichols, she had felt overwhelmed by the size of the city and had no sense of whether or not she would truly be welcome at her cousin's home or if it had simply been a perfunctory invitation that had been offered with no real desire for it to be accepted. She had been someone without a job. She had been utterly absorbed in grieving the loss of her mother. She had been fleeing from the unwanted advances of a suitable, worthy and utterly boring young man.

Although it had only been a few days, it felt like weeks or even months. From the look on Sally Nichols's face when she opened the door, Sally seemed to have aged years rather than only the few days it had been since Billie had last seen her.

'It's nice to see you again, WPC Harkness. But I can't imagine what business you have with me,' she said, holding her shoulder against the door of the residence as if to keep Billie from entering. Her body language was clear. She had no interest in speaking with a member of the constabulary.

'It's best I come in. The conversation we need to have is not one I expect you want the neighbors to overhear. Is your mother home?' Billie asked.

Sally's eyes widened and she took a step backwards, holding the door wide for Billie to enter.

'No, my mother is at the café trying to see what can be done to get it open once more. What's this all about?' Sally asked.

'I think maybe we ought to sit down,' Billie said.

Sally drew a sharp breath and put her hand over her stomach

as if she felt suddenly nauseated. 'Let's go to the kitchen,' she said.

Billie followed her to the back of the small house and looked around. A canister of flour sat open on the tabletop, and it was obvious that Billie had interrupted Sally in the middle of rolling piecrust. From the savory smell on the stove, meat pies were on the menu. Billie's stomach gave a growl and she remembered it had been hours since her last meal.

'I'd like you to tell me about your activities at the art college and your relationship with Orson Hewitt,' Billie said, taking a seat at the kitchen table.

She kept her notebook in her pocket, wanting to put the other young woman at ease to the best of her ability. If what she suspected was true, there was nothing to be gained by making her even more distressed.

Sally sank into the chair opposite her and propped her arms on the table. She sagged against her hands, holding her face up as if she might collapse if she did not do so.

'How did you find out about that?' she asked.

'I'm a police constable. It's my job to investigate, and one thing simply led to another. You're in serious trouble, Sally. If you cooperate, I will be sure to mention that fact to whoever's in charge of what happens next,' Billie said.

Sally ran her finger over her patch of discolored skin. 'I didn't go through with the leafleting. I meant to. And at first I wanted to, but when the time came, I simply couldn't do it.' She pulled her hand away from her face and cradled her arm around her midriff.

'Does your mother know about the baby?' Billie asked.

Sally gasped. 'How did you guess?'

'You looked decidedly green about the gills that day in the café when you were serving me, and the discoloration on your face is something I've seen before in expectant mothers. The photograph your mother had at the café didn't show you having that dark patch on your cheek, so I knew it wasn't a birthmark,' Billie said. 'Is Orson the baby's father?'

Sally shook her head. 'No. It's a man I met in the café about a year ago. I know it looks like I'm an unwed mother, but I married him secretly before I became pregnant.'

'Why was it a secret?' Billie asked.

'He's German. My mother would've been horrified for me to have fallen for a German, so I didn't tell her, and he was interned before I found out I was expecting. It's all so unfair. He came here as a small boy after the last war and the government just decided that Germans couldn't be trusted, so they locked him up and I haven't seen him since,' Sally said.

'Is that why you were working with Orson on fascist leaflets?' Billie asked.

'The leaflets were Orson's idea. I'm not saying I wasn't at all involved, but when the time came to distribute them, I lost my nerve. I just kept thinking about what Audrey said about getting caught and how we needed to be really careful,' Sally said.

Billie felt excitement like an electric shock running through her body. Had Audrey been involved with aiding the Germans? Is that what had got her killed?

'Audrey was involved, too?' Billie asked.

'Involved? She was in charge,' Sally said, her eyes widening slightly.

The notion of vivacious and lovely Audrey being a traitor shocked Billie to the very marrow. After all her parents had to say about patriotism and the loss of her own brother at the hands of the enemy, she found it incomprehensible.

'In charge of what, exactly?' Billie asked.

'She worked as an intermediary between higher-ups who were working towards a revolution by supporting the Germans and those of us who had the same ideals,' Sally said.

'Was that the real reason you let Audrey use the café after hours without telling your mother?' Billie asked.

Sally nodded. 'Audrey told me she needed a place to meet some people in secret. She definitely met with an older man who was married. Other people simply assumed they were carrying on a romantic liaison. She never told me exactly what his role was. I had assumed that he was one of the people she reported to about our activities.'

'Was the man a professor at the art college? A Professor Trent?' Billie asked.

Sally nodded. 'Audrey never said what his name was, but

Orson told me. He was one of the people who believed she was
having an affair, and it drove him mad.'

'Were only the four of you involved?' Billie asked.

'I don't know. Orson was the one who recruited me. He had
been a customer and one day he brought Audrey in. It wasn't
long afterwards that I found myself offering the café to use
after hours. Just something about her made you want to do her
favors.'

'You say that she warned you not to be hasty with the
leafleting?'

'Orson was the one who wanted to distribute the leaflets at
the docks. On the day of the air raid, we went to the art college
and printed them in the newspaper office. He used to work on
the staff there and still had a key to get in. I was worried about
getting caught, but he said I should just think about my husband.
But when we took the leaflets and showed them to Audrey, she
didn't seem as excited about distributing them as Orson had
thought she would be,' Sally said.

'What did Audrey say about the leaflets?' Billie said.

'She needed to wait for authorization from upper levels before
doing something so brazen. She tried to convince Orson to leave
the leaflets with her for safekeeping, but he refused.'

'Did they argue?' Billie asked.

Sally nodded vigorously. 'It was quite a row. Orson stormed
out not long before the sirens went off. I wouldn't have been
unhappy if he had ended up dead, too. That way, nobody
would've been able to say what I had done,' Sally said.

'What exactly did you do?' Billie asked. She wondered if
she was looking at Audrey's killer.

'I stole the bicycle from the butcher's delivery boy so that
we would have something to use to distribute the leaflets.
And I stole a map of the docks from the public library,' she
said.

'*You* stole the map?' Billie asked. 'Why did you do that?'

'Audrey asked me to. She said it was a request from her
superiors and that she couldn't take care of it herself because
she knew the librarian personally.' Sally started to shake and
cry quietly. 'But I didn't distribute the flyers. I told Orson he'd
have to do it on his own and that I didn't want anything more

to do with any of it after Audrey died.' She looked pleadingly at Billie. 'Will they hang me? What about my baby?'

Billie felt overwhelmed by nausea. On the one hand, she found it hard to fathom that someone with so much in common with her would see the world so differently and seek to betray her own country based on a short relationship with a man. On the other, the idea that someone might be executed for taking a map from the library and stealing a priest's bicycle in aid of the enemy felt like a tragedy.

She understood the government needed to crack down on such things, but was any of it so very bad in the long run when one considered all the atrocities occurring every day across the globe? She wished she had some sort of comforting words to share with Sally, but nothing came to mind. The badge of a police constable meant nothing in the face of the high-ranking officials who made those sorts of decisions.

'I have absolutely no idea. I certainly hope they won't. Perhaps if you are willing to testify against Orson, you might be shown some leniency. In the meantime, I would tell your mother about your husband and your baby. You're going to need her, no matter what happens,' Billie said.

'It's not the sort of secret you want to burden your mother with,' Sally said.

'I know from hard-won experience that keeping secrets from your mother only leads to misery. I kept one from mine, and when she found out, we had a terrible argument. I never had the chance to make up with her before she was struck down by a car and killed,' Billie said.

She slid back her chair and left Sally sitting at the table with a great deal to think about. She let herself back out on to the street with much pondering, too.

Audrey Chetwell was the one behind the theft of the map. And Audrey Chetwell was the one who was in charge of a small group of people aiding the enemy. She knew that Audrey had been murdered. What she didn't know was how Avis was involved. Was she one of the superiors to whom Audrey reported? There was only one way to find out.

FORTY

Kingston upon Hull
Dear Mrs Thomas,
    Your letter reporting the goings-on in Barton St Giles
could not have been better timed! I must admit to being
rather homesick of late. I had been thinking of my mother's
sweet peas at the rectory and wondering what had become
of them. It was so kind of you to see to trellising them up
over the garden fence. I am sure my mother would be so
pleased to know that they have had the chance to go on
spreading their delicious fragrance and cheerful colors
even without her guiding hand. Such things matter more
now than ever, don't you think?
    Love,
    Wilhelmina

Billie checked in at the nearest police call box for any messages. Upon hearing the one left by Peter, she retraced her steps to the college. They tracked Orson to his room. He looked none too happy to see them, and Billie herself wished that the interview was already over. Her heart fluttered in her chest as she wondered if Orson would admit to Audrey's murder or if she was going to need to have a terrible conversation with someone about Avis.

Still, there was nothing for it but to get it over with. She and Peter had discussed who would take the lead in the conversation and had decided that she would be the one to do it. As soon as he admitted them to his small, cramped room in the dormitory, Peter stood with his back to the door, effectively blocking it. Billie perched on the edge of Orson's unmade bed.

'I have a lot of studying to do for my exams, so I hope you won't take up much of my time,' Orson said, folding his slim arms over his chest.

'I don't think you're in any position to dictate the terms of our conversation. Under the Treachery Act, you're already in far more trouble than anyone would want to be. The only question that we have is whether or not you are also responsible for Audrey Chetwell's murder,' Billie said.

Orson opened his mouth and snapped it shut again. His face turned the color of a plum, and he began to hyperventilate. Billie looked around the room for a paper bag; spotting one nearby, she handed it to him. He breathed in and out until he was able to recover himself.

'Should I take that as an admission of guilt?' Billie asked.

'I didn't kill Audrey. I would never have harmed her,' he said.

'We know all about the leaflets and the argument you had with her on the night she died. We even know that Audrey urged you not to distribute the leaflets. The only thing we don't know is why you would have killed her,' she said.

'I wouldn't have killed her. I loved Audrey. She would have come to care for me too in time, I'm sure. After all, we were perfect for each other. We believed in the same causes and were willing to take the same kinds of risks. I was completely devastated when I heard about her death,' he said.

She didn't like the feverish look that had come into his eyes. She flicked her gaze over at Peter who gave her a reassuring nod. She felt comforted by his presence and by his larger size. If it came to it, she and Peter would be able to take Orson on, no matter how crazed he became or how little he had left to lose. She took a deep breath and continued.

'How did Audrey recruit you?' Billie asked. There was something rather sickening about the notion of Audrey using her charm to convince others to support her treachery.

'She didn't convince me. I've always thought the Jews need putting in their place and said so one evening when a few of us met up after a drawing class. Audrey pulled me aside and told me she agreed. We started working together not long after that.'

'It sounds as though maybe she was not quite as dedicated as you, considering that she didn't support distributing the leaflets.'

Orson shook his head vigorously. 'It wasn't that she didn't believe in distributing them. We just disagreed about the timing. She said that she needed to get permission from her superiors to take that sort of risk. I told her I didn't see why we had to wait for permission since we were the ones taking responsibility. I also pointed out that I couldn't give anyone away even if I was arrested since she never told me the names of those she reported to.'

'But you had your suspicions about who one of them at least might be, didn't you?' Billie asked.

A look of misery flooded Orson's face. 'Of course, I knew it had to be Professor Trent. I thought that maybe if I did something on my own initiative, she would find me as appealing as she did him. But when I arrived with the leaflets, she told me I was getting ahead of myself. She didn't understand how much I had risked by printing the leaflets. I was furious,' he said.

'Is that when you decided to kill her?' Billie asked.

'I didn't kill her. The last time I saw her, I was sure she would be fine,' he said.

'The last time you saw her?'

'I doubled back after our argument. I wanted to apologize for losing my temper. So I took the bicycle and doubled back to the café. When I got there, I saw she had another visitor,' Orson said.

'Who was the visitor?' Billie asked.

'Professor Trent. She seemed surprised to see him, but she opened the door and let him in, so I assumed she wouldn't want to see me. I was too angry and frustrated to trust myself to speak to her, so I stayed outside.'

'When exactly did this happen?'

'Just before the air raid. I wanted to wait for him to leave before I apologized, but the sirens went off before he came out, so I took off to seek shelter. I rolled the bicycle under a bridge and stayed there until the sirens stopped.'

'You didn't try to go into one of the public shelters?' Peter asked.

'No, of course not. I had all the leaflets on the bicycle. I couldn't risk being discovered with them, but I certainly didn't want to lose them either. Do you know how difficult it was to print all of them without being discovered?'

'And you didn't go back into the café to seek shelter there?' Billie asked.

'No. I didn't want to know exactly what they were up to in there, if you know what I mean. Besides, I guess I'm grateful I didn't. If I had gone into the café, I might've ended up killed in the air raid like Audrey,' he said.

By the time they reached the station, they had worked out what they would do. They'd ask to speak to the sergeant on his own if possible and present him with the evidence gathered during the course of their investigation. If they were very lucky, they might manage to keep their jobs. If not, Billie was sure she could find a place in the information bureau. What Peter would end up doing, she didn't know. There were always calls for additional fire wardens and firefighters and ambulance drivers, although she wasn't sure that Peter knew how to drive. She gave him an encouraging smile as he held the door of the police station open for her to step on through.

The only thing she was sure of was that she didn't want to trust the information they had uncovered to Avis. On the journey back to the station, the memory of Avis lying to her about Professor Trent's visit to the station ran through her mind like a newsreel at the cinema.

'Here goes,' she said, taking a step towards the desk.

Sergeant Skelton was nowhere to be seen. She had just asked another officer if he knew where to find the sergeant when she heard a voice calling out to her over her shoulder. She turned to see Avis Crane. A wave of fear washed over her as the older woman's eyes narrowed and she took a step in Billie's direction.

'What in the world are you so desperate to speak with Sergeant Skelton about, Constable? After all, you are supposed to report to me, aren't you?' she said, closing the gap between them even more.

Peter stepped to her side and intervened.

'WPC Harkness and I have been conducting an investigation

into Audrey Chetwell's death. Things are simply not adding up, but we are quite sure we've got to the bottom of it. Knowing how Sergeant Skelton takes offense if he's not the first to know any police business in his station, we thought we would approach him first,' Peter said. 'It was my idea. Don't blame WPC Harkness.'

'That's very commendable of you, Constable. Sergeant Skelton has gone out on an urgent call and is not expected to return to the station today. I'm sure that WPC Harkness can fill me in on all the details while you get back to the important work of patrolling your beat,' Avis said.

Without awaiting Peter's response, Avis grabbed Billie by the arm and propelled her down the hallway towards her office.

FORTY-ONE

Kingston upon Hull
Dear Mrs Barclay,

Thank you so much for letting me know how much my mother is missed by all of you. I am certain she would have been pleased to know that you so enjoyed the eggless cake she brought to WI meetings. I am equally certain she would have been delighted to share the recipe with you. I am afraid I do not have it with me here in the north; however, if you stop in at the rectory, I am sure you will find it in my mother's recipe box. Please do make a copy for yourself and anyone else you believe would enjoy it.

Love,
Wilhelmina

Billie was struck once more by how far away from the rest of the hustle and bustle Avis's office seemed to be. She felt as though her blood was turning to slush with each step that pulled them farther and farther away from any witnesses to what Avis might have in mind.

'Take a seat,' Avis said. She shut the door behind them and turned the lock before taking her own place behind the desk. 'Now, what is it you have to report?'

Billie wasn't sure what she ought to do. Was there any possibility that the map she had seen in Avis's supply closet was not the one Audrey had instructed Sally to steal? Billie couldn't believe in such a preposterous coincidence as that. She was going to have to confront her with her involvement. She took in a calming breath and hoped she would be able to keep her nerve.

'Constable Upton and I have discovered that there was a spy ring operating out of the café where Audrey's body was found. In the course of our investigation, we determined that Orson Hewitt and Sally Nichols were involved as operatives. Orson was responsible for printing and distributing the leaflets that were found at the docks. Sally stole a map from the public library, the one that I reported to you as missing,' Billie said, trying to keep a tremor from her voice.

'You have been busy. I was right to believe that you are exactly the sort of young woman who would make a very fine addition to the constabulary. Is there anything else?'

'Orson Hewitt reported that he saw Professor Trent entering the café not long before the air-raid siren went off. I can't help but wonder if he was involved in her death,' Billie said.

Avis leaned over the desk, an eager look on her face. 'Are you quite sure about Mr Hewitt's statement?' she asked.

'I'm inclined to believe him. It doesn't make any sense for him to mention that if it wasn't true. He claims that was the reason he didn't return to the café in an attempt to reconcile with Audrey after their argument. Do you think it's possible that he's the one who killed her?'

'Perhaps. Was there anything else you think I should know?'

'There's one more thing,' Billie said, taking a deep breath. 'I found the map that's missing from the library in the storage closet here in your office. Can you explain that?' Billie asked.

Avis looked at her as if frozen, and then a small smile crossed her face. She nodded.

'Yes, I was right to think you'd make a very fine constable. You remind me very much of Audrey. She worked for me too, you see,' Avis said.

Billie felt her heart sink. She had hoped against hope that Avis had not been involved with enemy activity, but there she had gone and admitted it. Billie tried to keep herself from glancing over her shoulder and estimating the distance to the door. She had no idea what Avis might do if she felt she would be revealed for who she really was.

'Are you a spy for the Germans, too?' Billie asked. She tried to keep the quaking from her voice but was not entirely sure that she had succeeded. Avis's smile was not the reaction she had expected.

'As determined an investigator as you are, you've got your wires crossed somehow. Which I suppose is as good a tribute to Audrey as anything could be. And rather a compliment to me, if I do say so. Audrey worked for me, but not by spying for the Germans, at least not in the way that you mean. Considering how brave you were to confront me, especially since I locked you in here at the end of the hallway when you suspected me, I shall take you into my confidence,' she said.

Billie forced herself to release the breath she hadn't realized she had been holding.

'I would appreciate that.'

'Audrey was recruited to pose as someone who was coordinating German sympathizers. Her role was to uncover leaks in security on the home front. The map was one that Audrey asked one of her operatives to attempt to steal at my request. From that little exercise, we learned it was far too easy to access maps from public libraries. We had a letter printed in the local newspaper as a way to announce to librarians that such a thing might be taking place and to be on their guard against it.'

'So Audrey gave you the map herself?' Billie asked.

Avis nodded. 'Exactly. As soon as Sally provided her with it, she returned it to me for safekeeping. Eventually, I would have found a way to put Lydia's mind at ease that she was in no danger of losing her job, but you discovered it before I had the chance to do so.'

'What about your involvement with Professor Trent? Was he somehow a part of the operation, too? Is that why you denied he was at the station?'

'I didn't think you had quite believed me the other day. I had hoped you would have got a poor glimpse of him, but I suspected you were too sharp-eyed for that. My only other hope was that you might think that I was some sort of home-wrecking spinster, given Professor Trent's reputation,' Avis said. 'Oh, my dear, from the look on your face, I have to assume that's exactly what you thought. I suppose I should take it as a compliment that you don't think I'm too old to be getting up to such things.'

'So was Professor Trent involved in your operation?' Billie asked.

'Audrey reported to me and I reported to him. Professor Trent was a far more complicated man than it appeared, and his wife was kept entirely in the dark, poor woman. Unfortunately, at present, one must be exceedingly careful about whom to trust. Professor Trent and his wife did not have the sort of relationship where he felt he could let her in on his secrets. I am certain it has caused her a terrible amount of grief. Unfortunately, she's not going to be able to be told any differently. Do I make myself clear?' she asked.

'You do. Do you think she's the one who killed Audrey?'

'I wish I knew. Audrey was a truly gifted operative, and I am very sorry to have lost her. We need young women like her working on the home front. There are far more people who are willing to help the enemy than we would like to believe.'

'Is that the reason you urged me to take a look into what happened to Audrey without making it official? You didn't want for her role to come to light in the course of an ordinary investigation?'

'It would be better for the whole thing to get swept under the rug than for the Germans to know that we were running them ourselves. It's vitally important that we are able to continue to feed them misinformation and to use their own operatives to gauge their activity on our shores. As much as I regret what happened to Audrey, it is better to leave her death shrouded in mystery and to claim that she was a victim of the air raid than for that to get out.'

'You're the one who altered the report about the debris surrounding Audrey's body, aren't you?'

Avis nodded. 'It seemed the best way to support the notion that she was killed in the air raid. I do regret your suspicions of Constable Upton.'

'You are not even going to tell her family what happened to her?' Billie asked. 'Her father's a city councilor, after all. Shouldn't he be able to be trusted with that information?'

'Not even a city councilor can be trusted with such secrets. The fact that you've been privy to them should impress upon you how much I esteem your character. It's a rare thing for anyone to be admitted into that sphere of information. Can I count on you?' Avis asked.

Billie felt a wave of emotion wash over her. She had wanted more than anything to do her bit. She had not imagined it possible that she would be trusted with something so important.

'You have my word. Does that mean I should not share what you have told me with Constable Upton?' Billie said.

'I'm putting my trust in you to use your own best judgment. One of the most important parts of our business is knowing whom you can or cannot trust.'

FORTY-TWO

Kingston upon Hull
Dear Ronald,

I know it likely seems a frivolous thing in times like these, but I wondered if it would be too much bother to ask you to store my mother's recipe card box in the cupboard beneath the stairs? Mrs Barclay should be coming round sometime soon to make a copy of one of the recipes, so there is no hurry, but her request selfishly brought to mind how much I would hate to see it lost in an air raid. I live in hope that such raids as are happening here never darken the skies above Barton St Giles, but if it should come to that, the cupboard is the safest place for valuables. I would ask you to send it to me, but I

*believe it is far safer at the rectory than anywhere here
in Hull.*

   Appreciatively,
   Wilhelmina

I f Lydia had noticed that Billie was agitated that evening when she returned from her shift, she gave no sign. She chatted briefly about the news of the day and the little occurrences that had happened at the library. She sat on the sofa with her feet outstretched as she read through the evening paper, handing sections of it to Billie as soon as she completed them. It was the sort of cozy family evening that Billie had always enjoyed in Barton St Giles. The furnishings at the rectory had been very different from the ultramodern surroundings of her cousin's home, but the sense of belonging was the same. Billie's heart gave a squeeze as she thought of her father spending the same moments in far less comfortable circumstances.

'Take a look at this letter to the editor. Some man is up on his high horse about shoddy workmanship from the city.' Lydia peeled off another section of the paper and handed it to Billie. 'Although I must say he makes a better point than many other letters to the editor. Often they simply complain about loose dogs or children running about in gangs. At least this one is about public safety.'

Lydia tapped the headline as she handed it over to Billie. Something nagged at the back of her mind as she read the writer's complaint. He was one of the many people out in Victoria Square when the sirens went off during the second raid and he attempted to enter the nearest shelter. Arriving at the door, he found it bolted shut with no way for anyone to open it. He berated the city government for constructing shelters in public spaces if they were to be barricaded against the very people who paid for them in the first place. He went on to say that it was a wonder that no one had been killed standing on the doorsteps of the building that was supposed to ensure their safety. Billie lowered the paper to her lap in a daze. She knew the name of that shelter. What she didn't know was why anyone would lie about it.

'I'm going to have to go back to work for a little while. I think you had best not wait up for me,' Billie said. Lydia looked at her with a mild flare of concern before turning back to the paper in front of her.

'Be careful if you're coming home after dark.'

Billie used the telephone in the hall to ask the boys at the switchboard to locate Avis. She hung up and rushed out of the house without regard to the darkness or the traffic. She ran most of the way to the station and arrived out of breath and relieved to see that her superior had arrived ahead of her. She quickly explained what she had realized.

'Are you quite sure about that?' Avis asked.

Billie held out the newspaper for Avis to read for herself. 'I think we have to bring him in for questioning,' she said.

Avis read quickly through the letter to the editor, then reached for the telephone on her desk.

In less time than Billie would have thought possible, she and Avis were sitting across the interview table from Councilor Chetwell. His body language spoke volumes, and all of them were words of complaint.

'I certainly hope you have a good reason for hauling me out of the council meeting and dragging me in here like a common criminal,' he said.

'I'm going to read to you your statement concerning the death of Professor Trent. You claim to have been in a public air-raid shelter after leaving a social club meeting – is that correct?' Avis asked. She pointed to a typewritten report placed on an open folder in front of her.

A vein throbbed in the councilor's throat, and he strained forward as if he wished to read over the report once more himself to be sure what was written matched his statement.

'That's right. What sort of person would not take cover when the air-raid sirens went off? I see nothing wrong with that in the least.'

'It seems a perfectly reasonable thing for you to have done. In fact, many people attempted to do just that but seem to have had far less luck in doing so than you claim to have had,' Avis said.

'I don't follow you,' the councilor said.

Avis slid the newspaper across the table at him. 'My constable here has pointed out to me that there was a problem with the very shelter you claim to have been in for the duration of the air raid. Since you could not possibly have been in the shelter as you stated, would I be right in assuming that you were in fact at the art college stabbing Professor Trent?'

The councilor sagged back against his chair. All the fight seemed to evaporate from him. Billie thought he looked as though he had shrunk by half his size.

'You don't understand. I did the country a favor. That man was a monster,' he said.

'What do you mean by that?' Avis asked.

'He completely corrupted my daughter,' he said defiantly. A glimmer of fight returned to his face after the initial shock of being discovered wore off. 'Something had to be done.'

'How exactly did he corrupt her? Were you under the impression that he had seduced her?' Avis asked.

Color rose to the councilor's face. Billie could tell he was deeply uncomfortable with discussing such things with members of the opposite sex. He swallowed and nodded.

'He had an undue influence over her and was able to convince her to behave in a manner that was completely outside her usual character,' he said.

'I assume you're talking about Audrey's work as an enemy operative,' Avis said.

Billie stiffened, as did Councilor Chetwell. His eyes grew wide in his face and he stammered.

'You knew about that? My Audrey never would have done such a thing if he hadn't convinced her to do so,' he said. 'Especially not after what happened to her brother.'

'You're right about that. She wasn't working for the Germans. Professor Trent was her handler. He was running an operation that was rooting out those friendly to the enemy on our shores. Audrey was posing as someone coordinating such efforts for people above her and was remarkably talented at the job. Professor Trent was not involved in any sort of romantic liaison with your daughter,' Avis said.

Billie thought she had never seen someone look so stricken in all her life. Even the look on her mother's face when she confronted Billie with her enlistment in the services could not have compared with what she was seeing forming on Councilor Chetwell's.

'Do you mean to tell me that Audrey had not betrayed her country?' he asked.

'No, sir. She was a devoted servant of the Crown and put herself at considerable risk in her efforts to help protect our interests both at home and abroad. You have materially damaged her efforts by what you did to the professor. Not only have we lost your daughter but also the organizer above her. You have done irreparable harm to the country's efforts,' Avis said.

Councilor Chetwell began to shake with great wracking sobs. His level of remorse seemed to Billie to be quite out of proportion to what he had done to Professor Trent. It sounded like despair. In fact, it sounded to her ears like the sobs she had heard coming from her own throat when she knew she was the reason her mother had died.

'It was you, wasn't it?' Billie asked. 'You're the one who killed Audrey.'

Billie felt Avis's gaze riveted on her. But she couldn't pull her own away from the councilor's face. After another sob heaved up from deep within him, he nodded.

'I followed her to the café and watched people coming and going. She would never tell her mother or me where she was going, and she was out all hours. It was my duty to look after her.'

He looked from Avis to Billie and back again, as if to seek their approval for his fatherly judgment. Avis nodded that he should go on.

'You were only doing what you thought was right to protect your daughter,' Avis said.

'Exactly. After that young engineering student and a girl left, I determined to confront her about what she was doing at a closed café. But before I could cross the street and ask her to account for her actions, Professor Trent showed up. When she opened the door, she just beamed at him and pulled him quickly inside. I didn't want to see what they might be up to and so I waited until he left before I went in.'

'Were you there during the air raid?' Billie asked.

He looked over at her once more and nodded.

'I was crossing the street when the siren went off. I had grown tired of waiting outside and decided that maybe it would be better if I caught them in the act. Audrey looked completely shocked to see me. She was the only one still in the café. The professor must have left by a back door. That's when I spotted a leaflet next to her handbag on the counter. Can you imagine my disgust when I saw what it said? Her brother's body hadn't even been found to be properly buried and I discovered that she'd been aiding the enemy?'

'What happened then?' Billie asked.

'She said I didn't understand, and she reached for the leaflet and tried to pull it away from me. I completely lost my temper and snatched up something close at hand. Before I realized what happened, I hit her, and she fell to the floor. I couldn't believe what I had done when I looked at my hand and saw that it held a marble rolling pin smeared with her blood. I dropped down and scooped her into my arms, looking for any signs of life. I sat there holding her body while the bombs kept dropping out of the sky. I prayed that the building would collapse on the two of us and that it would put an end to my misery. No one would know what either of us had done.'

'But you didn't stay until that happened, did you?' Avis said. Billie thought she heard a trace of bitterness in Avis's voice. The councilor shook his head.

'When the sirens ceased, the building was still standing, and my daughter was dead. Beside her was a leaflet announcing to the world that she was a traitor. That's when I knew what I had to do. I gathered up the leaflet and the rolling pin and tidied up any sign of my footprints. I left through the back and joined the crowds of people milling about in a daze. One more man who looked shocked and horrified attracted no attention. I threw the marble rolling pin into the debris of one of the buildings that had taken a far worse blow from the bombing and crumpled up the leaflet and threw it in a blaze that had started up in a building nearby.'

'That explains what happened to Audrey, but what about Professor Trent?' Billie asked.

'I decided the one thing that I could do for my daughter was to kill the man who had convinced her to betray everything she was raised to hold dear.' He let out a deep sigh.

'During the night of the next air raid was when you decided to kill him?' Avis asked.

The councilor nodded. 'I made my way to the art college where I knew that he had classes. After all, I knew Audrey's timetable at the college, and he was one of her teachers. It was an easy enough thing to wait until the students left and then to attack him in his own classroom. As I was making my way home, another siren went off. I thought it was fate's way of having a second chance at taking me out at the hands of the enemy. I thought it would be a form of justice. But somehow I wasn't one of the people injured that night even though I continued to walk about the streets in the open. What's going to happen now?'

'I suppose that depends on what you're willing to admit to formally,' Avis said. 'I suggest that we continue to allow Audrey's death to be blamed on the enemy. You could officially confess to having killed Professor Trent because you suspected him of having an affair with your daughter. That way, the work she gave her life for is not undermined,' Avis said.

The councilor nodded and sank back against his chair. 'It will hurt my wife, of course, but she is grieving so badly that one more blow likely won't make much difference.'

FORTY-THREE

Hull
Special Constable Upton's PNB

The station was abuzz with chatter when Peter arrived for his shift. Everyone in the department had something to say about the arrest of the councilor. Man after man stopped Peter to add their twopence to the story, but there was only one person he wanted to talk to about it.

He found her in the vacant lot behind the police station, leaning against the brick wall of the building and soaking up a bit of sun. Her face was tilted towards the sky, and she looked as though she had been through a clothes wringer like the one his mother had set up in the small bit of waste ground behind her home.

'I heard you sat in on the interview with Councilor Chetwell,' Peter said. 'The rumor is that you're the one who spotted the hole in his alibi. Good work.'

'It was just a bit of luck, that's all,' Billie said. 'My cousin Lydia was the one who called my attention to it.'

'But you're the one who put two and two together. I guess the councilor was right about one thing.'

'What was that?'

'He was right not to want women to serve as police constables. If you hadn't been here, he probably would've got away with it,' Peter said.

He patted her on the shoulder. Her eyes widened in surprise at his friendly gesture.

'Does this mean you think women serving on the force is a good idea?' she asked.

'It does if they are all like you,' Peter said. 'But somehow I'm inclined to believe you might just be one of a kind.'

> *Kingston upon Hull*
> *Dear Father,*
>
> *I wish I could write you a distractingly breezy letter filled with light-hearted news of life here near the seaside. But the fact of the matter is that my heart is heavy, and I wish I could look upon your face just now.*
>
> *Tonight, I sat across the table from a man who destroyed his family with his own two hands. As I realized what he had done, all I could think of was how much you and Mother showed your love for Frederick and me. No matter what, I knew, deep down, that you had my best interests in mind and that you both were always trying to keep me safe.*
>
> *I just wanted you to know that I appreciate your care*

and love more and more with each passing day and that
you are in my heart always.
   All my love,
   Wilhelmina

'What will happen now?' Billie asked.

'As long as you're willing to be discreet, and if the councilor is, too, I expect that the secret of the operation will be safe. I don't expect that the councilor will have to keep the secret very long. Murder is a hanging crime, after all, and he's made a full confession.'

'I think that the look on his face when he realized that Audrey hadn't been involved in spying for the enemy was the most horrible thing I have ever seen in my life,' Billie said.

Avis reached out and patted her on the shoulder. 'This is not a business for the fainthearted. I'll understand if you want to go back to the library. There is a great deal of good you could do by serving at the information bureau. There's no shame in that and I won't think less of you if you decide to leave.'

Billie stood there for a moment considering the options. The library was beautiful, and she could provide real assistance there. Certainly, there would be days that would challenge her patience and also prove difficult as suffering people arrived with questions and concerns about their loved ones. But she thought, too, about Councilor Chetwell and his belief that women didn't belong on the police force. And now, as his crimes came to light, there would be no better time for his opinions to be something people became less inclined to heed. Besides, she was good at her job and not everyone would be. She thought probably even her mother would be proud of her.

'If it's all the same to you, I'd rather stay,' Billie said.

AUTHOR'S NOTE

This novel was inspired by the extraordinary bravery, stalwartness and community spirit of the people of Hull, UK, during WWII. With ninety percent of its buildings damaged or destroyed, it was the second most bombed city in England during the war. For insight and information about their day-to-day experiences I relied heavily on several sources, particularly the May and June 1940 editions of the *Hull Daily Mail* as provided by the British Newspaper Archive. Other vital resources included *Hull at War 1939-45* by David Bilton and Malcolm K. Mann and *A North-East Coast Town, Ordeal and Triumph* by T. Geraghty. For a more general understanding of life on the home front, I turned to *Wartime Women, A Mass-Observation Anthology 1937-45*, edited by Dorothy Sheridan.

I kept as many of the details of life during the early war period as close to the facts as the novel's story would allow. The one real liberty I took with the truth was the start date of women serving as WPCs in Hull. While the first female constable was sworn in in September, 1940, I wanted to place Billie in Hull as the period of bombings basically began. So, for the sake of the story I fudged the dates a bit. However, other details are firmly rooted in reality. More pedestrians were killed in the early months of the war than combatants, as a result of blackout conditions. Access to areas along the coast was severely restricted beginning in the summer of 1940. Anglican clergy was encouraged to head off with the troops to provide moral and emotional support at the front.

While all of the characters in the novel are works of fiction, the roles I have assigned to Billie and Peter, as well as the more minor characters, were also based in reality. Women, as well as men in reserved occupations, threw themselves into volunteering opportunities on the home front. From priests providing shelter in churches to librarians coordinating

information bureaus, people of all sorts shouldered innumer-
able extra duties to make survival possible. Without their
unstinting efforts the war might well have turned out very
differently.

ACKNOWLEDGMENTS

No novel reaches readers solely as a result of the author's efforts, and this one is no exception. I owe a great deal of thanks to several people for their assistance in this project. Firstly, I wish to thank my literary agents Meg Ruley and Christina Hogrebe for believing in Billie from the very beginning. I also would like to thank all of the other team members at the Jane Rotrosen Agency, particularly Sabrina Prestia, for their support and expertise.

Thanks also is due to Victor Wakefield for the information, inspiration and insights he shared. I am so grateful he was willing to take the time to give me his perspective as someone who lived in England during the war years. The novel is better because of his generosity.

I also wish to thank my children, Will, Max, Theo and Ari, who provided encouragement whenever I needed it. And, as always, I want to thank my husband, Elias Estêvão, the hero at the heart of all my stories.